Riches to Rags

Dana Gricken

ISBN: 979-8-88653-457-3

Published by Satin Romance
An Imprint of Melange Books, LLC
White Bear Lake, MN 55110
www.satinromance.com

Published in the United States of America.

Cover Design by Caroline Andrus

Dedicated to Whitey

Chapter One

My girlfriend's birthday party was going to be amazing.

I had stayed up all night at my mansion in Malibu, stringing lights, blowing up birthday balloons, and getting the food and drinks ready. Then I had texted my girlfriend happy birthday, sent her roses and chocolates through Uber, and told her I was excited to see her tonight.

What more could a lady want?

I checked myself out in the foyer mirror. I smoothed my brown hair, then fixed my tie. I put my birthday gift on the table and waited for the guests to arrive.

When the bell rang half an hour later, I opened the door. The hot California air wafted inside. My parents stood there, as chipper and luxurious as always. Mom wore a grey fur coat with heels—I wasn't sure how she stayed cool in this heat—while my dad wore a blazer with dress pants. They were both carrying birthday gifts.

"Ah, Ethan! So nice to see you," Mom gushed, leaning in and kissing my cheeks. "Is Anna here yet?"

"Nope, not yet. Here, I'll take those," I replied. "You're

the first ones to arrive. Come on in—make yourselves at home."

Mom entered first, followed by Dad. He stumbled a bit as he entered my house but regained his balance by holding onto the wall. Ever since Dad had been diagnosed with Parkinson's, he had decided to turn the family business over to me. He'd spend his golden years getting some much-needed rest.

"Everything going well with the company?" Dad asked as I set their presents down. "You and your brother getting along?"

"Yeah, everything's been pretty smooth so far. No need to worry, Dad. I'll take care of it."

Dad grinned, patting my shoulder. "I know you will, son. I'm very proud of you."

Just as I thanked him and turned to close the door, someone's foot wedged inside. It belonged to my brother, Nathan —two years older than me and almost identical. We had the same brown hair and wore similar suits, but he had brown eyes instead of my green.

"You talking business without me?" Nathan joked. "I'm hurt. Nice to see you outside work, little brother."

He gave me a fist bump, then nodded at Dad. We were all a little more careful around Nathan lately. Since he was the oldest, he always expected to inherit Dad's company and all its responsibilities. But Dad had passed the company onto me instead. Now I was Nathan's boss. Despite his jealousy and frustration, he still got along with me.

"Good to see you, son," Dad boomed. "Everything going well at work?"

"Well, it's not the job I thought I'd have," Nathan began, stealing a glance at me, "but it could be worse. I hate to admit it, but...Ethan's doing a pretty good job. He's a great boss."

I smiled. "Thanks, I appreciate the vote of confidence.

Well, come on in. We're just waiting on a few more people to show. And the birthday girl herself."

Nathan nodded, entering the house and chatting with Mom and Dad. They helped themselves to the refreshments as I waited near the door. When more people trickled in, including some of Anna's friends and my co-workers, I let them in and took their coats and gifts. As my house became more crowded, I spied Anna's convertible pulling into my driveway.

This was it—showtime! I hoped she liked my gifts and the party I had planned for her.

"She's coming," I called, turning to everyone inside. "Get ready."

Everyone nodded, hushing as I opened the door. Anna walked inside with a big grin and kissed my cheek. She looked as gorgeous as ever in her designer red dress, high heels, and Gucci purse.

"Happy birthday, babe," I whispered. "And some other people want to wish you a happy birthday too."

When I gestured over my shoulder, everyone yelled, "Happy birthday!" Anna was beaming when I glanced back at her. So far, so good.

"Did you do all this?" Anna cried, glancing around. "The house looks incredible."

I nodded, shutting the door. "Thanks—yeah, it was all me. Anything for my best girl."

She kissed my cheek again. "You're too good to me. Ooh, gifts!"

Anna rushed to the table where I had put the gifts, her eyes widening. I walked over and pointed at a small box and a card. "There's mine—open that first."

"Okay." She smiled, reaching for the box. She held it up to her ear and shook it. "Sounds fancy, whatever it is. Maybe...a diamond bracelet or earrings?"

"Well, n-not exactly," I stammered. "But I hope you'll like it anyway. Go on, open it."

Anna giggled and unwrapped the gift, peeking inside. Everyone was staring at us while sipping their drinks as she reached into the box and pulled out a small mixtape. She frowned.

"Um, what is this?" she hissed.

"It's a mixtape," I explained. "Kind of an old thing to do, but romantic. I copied music on there that reminds me of you. And all the adventures we've been on."

"Huh." She put the mixtape down. "I see. Is this card from you too?"

"That's right—I made it myself."

She opened the heart-shaped card, reading the dedication. I had written something sappy about how meeting her was the best day of my life. She read the card for a second, and then put it down, still frowning.

"There's...nothing in there." She stared up at me in confusion. "No gift card, money, jewelry, or sports car."

"Oh." I scratched the back of my neck nervously. "I didn't know you wanted that. I wanted to give you something special—something heartfelt. Something better than money."

Everyone at the party was staring at us now, murmuring. Shame seized me. Even if Anna didn't like the gifts, did she have to humiliate me like that?

"Oh, babe. You're so silly." She shook her head. "Okay, what else is there for me?"

"I got you a Rolex," Nathan answered, reaching onto the table for a small box.

I hung my head. My cheeks reddened as Anna ripped open his package. She gasped when she saw the gold watch and put it on immediately.

"Oh, thank you, Nathan!" she squealed. "You're the best. It's so shiny. See?"

As she waved it around, other people stepped forward, giving her their gifts. They were all expensive—perfume, makeup, jewelry. Things you could buy at a store. I wanted to give her something more personal. Once she had unwrapped the rest of her presents, Anna turned to the crowd.

"Thank you for coming, everyone," she began. Then she glared at me. "I know you tried, babe, but it's not too late to get me a better gift. There's a new car dealership just a few miles from here."

"Don't blame my brother," Nathan chuckled, shaking his head. "He's still learning about business *and* women. I'm sure what he gets you for Christmas will be much better. Right, brother?"

As he patted my shoulder, I cleared my throat. "Yeah, yeah...much better. Excuse me, I need to use the bathroom."

I wiggled out of my brother's grasp, heading down the hall. I overheard Anna thanking everyone for the gifts as she tried on her jewelry. As they had a great time without me, I locked myself in my bathroom and splashed some water on my face.

When I looked up in the mirror, I felt so stupid. Did Anna even like me for who I was? I had met her at a party, one of those rich, swanky events that my father had hosted. She had come off so polite and sweet. Although the past six months were fun, we didn't have a future together. Not when we were so different.

It was time to let her go.

Just as I dried my face, I heard a knock on the door. I spun around and hoped it was Anna, sorry for humiliating me. But it was only my mother.

"Darling, there you are," she scolded. "You sure made a scene when you rushed off."

I sighed. "It's nothing, Mom. Don't worry about it."

She reached for my hand. "A mother can always tell, Ethan. What's going on?"

I leaned against the sink. "I just...I worked so hard on those gifts. I spent hours making the card and putting together songs that reminded me of Anna. Why can't she see that? Or appreciate it?"

"Oh, I'm sure she does," Mom murmured. "She just has expensive taste, that's all. Nothing wrong with that."

"Unless that's all she's after." I faced my mother. "Is Anna only interested in me for my money?"

Mom shrugged. "And if she was? Would that be so bad?"

I blinked. "What? Yes, of course it would be! I want *real* love. I don't want a gold digger."

Mom crossed her arms. "I married your father for his money. And I don't regret a thing. He bought me nice things. I raised you and your brother. An even trade, I think."

"Do you...do you even *love* Dad?"

"Of course I do. I came to love him in time," Mom explained. "But you need much more to make a relationship work, darling. I like Anna—she fits in well with the family. It would be a shame for you to end that. So why don't you stop sulking and come back to the party, hmm?"

Mom gave me a side hug, then walked back out to join everyone else. I couldn't believe what I was hearing. My own mother only married my father for money. And he was okay with it. I knew I wasn't—that I wanted something different.

I wanted something real.

After taking a deep breath, I walked out of the bathroom. The party was still in full swing. Anna chatted with my brother in the corner while staring at the watch. Maybe she should've dated him instead.

When Nathan noticed me approaching, he smiled. "There he is—Boss of the Year. Where did you run off to?"

"To the bathroom. Sorry, wasn't feeling well." I glanced at Anna. "Can I talk to you for a minute? Alone, upstairs?"

Anna nodded. "Of course. Excuse me, Nathan."

Nathan understood, and headed back to mingle with everyone else. I led Anna to the porcelain staircase and took her upstairs. When I shut the door, she scanned my room.

"What are you looking for?" I demanded.

Anna turned back to me. "For my gifts, silly. I mean, that stupid mixtape can't be the only thing you bought me, right? It was pretty lame. No offense."

"I worked hard on your gifts." I gritted my teeth. "The least you can do is be grateful."

She scoffed. "For what? For gifts I never wanted? Sorry, but if you buy someone a crappy gift, you deserve to be told. And yours sucked. No one makes mixtapes anymore, Ethan. Not since, like, the nineties."

Maybe not. But there had to be someone out there who appreciated my homemade efforts. And now, I just had the difficult task of finding them. But first things first.

I cleared my throat. "Anna...I'm sorry, but I don't think this is working out. We're just not compatible."

She blinked. "I...don't understand, Ethan. What are you saying?"

"I'm saying...I think we should break up. Move on and date different people."

"Breaking up with me on my birthday?" she snarled. "Are you serious?"

I sighed. "I know. It's not the way I wanted this night to go, but—"

She reached over to my dresser, grabbing a vase. She poured water over my head and threw the vase at the wall. It shattered as water and rose petals leaked down my suit, dripping onto the floor.

"You jerk!" she cried. "I hate you. I never want to see you again!"

She stormed out of my room, heading downstairs. I followed and leaned over the handrail as people gaped. Anna headed to the door and rushed outside. A minute later, she returned to the table, snatching as many gifts as she could carry.

The gifts were her real love, anyway. Who cared about me or the party?

She stormed outside again, hopping into her convertible and speeding off. As I walked down the stairs, everyone was staring at me, wondering what was going on. Dad stepped forward first.

"What happened?" he demanded. "Why are you soaking wet?"

"Anna and I...we just broke up." I muttered, reaching for a kitchen towel. "The party's over, by the way. Just like our relationship."

Everyone gasped, then began murmuring again. Mom glowered at me. But what was I supposed to do? Marry a gold digger? I wouldn't end up like my father.

People began to scatter outside, saying how sorry they were that Anna and I had broken up. But I wasn't. Now I was free to find someone who loved me for me, wherever she was.

When it was just me, my parents, and my brother left, the house grew silent. Nathan was the first to clear his throat. "So...that was the worst birthday party I've ever been to."

"What happened, Ethan?" Dad cried.

"What happened is that we aren't right for each other. At all," I spat. "She was only into me for my money. She proved that today with the gifts. And I want something more, something deeper. I want true love."

Nathan scoffed. "True love? Jeez, you sound like a Disney movie."

"Maybe I do. But I still believe in it. Grandma and Grandpa loved each other, didn't they? When they started our company?"

"Well...yes," Dad faltered. "But that was different. They were the exception, not the rule. True love is very, very rare."

So everyone was telling me. I glanced between Mom, Dad, and Nathan, wondering when they had become such cynics. Did they want me to end up with someone who only wanted me for my money?

I cleared my throat. "Look, no offense, but I think I want some alone time. So, if you wouldn't mind..."

Nathan nodded, heading to the door. "Of course. See you at work tomorrow, Eth. And sorry about Anna."

As Nathan left, Dad did the same. "Yes, I'm sorry too. You were great together. It's just a shame, that's all."

As Dad stumbled out, heading to his SUV, Mom hung back with a sigh. "So, you broke up with Anna."

"I did—and I'd do it again. I'm sorry, but I'm not like you or Dad. I won't marry for money. I want to marry for love, for companionship. I want a soulmate."

"Darling, that's going to be a bit difficult with the kind of money we have." Mom gestured toward my house. "Our reputation precedes us. And I still think you and Anna were a great couple. I was hoping you two would get married soon. You seemed so compatible. Same sense of humor, snappy dressers, a good bond."

What was the point of getting married? So Anna could take more of my money? I'd had enough of that already. From my point of view, we didn't seem as compatible as Mom thought.

"Just think about it, okay? Maybe it's not too late to fix

things with her." Mom kissed my cheek. "Anyway, I'm only a phone call away if you need to chat."

As Mom left the house, I realized I couldn't call her. She didn't understand—and I was sick of repeating myself. Why was it so hard to believe that I wanted true love?

I sat down on the staircase in my empty house. The place was a mess—torn wrapping paper and deflated balloons scattered everywhere. Someone needed to clean it up.

I rose to my feet, reached for a trash bag, and tried not to think about my tragic love life.

Chapter Two

I spent the next hour silently cleaning up my house. When I checked my phone before bed, Anna had texted and called a hundred times. She kept yammering on and on about how I'd regret it.

Maybe I had dodged a bullet.

When I went upstairs to change into my pajamas, I found my grandma's engagement ring in my top drawer. I dreamed about finding someone to give it to as it gleamed in my bedroom's dim light. Someone who loved me for me.

Maybe my brother was right—maybe that only existed in Disney movies and fairytales.

After putting the engagement ring back, I climbed into bed, watching another episode of *Love Always Wins*. It was a soap opera with a cult following. Most people called it cheesy because it targeted women, but I adored it. I kept that fact to myself though, lest my brother tease me. The show took place in a small town, centered around multiple generations of families. Love always saved them in the end.

No wonder I believed in happily-ever-afters.

I fell asleep shortly after that, waking up to sunlight

poking through my curtains. Alone. Even when I had Anna over, I was lonely. Love wasn't supposed to be loneliness.

I headed downstairs, ate breakfast by myself, and dressed myself. I decided on a navy blue suit before putting on my watch and grabbing my briefcase. As I left the house, locking the door behind me, I noticed someone had stomped on my flowers in the front yard and smeared mud everywhere.

Anna. Hell hath no fury like a woman scorned. I debated calling the police or telling my parents, but I wanted to give her a chance to calm down first. To act more like an adult.

Shaking my head, I stumbled into my SUV, pulling out of my laneway. I listened to the radio as I drove to work. I had inherited my father's company, The Miles Marketing Group, just a few months ago. It was located in a tall skyscraper in downtown Los Angeles. Big corporations paid us hand-somely to market their products. My father had made millions. It was my job to do the same.

No pressure, right?

After parking in my CEO spot, I nodded politely at the security guard and headed for the front doors. I had to scan my work ID to get inside the building. When I did, hundreds of employees were walking around, answering calls and working on their computers. Typing and mindless chatter filled the air. They all greeted me as I headed to the elevator.

My office was on the top floor—level fifteen. It had a gorgeous view of Los Angeles, especially at dawn and dusk. I wished I could share those sights with someone. I had taken Anna there a few times, but she seemed more interested in my salary.

Once the elevator had let me off on the fifteenth floor, I stepped out, noticing more people in cubicles typing away. When I heard my brother's loud voice near the photocopier, I knew he had beaten me to work. Everything was always a competition to him.

"...yeah, things are over between them," Nathan was telling one of my employees. "And it was a pretty nasty breakup. She stormed off and everything."

I marched toward the photocopier, clearing my throat. "Morning, Nathan. Telling everyone about my relationship woes?"

Nathan spun around. "Just trying to make Jimmy here feel better about his love life. His wife just cheated on him."

The man glowered toward the floor. I sighed. "I'm so sorry. I hope you find someone better."

I desired the same.

Jimmy nodded before scurrying away. Ever since I took over the company, employees were afraid to talk to me. I thought of myself as a fairly easy-going boss, but they were still a bit hesitant. All of them except Nathan.

He was as outspoken as ever.

"Hey, Mr. Boss Man," Nathan began. "You feeling okay this morning? Last night was...something."

I sighed. "I'm as good as I can be. Anna came by and stomped on my flowers. She's been sending me a bunch of angry texts too."

Nathan whistled. "Damn, she sounds like a psycho. Maybe it's a good thing you broke up with her. Speaking of that...she's not off-limits, is she?"

"Off-limits?" I frowned. "What are you talking about?"

Nathan grinned. "Come on, Eth, don't be dense. Would you be mad if I asked her out?"

"Dude, I just told you she's been sending me threatening texts. Did you not hear that?"

"Of course I did." Nathan smirked. "She's a psycho. But psychos are beasts in the sack. And she *is* pretty hot."

I rolled my eyes. "Fine, whatever—ask her out if you want. Just know that she's probably a gold digger and a little unstable."

"Just my type." Nathan grinned. "You're the best, Eth. Well, I should get back to work. But I've got a little something that should cheer you up."

I raised an eyebrow. "Oh? What is it? Please don't tell me it's a trip to the strip club again."

"Nope, not that. Something I know you'll like. Catch you later!"

As Nathan sauntered off to his cubicle, I shook my head. I had no idea what my brother was up to now, but I hoped it wasn't too crazy. I made my way to my office near the back window, nodding politely at more employees. My secretary Cheyenne Nichols was at her desk just outside my office, taking phone calls and scribbling down notes.

I was always happy to see Cheyenne. She was one of the few people I trusted in the office. She had worked for my dad originally, staying on when I took over. We had grown close ever since. As friends, of course, since she was in a relationship and I wasn't her type. She had dark hair in braids, piercing brown eyes, and a classy pencil skirt and blouse.

"...yes, Mr. Vaughn, I'll tell him," Cheyenne continued, looking up from her desk and noticing me. "He just got in now. Okay, he'll see you soon. Buh-bye."

I walked over, smiling. "Hey, Cheyenne. Who was that?"

"Oliver Vaughn. That businessman who's setting up a hotel chain?" she replied. "He's coming in soon to talk marketing. He'll be here shortly."

"Got it. I'll be ready for him, thanks. How are you this morning?"

Cheyenne beamed. "Perfect, actually. I haven't told anyone yet, but...I got engaged last night."

Cheyenne held out her hand, showing off a gorgeous engagement ring. It sparkled. I took her hand, inspecting the ring.

"Wow, that's a real diamond," I exclaimed. "Congrats, Cheyenne. I'm happy for you."

The only kind of pure happiness that love could bring shone on her face. "Thanks, Ethan. Alicia popped the question last night. We were eating dinner on a boat when she pretended to drop her napkin. When she reached down for it, she pulled out the ring."

"Romantic." I smiled. "How long have you been dating again? Two years?"

"Three, actually. We met through mutual friends. She's a teacher—good with kids. Which is perfect for us if we want to have a child."

I swallowed hard, trying not to be jealous. "That's amazing. You'd make a great mom. You have a date for the wedding planned yet?"

She shook her head. "Not yet—it's still early. But we were thinking of having a private ceremony. Maybe on the beach."

"That's a good idea. If you need a place for the reception, you can use my house. Free of charge."

Cheyenne beamed. "Thanks, Ethan—we appreciate that. Don't worry, you're definitely getting an invitation. Or maybe we'll have the ceremony in a small town. We stayed at a nice place in Maine not that long ago."

"That's a cute idea. Wherever it's happening, I'll be there." I leaned closer. "Say, Cheyenne...can I ask you something?"

She nodded, reaching for her coffee cup. "Sure, what's up?"

"I, uh, kinda broke up with my girlfriend last night," I muttered. "At her birthday party."

"Yeah, I heard about that. Your brother's been telling everyone around the office. I'm so sorry, Ethan. That's tough."

My brother. He was a nuisance most of the time, airing my dirty laundry. He was worse than those tabloids.

"Thanks. Anyway, I guess I was just wondering...how did you find someone?"

"Trust me, it wasn't easy. I went on a lot of dates with idiots. Guys and girls alike. It took me years to meet Alicia. But I'm glad I waited—I can't imagine being with anyone but her."

"Do you have any advice for someone like me? Who wants to get married and have kids one day?"

Cheyenne smiled, holding my hand. "It'll happen for you, Ethan. You're a great guy—caring, thoughtful. And you have your own company. A total catch. You just have to be patient."

I sighed, leaning back from the desk. It wasn't the answer I was hoping for. "Yeah, maybe you're right. But I'm thirty-two. I just...I don't know. I feel like I'm running out of time."

"Hey, love arrives exactly when it's meant to," Cheyenne told me. "So don't worry, it'll happen. Just don't give up, okay? Keep going with it. You'll find someone amazing."

"Hopefully it'll happen sooner than later. While I still have hair," I joked, patting my head. "See you later, Cheyenne. Tell Mr. Vaughn to come in when he gets here."

"Will do. And Ethan?"

I turned around. "Yeah?"

"It was her loss," Cheyenne reminded me. "Not yours. Remember that."

"I'll try." I faked a smile. "Thanks for cheering me up."

"No problem. What are secretaries for?"

I chuckled, shaking my head as I entered my office. For so long, it had my father's name on the frosted door. Now, it was mine—ETHAN MILES, CEO. It felt good, even if my brother had been first in line to inherit the company.

I placed my briefcase down on the desk, turning my

computer on. I had several leather chairs for guests and tall bookshelves around the room. I answered a few emails and watched the sunrise for a bit before I heard a knock.

"Come in!"

Cheyenne opened the door. "Mr. Vaughn is here, sir. Shall I send him in?"

I rose to my feet. "Yes, please do. I'm eager to talk business."

She nodded, turning around and gesturing for someone to enter my office. He was young like me—in his mid-thirties —who had probably inherited his fortune. Oliver Vaughn had blond hair, wore a designer black suit, and swaggered in.

"Ah, Mr. Vaughn." I held out my hand. "Nice to see you. How goes the hotel development?"

He shook my hand, grinning. "Well so far—I've got most of the details planned out and the workers booked. My grandfather would be proud. So, I was hoping we could go over some ideas. I'm hoping to launch an aggressive marketing campaign..."

After Oliver sat down, we discussed his plans. We signed a contract that stated The Miles Marketing Company would fund commercials and billboards. In return, we'd get a percentage of his profits. Easy money.

Oliver rose to his feet, grinning. "Thanks for all your help, Ethan. I'm confident these new hotels will be a success. My company plans to put a Vaughn Hotel in every city in America."

"Ambitious. With our help, we'll make it happen." I shook his hand again. "We'll talk again soon. Have a good day."

He thanked me once again, leaving my office. After answering more emails and taking phone calls, I departed for lunch. Anna still sent me threatening texts, so I blocked her number. I didn't need that kind of negativity in my life.

I wanted a fresh start—a new chance at love. Which meant I'd have to leave her behind.

Just as I rose to my feet, I heard a knock. I opened the door and found my brother standing there and grinning.

"What?" I snapped. "Do I have something on my face?"

"No, silly. I have a surprise for you, remember? Come on —follow me. They finally showed up."

I grimaced. "Who showed up?"

"No questions! Just come on—hurry."

In confusion, I followed Nathan through the cubicles. He led me toward the elevator and pressed the button for the third floor. That was where we held our more important presentations and meetings. After we stepped off, greeting more employees, Nathan gestured down the hallway.

"This way. To conference room B. And you can thank me later."

Puzzled, I followed my brother, wondering what he had gotten me into now. He was always up to something. Even when we were kids, he was always pulling pranks on me and getting me into trouble. How little had changed.

After we turned down the hall, entering the large conference room, I realized what Nathan had done. He had strung up a sign that read OPERATION: FIND ETHAN A WIFE. And the conference room was filled with lovely women, all of them dressed to the nines and holding drinks.

"What is this?" I cried, turning to Nathan.

"I'm helping you find a wife, Eth. What does it look like?" Nathan smirked. "You want to get married so bad, I thought I'd help. So I put out an ad in the newspaper last night. See for yourself."

Nathan picked up a nearby newspaper, showing me the headline. It read: MILLIONAIRE BUSINESS OWNER SEEKS WIFE, TRUE LOVE. It listed the time and conference room to meet me.

"Are you crazy?" I exploded, turning to Nathan. "Putting an ad in the newspaper? Holding a conference at work? This is beyond unprofessional."

"Hey, it worked, didn't it? Look at how many women showed up, all eager to meet you," Nathan chided, gesturing toward the room. "Go on—talk with them, see if anyone catches your eye."

I threw the newspaper down, shocked. "I just...I can't believe you'd do this. That you'd try to help me. I thought you didn't believe in true love?"

"I don't, but you do. And I can't have you moping around all the time now that you broke up with Anna. This company needs you at your best, Eth. Don't be scared—chat with the ladies. I see a few from here that look divine."

Nathan, always the womanizer. I took a deep breath and entered the conference room. What if I was going to meet my future wife today? Someone I had a real connection with?

I approached one woman first, a blonde in a red cocktail dress. She beamed at me. "Ethan, right? I've heard a lot about you. I'm Chelsea."

"Nice to meet you," I squeaked, shaking her hand. "Thanks for coming. So, what do you like to do?"

"Oh, this and that. I like surfing and sunbathing." Then she paused. "Is it true you're the wealthiest CEO in LA? That's super awesome. What's it like running a company?"

My smile faded. Chelsea wasn't too different from Anna. I scanned the room, wondering if all the women here were the same. Was there anyone in Los Angeles who wanted love and not just money?

"Uh, it's a lot of work," I stammered. "It all started when I inherited the company from my father..."

I chatted with Chelsea for a while, then made my way around the room to speak with the other women. Nathan watched from the doorway while checking out the ladies. But they were all the same—more interested in my money than me. And they weren't subtle about it. One woman even asked if I had a yacht.

"All right, ladies. Lunchtime is over. We gotta get back to work," Nathan called, checking his watch. "My brother will contact you if he liked what he saw. Thanks for coming!"

All the ladies nodded, saying goodbye and leaving the building. But I was more dejected than ever. I wasn't going to find someone like Cheyenne had. As I watched them go, the room turning quiet. Nathan walked over with a smirk.

"So? Which one caught your eye?"

"None of them." I sighed. "This was a terrible idea, Nathan."

Nathan winced. "What? But some of them were nice. I like that Chelsea girl. Nice hair, nice hips—"

"Then you date her!" I spat. "You can date them all, Anna included. Because I'm done. And I don't want any more of your help."

Nathan's face fell. "Oh, come on, man. Don't be like that!"

But I had already stormed out of the conference room, more convinced than ever that love just wasn't in the cards for me.

Chapter Three

As I rode the elevator back up to my office, I feared I had been too hard on my brother. He was only trying to help—as unusual as that was. Growing up, he had been my biggest competitor. Maybe he had changed. And maybe this time, I had been a jerk.

Sighing, I stepped off the elevator, heading toward my office. Cheyenne was still gone for lunch as I walked past her empty desk into my office and sat down. As I read through some more emails, I heard a knock. I hoped it was Nathan so I could apologize, but then Cheyenne's head appeared through the crack.

"Ethan? Sorry to bother you." She peered into my office. "But someone's here to see you."

I frowned, glancing at my calendar on the wall. "Oh. But...I didn't have any appointments this afternoon."

"I know, sir. And I told her you're busy, but she's insisting to see you."

She? I hoped it wasn't Anna. I'd had enough of her harassment and moneygrubbing for a lifetime.

I rose to my feet. "Okay, then. Send her in."

Cheyenne nodded, then opened the door a little wider. A

gorgeous blonde woman walked into my office, smelling of vanilla and roses. I knew who it was—my ex-girlfriend, Diana Fortuna. And she was as elegant as ever in a black halter dress and heels. She smiled at Cheyenne, and then shut the door behind her.

Cheyenne knew who Diana was—everyone did. She was a businesswoman in her own right, founder and owner of an advertising company. Unlike me, she wasn't rich off her family's money but her own. Something I found very attractive about her. And although we were rivals, that didn't stop us from hitting it off at a marketing convention in Sweden a few years ago.

As she stared at me, all our petty arguments came flooding back. The competitiveness. Her need for success and power. And how she wasn't ready to get married and have kids like me. I had planned to give her my grandmother's ring before she broke up with me.

So yeah, my track record with love wasn't the best.

"Ethan," she began. "It's been a while."

"Diana, hi." I strode toward her. "Why are you here?"

"I heard about your breakup. Your brother's telling everyone. It's making its way around town."

I shook my head, unsurprised. People loved to gossip in Los Angeles. The tabloids were vicious.

"Yeah, it's true," I clipped. "Anna...she was just into me for my money. I feel stupid for taking so long to figure it out."

"Ah, Ethan. Always the hopeless romantic," she drawled, stepping closer. "Anyway, I wanted to check you on. See how you're doing since the breakup."

I shrugged. "As good as I can be. Trying to stay busy with work. My brother tried to set me up with a few women, but none of them felt right."

"That's too bad." Diana crossed her arms. "I'm single too."

Uh-oh. I knew where this was going.

"Di, we've been down this road before—"

"And we were good together," Diana interrupted, reaching for my hand. "And the sex was incredible."

"I know," I lamented, "but things ended between us for a reason. We weren't right for each other—we didn't want the same things. I think we should leave it in the past."

Diana scrunched her face, ripping her hand away from mine. "You always were stubborn, Ethan. Anything I can do to change your mind?"

Staring at her—having her this close—disoriented me. I couldn't tell if that was Diana's effect or her perfume, but I found it hard to say no. Then I forced myself to remember all the bad times and held my ground.

"I'm sorry," I replied, "but I don't think it'll work."

She stepped back. "That's disappointing. But I respect your decision."

"Thank you. Say...my brother didn't put you up to this, did he? He's been scheming a lot lately."

More than usual.

Diana chortled. "Ethan, we both know no man can make me do anything. No, your brother didn't send me. I'm here for my own reasons."

"All right, just checking. But it was nice to see you. I think we should keep in touch."

"I'd like that." She cleared her throat. "Do you think you could get me a glass of water? Nasty bug going around. My throat's still a bit sore from a flu I had last month."

"Yeah, of course. We've got tons of drinks in our break-room. Wait here."

Diana nodded, taking a seat in front of my desk as I left my office and shut the door for privacy. Cheyenne was watching the door curiously when she saw me come out. Her eyes flickered to the office—looking like she wanted to know what was going on—but we could gossip later. For now, I needed to get Diana a drink.

Then I paused, wondering if she would've preferred tea instead. That always soothed my throat. I turned around, quickly opening the door and poking my head inside the crack.

"Hey, Diana, you want a tea instead—"

I froze when I saw Diana bent over my desk, leafing through the paperwork in my top drawer. And I could see the words VAUGHN HOTEL PROJECT at the top of the folder she was holding.

When she realized I had come back, she froze like a deer caught in the headlights. "Ethan! I was just...uh..."

"Snooping through my files?" I growled, walking toward the desk. I took the file out of her hands. "This is private information. Between Oliver Vaughn and the Miles Marketing Company only."

She giggled nervously. "I know that. I was just, um... looking for something to do. I got bored waiting for you to get back."

I sighed, keeping the folder under my arm. "Diana, you're a much better liar than that. I'm disappointed."

She nodded. "That was quite pitiful, wasn't it? I need to do better."

"Is that the real reason you came here? To look through my files?"

Diana glanced at the folder under my arm. "Yes—I wanted to see what you and Oliver Vaughn were working on. I was hoping to make him a better offer. His hotel corporation is going to be huge, and I want a slice of that pie."

"So you wanted to steal my client," I sneered. "You were only using me—pretending to care. I shouldn't even be surprised."

"It was your fault for leaving me alone with all these files hanging around. We *are* rivals. Even if we shared a bed once." Diana crossed her arms. "Besides, you would've done the same thing. Business is business. Companies steal clients from each other all the time. That's the way the game is played, babe."

I shook my head. "I refuse to believe that—and don't call me babe. We're done here. I'd like you to leave. Now."

"So, no drink?"

I crossed my arms.

"Fine, fine. I'm leaving." She headed for the door. Then she turned back to me. "Despite what you think, I do like you, Ethan. And if you ever want to get back together, you have my number. I'm always around."

She left my office, walking down the hall, hips swaying. She was mesmerizing—but I tore myself away. Not even a perfect figure like hers could make me forget that Diana was a rival. And a lying seductress at that.

I plopped back down, putting the folder back in my desk. Maybe I needed a lock and key for my files. Were these women my only options? A money-hungry Valley girl like Anna or a conniving rival like Diana?

If so, I'd happily stay single for the rest of my life.

When the door creaked open, I sprang to my feet, hoping it wasn't Diana. But it was only Cheyenne peering in at me, her eyes wide. "Sorry to interrupt, but...what was Diana doing here?"

I nodded, adjusting my tie. "She supposedly wanted to get back together. But the second I stepped out of my office, she started rummaging through my files. Specifically, the one on Oliver Vaughn. She wanted to steal him right from under me."

Cheyenne shook her head. "That two-timing snake. Oh, sorry."

"No, it's okay. I totally agree with you." I rose to my feet, walking toward the door. "I sure know how to pick 'em, huh?"

Cheyenne sighed. "Ethan...I'm so sorry. You deserve better. Seriously. Anna and Diana are both way beneath you."

"Are they? Maybe I'm starting to think I deserve it. Maybe I did something in a past life."

"Don't talk like that. You're a good man. And you deserve great love. You'll find it—and then you can tell both Anna and Diana to take a hike."

I smiled. "Thanks, that'll be a good day."

"It'll happen soon." Cheyenne winked at me. "Come on —let's get a coffee at that nice place down the street. It'll take your mind off everything."

Thank God for Cheyenne. Without her, I would've lost my mind. She always knew how to bring me back down to Earth.

"I'd like that. Let me just put the file in a safe place."

Cheyenne nodded, waiting for me near her desk. I stuffed the file on Oliver Vaughn's hotel development into my safe and locked it tight. No one was going to steal my marketing secrets—no matter how killer their curves were in a dress.

Once I was ready, I walked out of my office, heading toward the elevator with Cheyenne. My brother poked his head out from his cubicle, sniffing the air.

"I remember that scent," he began. "Vanilla and roses. Was...Diana Fortuna here? Your ex?"

I rolled my eyes, leaning on Nathan's cubicle wall. "That's right—but not for long. I kicked her out when she tried to steal a file on Oliver Vaughn."

Nathan snickered. "Damn, Diana hasn't changed one bit. I'll keep an eye out for her, though, and let you know if she comes back. I'll make sure she doesn't have a chance to steal anything else."

"Thanks, man. I owe you one." I turned to Cheyenne. "Hey, can I talk to Nathan alone for a sec?"

Cheyenne nodded. "Of course, I'll meet you downstairs when you're ready."

I thanked her, waiting for Cheyenne to walk off toward the elevator before I turned back to Nathan. "So...I owe you an apology."

Nathan raised an eyebrow. "For what?"

"What do you mean, for what? For losing my cool on you. That wasn't right. I'm sorry, Nathan. I know you were only trying to help."

"I was, but I see what you mean. Now that I think about it, I don't think those women were right for you. Maybe you're better off. And I promise, no more scheming. Well, unless you give me the green light."

"Ha, thanks. I do appreciate you trying. I just...I don't know. I'm not sure anyone in this city wants what I want. Real love. I think everyone's just chasing money and fame."

Nathan nodded, reaching for the coffee on his desk. "You could be right. This is Los Angeles, after all. A lot harder to find something real here."

"True. I wish...I wish for just a little while, I could lose all my money and fame. Just be a normal guy with a normal job and live in some small town. Maybe I'd have better luck finding love like that. At least, I wouldn't worry if my girl-friend only wants me for my money."

Nathan's face lit up. "Wait a second...maybe there's a way to make that happen. Dude, you've just given me a great idea."

"Huh? What are you talking about?"

"Are you giving me permission to scheme?"

I paused. "Only if it's a *good* scheme."

Nathan grinned. "Great—then give me some time. Go,

have coffee with Cheyenne. I'll be here, trying to make your dream happen."

I had no idea what Nathan was talking about, but he looked happy. And I still felt bad for snapping at him earlier so I let him plan. I just hoped it was better than his last idea.

With a nod, I turned away from his cubicle, watching as he pulled up a contract template on his computer and started typing. I shook my head as I got into the elevator, riding it down to the lobby. Cheyenne was waiting for me—as promised—by the revolving doors. We left our building, heading down the street to a local coffee shop.

Cheyenne and I sat there for a little while, chatting about normal things. We completely left love out of the equation, and it felt good. After an hour of shooting the breeze, we remembered that we both had work to finish up. We paid for our drinks and left the coffee shop to head back to the building.

After we rode the elevator up to our floor and stepped off, Nathan came running up to me with several papers in his hands. They looked official, with legal jargon and lines for signatures. As Cheyenne headed to her desk, Nathan grinned at me.

"There you are," he chirped. "Ready to see what I've been working on?"

"All right—lead the way."

Nathan nodded, heading to my office. He shut the door behind us and set the papers down on my desk. When I looked closer, I realized I was right—the papers *were* legal jargon. A contract transferring the ownership of the Miles Marketing Company from me to Nathan.

"Nate...what is this?"

"The solution to all your problems. You wanna be poor and find true love? I've got you."

I blinked. "You've lost me."

"Okay, let me paint you a picture. You sign this contract and hand the company over to me for one month. I'll run it while you're gone. In that month, I'll put a story in the newspaper that you lost all your money from a bad business deal. I'll tell everyone Dad fired you. Hopefully, in that time, you'll be able to find someone who likes you for who you are. No money, no problem."

I sighed. "Oh, I don't know. Being away for a month is a long time. Plus, I have a bunch of contracts to look over."

"What, you don't think I can handle it? That I'm not smart enough?"

I scoffed. "I didn't say that."

He leaned closer. "Come on, Ethan—you wanted a change. This is it. Pretend to go broke, find love, then come back to work. Who knows, maybe it'll work out. You won't know if you don't try."

Nathan had a point. And although the plan was way out there—the craziest thing I'd ever heard—maybe it was just crazy enough to work. Before I could stop myself, I already lifted my pen and signed my name on the dotted line.

"Done," I declared. "For one month, you've got the company. Good luck, brother."

Nathan grinned, picking up the paperwork. "You won't regret this, Ethan. And good luck to you too. Keep me updated on the hunt for love, all right?"

I chuckled. "The hunt for love. I will."

"That's what it is, isn't it? Searching for love's true kiss?" Nathan teased. "You got any idea where you're going to start looking for Mrs. Right?"

I thought back to something Cheyenne had told me. "Actually...I think I do. I need to talk to my secretary. And tell her you'll be her boss for a little while. Even if I don't find love, this might be a fun break. Honestly, Dad's ridden me hard since business school. It might be nice to have a month off."

Nathan stuffed the contract into his pocket. "I hear that. You're welcome, by the way."

"Thanks, man. I'll think of you when I'm relaxing."

"Just send me a postcard and we'll call it even," Nathan sang with a wink, walking toward my desk. "Well, I'd better get set up as the new CEO."

"All right. My computer's password is Toffee."

"Our childhood dog?" Nathan shook his head with a snort. "Man, you *are* sentimental. Some chick out there will eat that right up."

"The right one, hopefully. Text or call if you have any questions about the contracts. It should be fairly straightforward. And let me know immediately if there are any emergencies, okay?"

Nathan looked up at me from the screen. "You worry too much, Eth. Everything will be fine. Now, go. Your freedom starts now—and so does the search for the perfect lady."

Nathan was right. Now I just needed Cheyenne's help, and then I was ready to get started.

Chapter Four

"You're doing *what*?"

Clearly, Cheyenne was not a fan. I cleared my throat and calmly explained what was going on. "I'm leaving—just for a little while. My brother is taking over the company for the next month so you'll be working for him until I get back. Look, I know this is a big change, but I need you to do this for me, okay?"

"All right." Cheyenne sighed. "I just think it's a bit drastic. You're going to pretend you lost all your money?"

"Yep. That way, if I meet a special lady, I'll find out she likes me for me and not my fortune."

"I guess so. What about when she finds out the truth?"

"Well, I hope my money will be a bonus and she won't be mad. I'll cross that bridge when I get to it. I need to find her first. But I needed to ask you something. What was that small town you and your girlfriend went to? The one in Maine?"

Cheyenne raised an eyebrow. "Why? Are you planning on starting your search there?"

"Yeah, I think so. Small towns are friendlier, right? Maybe I'll find someone amazing. Do you have the name?"

Cheyenne pulled out her phone. "I can't remember—Alicia found it. Let me text her and ask."

"Great, thanks. Were the people nice? Anyone I might be interested in?"

Cheyenne giggled, finishing texting and setting her phone aside. "Are you asking me if there were cute women?"

"No. Maybe. Okay, yes I am."

"There definitely were. Especially the innkeeper's daughter. Oh, don't tell my girlfriend I said that." Cheyenne blushed. "I remember what it was called—the Cozybrook Inn. A lovely place to stay."

A cute innkeeper's daughter? I could get onboard with that. She'd understand how stressful running a family business was. But I was getting ahead of myself. For now, I'd focus on making it there and settling.

Cheyenne's phone buzzed a second later on her desk. She reached for it, glancing down. "Right, that was the name! Bridgewood, Maine. A far drive, but worth it. And she said good luck, by the way. I told her you were looking for something serious."

"That's nice of her. And thanks—I think that's where I'm heading. Better get home and pack."

"All right. But keep in touch, okay? You've got my number." Cheyenne paused. "Was this your brother's idea?"

"Yeah, it was. He thought I should hand over the company to him for a little while and pretend to give up all my money. He's trying to help me find love, surprisingly. Why?"

"It's just...okay, don't take this the wrong way, but I don't trust your brother. Something about him just never seemed right to me."

"What do you mean?"

Cheyenne glanced toward my office, making sure Nathan wasn't listening. "I don't know, I can't put my finger on it. I just feel like he's always been insanely jealous of you. He told me once that he wishes he was the CEO of this company. That he would do things differently if he was. And sometimes, he gives you these looks like...he hates you. Seriously, I'll have to take a picture sometime. If looks could kill."

I hated to admit it, but I felt it too. My brother had always been my biggest competitor growing up. He had to win every board game we played, constantly sucked up to Mom and Dad, and acted like a sore loser. He even went after girls I crushed on in high school. But he'd never do anything to hurt me. We were family—and family always stuck together. Right?

"Anyway, if I offended you, I'm sorry," Cheyenne continued. "I just needed to get that off my chest. Be careful, Ethan, okay? Especially now that your brother has control of the company. I don't think that was a good move."

"Everything will be fine, Cheyenne. I promise," I replied, trying to convince both of us. "Besides, it's only for a month and then I'll be back. So if my brother is up to anything, he won't have much time."

"Let's hope not. I'll keep you updated if I see anything strange. I'll be like...your little office spy."

I chuckled. "Thanks, Cheyenne—you're the best. Take care while I'm gone."

"You too. I hope you have a great time in Bridgewood, by the way. It is a lovely place."

So I'd heard. I thanked her again, then walked to the elevator. I paused when I sensed eyes on my back. When I turned, I noticed my brother watching me, the door to my office ajar. And he wore the widest smirk. It felt eerie.

I smiled at him, then stepped into the elevator. My smile faded. Was Cheyenne right? Was my brother up to something?

No, he couldn't have been. Even if he was jealous of me,

he'd never want to hurt our father's company. He loved Mom and Dad.

When the elevator arrived on the first floor, I stepped off and headed outside to the parking lot. I got into my SUV and drove home. When I unlocked the door, I realized Anna had called my home phone a dozen times. I deleted all her messages and took a much-needed hot shower.

I needed to wash Anna's stain off me. I wanted this small town to be a new start. I couldn't afford to bring any baggage along for the adventure. Whatever happened in Los Angeles stayed in Los Angeles, I promised myself.

Once I had gotten out of the shower and dressed, I headed downstairs, turning the TV on. The breaking news caught my eye. The headline on the TV read MILLION-AIRE CEO ETHAN MILES STEPS DOWN, CITING BAD BUSINESS DEAL. There was a picture of my face on the screen.

"Damn," I muttered. "My brother works fast."

I turned up the volume, listening to what the reporter was saying. "...and we've just gotten word from Nathan Miles that his brother, Ethan, has been fired from his role as CEO after losing money in a bad business deal. He's been kicked out of the family and lost everything. Nathan Miles is taking his place as CEO..."

"Didn't need to run my name completely through the mud," I grumbled.

But this was good. Hopefully, people would see it and think I didn't have any more money. If someone wanted to date me, there wouldn't be any fortune for them. I hoped it was a good plan.

When my smartphone buzzed, I reached for it, noticing it was my dad's number. I picked up immediately. "Hey, Dad—"

"What the hell is going on over at my company?" he

screeched, making me pull the phone away. "I just saw the news. You better start explaining!"

I winced. "Yeah, I know it looks bad. But it's not real. Nate and I made it up."

"Made what up? What are you talking about?"

"You know how I broke up with Anna last night? Well, after that, I mentioned to Nate that I was sick of women only dating me for my money. He proposed I pretend to lose all my money and hand the company over to him for a month while I look for someone special. Someone to love me for me."

It sounded cheesy, but I wanted that more than anything. More than my money and father's company and all the business deals in the world.

I heard Mom sigh in the background. "Are you still going on about true love, Ethan? Didn't we already have this conversation?"

"We did—and I've made my decision. Don't worry, I'll be back to work in a month. Nate's handling the business while I'm gone. I've never taken a vacation so it'll be fun, even if I don't find anyone special."

Mom and Dad were quiet for a few seconds. Did they not approve?

"Uh, hello? You guys are still there, right?"

"We're still here," Dad replied. "It's just...a little far-fetched. Why are you so sure you're going to meet someone within a month?"

"Well, I'm not. I just hope I will. Once my reputation spreads, everyone will think I'm a broke failure. Whoever wants to be with me after that will like me for who I am. I'll show them my personality, my sense of humor, my goals and passions. They'll see me for that instead of the money."

"I hope understand what you're doing, darling," Mom

quavered. "Because it sounds like you're looking for a needle in a haystack."

Why did I think Mom and Dad would understand? All they knew was money. That was the reason Mom had married my father, after all. What did they know about true love?

"Yeah, well, it's my life," I clipped. "I don't want or need approval. I'm leaving for a small town in Maine. My secretary told me it's a lovely place."

"Hmm," Dad replied. "Dear, could you grab me a drink from the kitchen?"

I heard Mom kiss his cheek. "Of course, honey. Be right back."

As Mom's footsteps faded, Dad whispered, "I don't want your mother overhearing this."

I frowned. "Dad, what's going on?"

"Didn't you ever wonder why I gave you the company instead of your brother? Even though he's the eldest?"

"I just...well, I didn't question it. It was your company."

"You're right—and I wanted you to run it. We both know your brother...he isn't the most reliable or mature person. You were the better choice, Ethan, and I stand by that. I'm concerned that you're leaving the business in his hands."

Dad wasn't the only concerned party. I thought back to what Cheyenne had told me. But it was too late now—the contract was signed. I wasn't going to tell that to Dad, though.

"Look, I'm sure everything will be fine. Nate isn't a total idiot. He wouldn't do anything to jeopardize your company," I assured him. "If you're so worried, why don't you stop by the office? Hang around until I'm back? A month isn't that long."

Dad sighed. "I wish I could, son, but my Parkinson's is worsening. I haven't told you kids or your mom that."

"Oh, no. Dad..."

"Don't worry, Eth. I'll be fine," Dad rasped. "Anyway, maybe I'm just overreacting. I'm sure your brother will do a great job. And if not, you'll be back in a month to run the company."

"Right. Dad...if you ever need to talk, about the illness, I mean, you have my number. I'm here for you. We don't just have to talk business all the time."

"Thanks, son. But I don't think I'm ready to talk about it just yet. I'll let you know when I am."

"Okay. Take care of yourself, Dad."

"I will. And look, if you need to do this...then I can't stop you. Have a good time, Ethan. I hope you find the woman you're looking for."

"You and me both. Talk to you later, Dad."

As I hung up, Mom was bringing Dad his drink. I hoped he would be all right. I knew Parkinson's was difficult, but it sounded like Dad was struggling. If he needed me, I'd drop everything in a heartbeat to help him.

For now, there wasn't anything I could do for Dad. Before making dinner, I decided to look up Bridgewood on Google. It seemed like a quiet, peaceful town—full of rolling hills, lakes, and plenty of sunshine. No wonder Cheyenne and her girlfriend loved it there.

I searched for the Cozybrook Inn next, landing on their website. It was run by a family and looked like a nice lodge to stay at. And Cheyenne was right—the innkeeper's daughter *was* beautiful. Long, dark hair, green eyes, freckles, and soft, porcelain skin. There was a picture of her smiling while working the front desk with her parents.

"Taylor Kennedy," I read off the screen. "Well, I'll meet you soon enough."

I shut my laptop, then made dinner. Once I had eaten, I packed two suitcases full of clothes and books for my adventure and went to bed. I was going to need my rest.

When the next morning came, I checked my home phone's messages, realizing Anna had stopped calling. Did it have anything to do with me pretending to lose all my money? What a gold digger.

After making sure I had everything, I dragged my suitcase out to my SUV and paused. I couldn't show up to a small town in such an expensive car. People might suspect I had money. I needed something more fitting.

So I drove to the bank first, taking out a few thousand and tucking it into my suitcase. I'd need that to afford my stay at the inn. Then I headed to a local car dealership, searching for something that screamed small town. A greasy-haired salesman came up to me while nervously fidgeting with his suit.

"Hello, sir," he began. "Can I help you? You look familiar..."

I nodded, glancing up from a sedan. "My name's Ethan Miles. My father started the Miles Marketing Company."

"That's where I know you from!" the man cried. "Hey, didn't you lose all your money or something?"

People had already seen the news. This was good, making me hope my reputation would spread to the smaller towns too.

I decided to play along, nodding. "Yeah, unfortunately. Anyway, I'm looking to sell my SUV and get something more affordable."

The salesman patted my car. "It's a nice vehicle—very expensive. I think I've got a few things to show you. Come with me."

I followed the salesman, heading to the back parking lot. I searched through the many vehicles before landing on a blue pickup truck. It was perfect—a four-seater with some room in the cargo bed to haul my things.

"I like this." I ran my hand along the hood. "Do you think it'd blend in well in a small town? I'm moving today."

"Yes, I think so. If you're interested, I could write up the contract right now. And you'd still have money left over from the sale of your SUV."

"Let's do it," I answered before I could doubt myself.

The salesman led me inside, writing up a contract for the truck. I traded in the SUV and signed my name. Then he handed me a few thousand. I tucked it all inside my suitcase. When everything was finalized, he handed me the key and wished me well. I put my suitcases in the back and hopped in the driver's seat.

I ran my hands along the smooth steering wheel, reaching for my smartphone. "All right, let's do this. Siri? Set my GPS to Bridgewood, Maine. And play some country songs on Spotify, will you? I need to get in that small town mindset."

As Siri turned on the GPS, *Life is A Highway* began playing. I stepped on the gas and pulled away from the car dealership. This was it—I was on my way to a small town, hoping to find the woman of my dreams. And if not, I'd still have a fun vacation.

As long as my brother wasn't scheming while I was gone.

Chapter Five

Forty-six hours.

That was the length of the drive from Los Angeles, California to Bridgewood, Maine. My butt went numb, and I had to pee, so I pulled over a bunch of times, finding cheap motels and truck stops. Eating breakfast with the bikers early one morning was definitely a highlight.

But I didn't mind. It had been eons since I had taken a road trip. My family and I rarely went on vacation when I was a kid—Dad was always too busy and Mom was always off shopping or attending some charity ball. For once, I felt normal.

When I crossed over into Maine, I realized how completely different it was from California. There were no palm trees but plenty of forests, ravines, and lakes. The air was fresher. The people were friendlier. The seafood smelled delicious. As I drove down a long road, I passed a sign that read WELCOME TO BRIDGEWOOD.

The sun rose. I smiled. I was almost there, almost at my new life.

Then I heard something crackle in my truck. When smoke erupted from under the hood, I immediately pulled over. Nestled between the trees and bushes, I jumped out and dashed toward the front of my truck.

When I opened the hood, smoke blasted into my face. I coughed, waving the grey fog away. I didn't understand mechanics, but I realized that wasn't a good sign. I pulled out my phone, but there was no signal.

Great. What was I supposed to do now?

The truck wasn't safe to drive—not when it was still smoking—and I was out in the middle of nowhere. There were no people or houses for miles. Not a good start to my love adventure. Just when I thought I'd have to start walking, I heard a car down the road.

When I spotted headlights, I jumped onto the road and waved my arms back and forth. "Hey, stop! I need help!"

The person slammed on the brakes, stopping inches away from me. I gasped. If they had hit the brakes a second later, I would've added injury to my list of problems. The door opened. A woman stepped out of the driver's seat of a red pickup truck. It was similar to mine, though hers appeared much better and cheaper.

"Are you crazy?" she squealed. "I could've hit you!"

I took her in for a second. She seemed around my age, maybe a few years younger. She was beautiful—and seemed familiar. With her long dark hair, green eyes, freckles, cardigan, and jeans, I knew I had seen her somewhere before. But where?

"Well?" she demanded, her hands on her hips. "You got anything to say for yourself, stranger?"

I cleared my throat. "Right, sorry. Thanks for stopping. My truck started smoking, you see, and I didn't think it was safe to drive. I flagged you for some help."

"You're right, you shouldn't drive a smoking truck," she scolded. "This yours?"

"Yeah—brand new too. Just bought it from a dealership."

She winced. "I think you bought a lemon. Here, let me inspect it for you."

I watched as she approached the hood, peering down. I stood behind her. "You know mechanics?"

She turned to me. "What, you think just because I'm a girl I don't know anything about cars?"

"No, I didn't mean that at all!" I stammered. Nice going, Ethan, way to insult the first woman you met. No wonder you're single. "I didn't mean to offend you at all—"

Then she started giggling. "I'm just kidding, stranger. Not offended. And yeah, I do know a few things about cars. Worked on them with my dad while growing up."

I sighed with relief. "Oh. Well, do you know what's wrong with it?"

She closed the hood. "Your engine's overheating. Can be caused by a number of things. You'll need a professional mechanic."

"Good idea. I don't have any phone reception, though. Can you help?"

"Sure, I can give you a lift. My parents own an inn not too far from here."

Then it hit me—she was the woman from the Cozybrook Inn's website. Talk about fate.

"Are you talking about the Cozybrook Inn?"

"Yeah, I am. You heard of us?"

"I have—one of my friends recommended your inn. Thought I'd come here on vacation. Do you remember her? Cheyenne and her girlfriend, Alicia?"

She paused. "I might. We get a lot of customers—it's hard to remember. And you're in luck since I'm heading back to the inn. I'll take you there where you can call a tow truck."

"Perfect, thank you. You don't know how grateful I am."

"No problem." She paused, eyeing me. "Before we go, though...you're not a serial killer or anything, are you?"

"I was, but I gave it up."

She blinked. "I sincerely hope you're joking."

I smiled. "I am. Don't worry—I'm not a serial killer. Just a guy looking for a nice vacation. My name's Ethan, by the way."

I didn't give her my last name just in case she looked me up. I was trying to leave the reputation of my family behind for as long as I could.

"Taylor. Taylor Kennedy," she replied, shaking my hand. "Nice to meet you, Ethan. Where you from?"

"LA," I answered, following her to her truck. "You've got a nice little town here. From what I've seen so far, at least."

"Trust me, it gets better. Hop in." Taylor leapt into the driver's seat. "You'll love Bridgewood. It's a nice town."

"So I've been told." I climbed into the passenger seat, shutting the door. I spied a bunch of fabrics in the back of her truck. "Wow, you got a lot of stuff back there."

She nodded, pulling away from the side of the road. "Yeah, I travel to the closest city to get some materials. Portland is just a few miles from here."

"I see. You planning on doing anything special with the fabrics?"

She shifted. "Nah. They're for the inn. So, Mr. LA, what do you do for a living?"

"Uh, just a boring corporate job," I lied. "Nothing special. But tell me a little about your inn. What's it like running the place?"

On the drive into Bridgewood, I chatted with Taylor. Our conversation was natural—and I made her giggle a few times. I learned that her inn was family-owned for generations and would be passed down to her one day. She didn't know it, but we had similar backstories.

"You'll meet my parents soon enough," she continued.

"Sharon and Mark Kennedy. And my cousin, Madison, is staying with us for the summer. Ugh."

I snorted. "Not too happy about that?"

"You can tell, huh?" She glanced at me before turning back toward the road. "She's just...a lot to deal with. Stay away from her if you can. Trust me, you'll thank me later."

I promised I would, though I sensed there was more to the story. I didn't want to pry and seem ungrateful. Ten minutes later, we drove through a quiet town. It was filled with quaint village homes, gorgeous parks, and little shops. My eyes were glued to the window.

"Welcome to the heart of Bridgewood." Taylor caught me gaping. "For a small town, there's always something going on. How long are you staying, city boy?"

"Only a month."

"Ah, good. Plenty of time to explore. We've got some festivals coming up that I think you'll like. Here we are, by the way."

She turned left, pulling into a parking lot. It sat next to a large forest with chirping birds and crickets. The inn itself was beautiful—like something out of the Middle Ages. The columns were rustic. There were wooden benches out front, plus a garden and a pond. The walls were painted brown with a stone sign that read WELCOME TO THE COZY-BROOK INN.

"The front desk has a phone you can use." Taylor turned off her truck. "Much better reception in there. Come on."

I nodded, stepping out of her truck and following her up the wooden steps. When she opened the double doors, she let me enter first. Then I stopped in the foyer and scanned the place. The inn wasn't what I was used to back in Los Angeles, but it had a certain charm to it.

There were deer heads on the walls as well as paintings of mountains and forests. The red carpet stretched around the foyer, beginning at the door before leading to the front desk and down a large hallway. A wooden staircase leading up to the upper level, which contained many rooms. An elderly woman stood at the front desk, speaking into the phone. She wore jeans and a t-shirt with an apron. Her red hair was turning grey.

Just as I approached her, somebody opened the door down the hall. Behind that door was a storage closet with supplies—toilet paper, towels, and other toiletries. An elderly man with a white beard and hair came out. He wore shorts, a Hawaiian shirt, and sandals. He spoke to a man around my age, who had blond hair, dark eyes, a t-shirt, and jeans. The blond carried a toolbox of hammers and lightbulbs.

"Thanks for coming on such short notice, Drew," the elderly man told him. "We're in your debt."

Drew shook his head, still clutching his toolbox. "Don't worry about it, Mr. Kennedy. Anything for Taylor and her family."

The two men noticed us and smiled at Taylor. Drew couldn't stop staring at her. Maybe he was her boyfriend or husband. Of course—a beautiful girl like that probably had a partner.

"Ah, Taylor. You're back," the elderly man said. "Who's this?"

"Ethan," Taylor answered. "His truck broke down outside Bridgewood. He just needs to use our phone to call a tow truck."

"Certainly—the phone's right over there. Once my wife is done using it, it's all yours." The elderly man held out his hand. "Nice to meet you, Ethan. My name's Mark Kennedy, Taylor's father and the owner of this fine inn. We live and work here."

"I know, Taylor told me a little about you on the drive here." I shook his hand. "Nice to meet you, sir."

"You gave this guy a ride?" Drew cried, his eyes widening. "What if he hurt you?"

"He didn't," Taylor snapped. "And I can take care of myself. Ethan, this is Drew Patterson, my best friend and electrician."

"Who saved us again when our light in the storage closet wouldn't come on," Taylor's father added. "He's a good soul."

"Just doing my best." Drew reached over to shake my hand. "A pleasure."

I tried not to wince at his strong grip. "Yeah, likewise. Anyway, thanks for the ride, Taylor. You really saved me back there."

She shrugged. "Don't mention it. Hope you can get your truck sorted out. Dad, Ethan's going to be staying with us for a month. He heard from a friend about our inn and wanted to check it out. Came all the way from LA for a vacation."

Her father's eyes light up. "Is that right? Well, I'm pleased to hear word of our inn has spread that far. I'll get a room ready for you while you use the phone."

I nodded. "Thank you, I'd appreciate that. Excuse me."

As I walked toward the front desk, I sensed Drew's eyes on my back. That guy clearly didn't like me. I wasn't in the mood for drama—having enough of that back home—so I ignored him and approached the elderly woman at the front desk. She had just hung up. Now she was writing something down on a notepad.

I cleared my throat. "Excuse me, but are you Taylor's mother?"

The woman glanced up. "That's right—Sharon Kennedy. My husband and I run this inn. Can I help you?"

"I just need to use your phone. My truck broke down outside town and Taylor gave me a drive."

"Oh, you poor thing! Of course, feel free to use the

phone. I've got a phone book right here if you need to find a tow truck."

I thanked her, reaching for the telephone. I was relieved to hear a dial tone when I picked it up. Searching through the phone book, I found the number of the only local tow truck and called their number.

"Yeah?" an elderly man answered gruffly.

"Uh, hi," I began. "My truck broke down outside Bridgewood. There's smoke coming from under the hood. Do you think you can tow my truck to the nearest mechanic?"

"You're in luck—I'm also the town's mechanic," he muttered. "Yeah, I can do that. Make and model?"

"Ford F-150 in blue. Trust me, you can't miss it. It's smoking like a chimney on the road into town."

"I'll find it. Meet me at Patterson's Mechanic in twenty minutes. And bring cash."

Before I could respond, he hung up. Grumpy old man. I hung up too, wondering if he had any relationship to Drew. They had the same last name.

When I turned around, Taylor's father had vanished. Taylor was still there with Drew, arguing in hushed whispers. I walked over, clearing my throat.

"Uh, sorry," I interrupted. "But if it isn't too much trouble, can you drive me to the local mechanic shop? Patterson Mechanic?"

"That's my uncle's business," Drew clipped. "He'll fix you up. In fact, I can drive you there myself."

"No need. I'll do it," Taylor responded quickly. "I just need to bring in the fabrics I bought in Portland. Give me a few minutes."

I nodded, watching as Taylor walked outside to her truck. Drew glared at me but didn't speak. I cleared my throat, changing the subject.

"So, nice town you got here," I chirped. "And Taylor seems nice."

"She's the best." Drew hovered over me. "And she doesn't need some stranger from out of town hitting on her. She's been through a lot."

She had? Like what? I was curious but didn't want to push it.

I scoffed. "Sorry, but I think you have the wrong impression here. I haven't hit on her."

"Uh-huh," Drew muttered. "Just stay away from her, all right?"

The guy reeked of hostility and jealousy. Before I could respond, Taylor walked in, carrying the fabrics. She gestured at the wooden staircase.

"Just need to bring these up to our attic," she explained. "That's where my bedroom is. I'll be quick."

"Take your time." I smiled. "I'm in no rush."

She nodded, then caught Drew still staring at us. I didn't like the way he eyed her. As she walked by, he grabbed her arm.

"Text me when you get back." Drew glowered at me. "I want to make sure you're safe."

She wiggled out of his grasp. "I'll be fine, Drew. See you later."

As Taylor stormed upstairs, Drew shook his head. He sneered at me and headed outside. Whatever was going on around here, I wanted to stay out of it. All I wanted to do was fix my truck so I could get back to finding love.

If it even existed in this small town—or maybe I was jinxed.

Chapter Six

I stood by the front door for ten minutes, patiently waiting for Taylor to return. What was taking so long? For now, she was my only ride. Fortunately, her mother kept feeding me cheese and crackers while answering phone calls.

A few minutes later, I decided to check on Taylor. I walked down the hallway, exploring the inn. I took the stairs to the second floor. The rooms were empty.

I poked my head inside one. It seemed cozy—silk sheets with a brown headboard, a small television, and little mints on the pillows. Whether I found love or not in this town, I was going to enjoy my stay. When I noticed the stairs to the attic, I climbed up and found Taylor.

She stood near a mannequin, adjusting a piece of fabric on it. She held a measuring tape and a pair of scissors. The attic was covered with fabric, sewing supplies, and more mannequins. Taylor was practically running her own little shop up here.

I cleared my throat. "Sorry to interrupt..."

Taylor jumped. "Oh, Ethan—you scared me! I guess I was taking a while, huh?"

"I don't mean to rush you, but it is important that I get to the mechanic. I'd like my truck back soon. If he can fix it, that is."

"Of course, of course. I'm so sorry. Sometimes I lose track of time when I'm up in the attic."

I took a step forward, eyeing the mannequins. "You've got some nice designs in here. Are you a fashion designer?"

Taylor blushed. "Nah, it's just a hobby."

"Well, you're great at it. Maybe you should pursue it professionally."

"Thank you, I appreciate that. The thought *has* crossed my mind."

"As it should—you're amazing." I pointed at a mannequin wearing a purple suit, fingering the fabric. "I'd wear that. Nice material too."

"Thanks, that piece is my favorite." Then Taylor sighed. "Anyway, I won't waste any more of your time. Let's get you to that mechanic."

"Sounds good. Hey, I don't mean to pry, but...is everything okay with you and that Drew guy? I caught you two arguing."

Taylor nodded. "Oh, yeah—we're fine. When you've been friends as long as we have, some problems crop up. I've known him since we were in diapers."

I whistled. "That's a long time. Are you two...together?"

Taylor was appalled. "Oh, no way. I love Drew—but as a friend. He's more like a brother to me than anything."

Ouch. I didn't respond, but I could tell Drew had feelings for her. But did Taylor catch on? It wasn't my place to break the news. I didn't come to this town to meddle in people's lives.

"You must have friendships like that," Taylor continued. "Where you've been friends so long that being with them romantically would just be weird."

I shifted uncomfortably. "Yeah, I guess so. Growing up...I didn't have many friends. It was just me, my parents, and my brother."

Mainly because people only liked me for my money. I closed myself off to friendships. Until I met Cheyenne.

Taylor frowned. "Oh, I'm sorry. That must've been hard. Well, I'll show you to the mechanic. Come with me."

I let Taylor go first, heading down the stairs. She nodded at her parents as we passed before leaving the inn. We got into her truck, then she pulled off and drove deeper into town. Taylor pulled into the parking lot of a small mechanic shop a few minutes later.

"Here we are," she announced, putting her truck in park. "Let's hope Mr. Patterson can fix your truck. He's pretty smart—I have faith in him."

"He sounded like a total grump on the phone."

Taylor snorted. "Yeah, Drew's uncle can be pretty unfriendly if you don't know him. Rest assured, he'll try his best to get you back on the road."

I reached for the door, taking a deep breath. "Let's hope. And hey, thanks again for the ride. You saved me."

"Don't mention it. It was my good deed for the day." Taylor smiled. "I don't have much planned today, so why don't I come with you? Maybe Mr. Patterson will treat you better if I'm there."

"Yes, please. A little backup never hurts."

As I stepped out of Taylor's truck, I heard a horn behind me. A large tow truck pulled into the parking lot, with my truck attached. It was still smoking. I hoped he could fix it. Otherwise I'd have to book a plane ticket to get home.

"There he is." Taylor hopped out of her truck. "Let's see what he has to say. Mr. Patterson!"

She rushed toward the tow truck, then I followed. The grumpy Mr. Patterson—balding, tired, and wearing overalls while carrying a toolbox—slid out of the driver's seat, spotting us.

"Taylor. And you must be the man who called me about the truck," Mr. Patterson drawled. "She's not in good shape. Where'd you get this truck from? A junkyard?"

"No, a car dealership back in Los Angeles. It lasted forty-six hours before giving out."

"Looks like you bought a lemon," Mr. Patterson grumbled. "Let me examine the truck. Wait there and stay out of my way."

I nodded, stepping off to the side as Mr. Patterson grabbed his tools and opened my truck's hood. Taylor and I watched as he checked under the hood and tinkered with a few nozzles. Then he stepped back, wiping his greasy hands on an oil rag.

"I see the problem," Mr. Patterson began. "Your truck's got a bad ground wire."

I didn't know what that meant, but it didn't sound good. "Oh no. Can you fix it?"

He nodded. "Yep, but it'll cost you."

"How much?"

"Several thousand. It ain't cheap."

I almost scowled. I had brought some money, but not that much. I was going to need some help.

"All right, I can get the money," I replied. "I just need to call my family. They'll loan me what I need. Can you get started right away?"

Mr. Patterson nodded. "Sure can. And you better have the money when I'm done."

"I will. Please, get started. Excuse me while I call some people. Hopefully I'll get some reception out here."

Mr. Patterson grunted, heading into his shop to grab some supplies. Taylor turned to me. "Your family's just going to give you the money?"

I didn't want to mention we were rich, so I just shrugged. "Yeah, we've got some savings. Then I'll pay them back when I get home. I have no choice."

"Right. Well, good luck. I'll wait for you in the shop."

It was nice of Taylor to stick around for me. I didn't know why she was doing it—if she just wanted to be a Good Samaritan or if she liked me. Maybe I was reading too much into things. And right now, my truck needed my attention.

I pulled my smartphone out of my pocket, relieved to see one bar. Hopefully that would be enough to call my family. I decided to call Nathan first, not wanting to stress out my parents. They disapproved of this plan enough.

I called Nathan. The phone rang and rang. Then it went to voicemail. I pulled my phone away from my ear, frowning. Nathan had never ignored my calls before. What was going on?

I knew there was a time difference between California and Maine, but still, he should've answered. I called twice more. Still nothing. Sighing, I dialed my dad's number and waited as it rang. He finally answered on the third ring.

"You have some nerve calling me," he grumbled. "Your mother and I are very angry with you right now, Ethan."

I frowned. "Angry about what? Me leaving? I thought you came to terms with it."

"Not that," Dad snapped. "Your brother called and told us your real feelings about the company. I'm hurt you didn't tell me first."

"Dad, I honestly have no idea what you're talking about. Nate called you? What did he say?"

Dad groaned. "I can't talk right now—I'm having a bad Parkinson's' flare-up. We'll discuss this another time. Good-bye, son."

"Dad, wait—"

But he already hung up. I pulled my phone away from my

ear, completely confused. Something was going on—something my brother was involved in. But what? And what had he told Mom and Dad that had made them so angry?

I shook my head, deciding to deal with that drama later. I needed the money to pay for the mechanic now. I headed toward the shop, opening the door with the chime of the bell. Mr. Patterson was still working under the hood of my truck. As I entered, scanning the room, I noticed some cars in the shop to be repaired. There was a front desk with a phone, a bank machine, and some chairs.

Taylor sat there, reading a gossip magazine. She glanced up when she heard me enter. "Ethan, there you are. Did you hear from your family?"

"Uh, no," I lied. "They're probably just busy. Does that ATM over there work?"

"Of course—Mr. Patterson installed it a few months ago."

I reached into my pocket, pulling out my wallet. "Good, I'll take some money out. Then I can pay off Mr. Patterson and finally get my truck back."

I walked toward the ATM, inserting my card. But there was an error. It kept telling me the card wasn't functional. I took the card out, blowing on it a few times before re-inserting, but it still wouldn't work.

"Okay, what the hell is going on?" I muttered.

Taylor stood up, setting her magazine aside and walking over. "Everything okay? The ATM not working?"

"No, I think it's my card. Hang on, let me call my bank."

Taylor nodded, heading back to her seat. I heard Mr. Patterson working on my truck outside as I reached for my phone. Luckily, it still had one bar. I dialed my bank and went through all the options before finally speaking with an associate.

"How can I help you today?"

"Hi, my name's Ethan. Ethan Miles," I whispered. "I'm trying to use my card at an ATM, but it keeps declining. Can you tell me what's going on?"

"One moment please." I gave him all my information, then heard typing before he spoke again. "Ah, I see the issue. The card was cancelled. You no longer have access to your account."

"I...what? Why not?"

"A man named Nathan Miles cancelled the card. He had access to your account."

I froze. Why and how would my brother have access to my account?

"That's...that's impossible," I wailed. "Are you sure about that?"

"Yes, sir. I'm afraid you no longer have access to any of your accounts."

Okay, things were just getting weirder. First my brother wasn't answering my calls. Then he said something to my parents. Now I couldn't access my bank account. I needed to speak with him.

I sighed. "Okay, well...thanks for letting me know. Goodbye."

As I hung up, I leaned on the front desk. The only money I had left was in my suitcase. And that wasn't enough to cover the cost of the truck repair. What was I going to do?

I'd never been this hopeless before. My family had never struggled with money. I was out of my element, miserable, and alone.

Taylor cleared her throat. "Um, is everything okay? You look pretty upset."

I turned around, sighing. "Yeah, it's just...I don't have enough money to fix my truck. I'll have to let Mr. Patterson keep it."

"Oh no. That's awful," Taylor cried, rising to her feet. "If

I had the money, I'd loan it to you. But I don't have that kind of cash."

But I did—or I was supposed to. And now it was in my brother's possession.

"Thanks, that's kind of you." I sat down. "I don't know what I'll do. Guess I don't have a ride anymore."

Taylor thought for a second. "I might have a solution. The inn's been looking for a new employee. Someone to help out with cooking and cleaning. You could get a job and pay off your truck that way."

"Would your parents hire me?"

"Why not? And you could have a room at the inn too. You wouldn't have to pay for it since you're working for us."

Without anywhere else to go, and no other way to make money, I had little choice. It wasn't the job I was used to, but it would pay the bills.

"Okay, I accept. And thanks," I replied. "You saved me. Again. You're a superhero."

Taylor blushed. "I'm not, but thanks. You do know how to cook and clean, right?"

"I do. I can make a mean grilled cheese, in fact."

"Perfect," she said. "Well, let's go tell Mr. Patterson. He'll have to wait to get his money, but it's better than nothing."

I nodded, leaving the shop with Taylor. We crossed the parking lot to reach Mr. Patterson, who was hunched over my truck's hood. At least it had stopped smoking.

Taylor cleared her throat. "Mr. Patterson? Ethan found a way to pay for your services."

Mr. Patterson glanced up. Some oil stained his collar. "Good. Just leave the money on my desk."

"Uh, actually, I'd like to pay in installments," I replied. "I'm going to work at the Cozybrook Inn for now. When I get paid, I'll send you the money. I hope that's okay."

Mr. Patterson began to argue before Taylor spoke up.

"Mr. Patterson, please. Go easy on Ethan. He seems like a good guy—I'm sure he'll get you the money as fast as he can."

I was glad I had Taylor on my side. Without her, I would've still been broken down on the side of the road with a smoking truck.

Mr. Patterson narrowed his eyes. "Hmm. Fine—as long as you don't miss a payment. If you do, I'll have to confiscate your truck."

I sighed in relief. "Sounds fair. Don't worry, I always pay back my debts. I'll get you that money."

"You better. And good news—it should be ready soon. Within the next hour."

"We'll wait around, then," Taylor offered, glancing at me. "At least you'll have a ride again."

It was one of the only things I had left.

"True. Though I did enjoy having you as my chauffeur. Five out of five stars."

Her giggle was a beautiful sound. It set off butterflies inside my stomach. Yes, men get butterflies too. Especially around beautiful women from small towns.

"Come on, there's a French fry truck just up the block," Taylor chirped. "Lunch is on me. We'll be back, Mr. Patterson."

The old man waved us off, then I followed Taylor down the road. She knew her way around Bridgewood pretty well. I was still a wide-eyed tourist.

"If you don't mind," I began, "I'll keep trying to call my family."

Taylor nodded. "Of course, go ahead. Just meet me at the truck when you're ready. It's just down that street to the left. You can't miss it."

As she walked off, I pulled out my smartphone again. I had two bars now. Instead of calling Nathan, I decided to text him. At least I knew that would go through.

ME

Dude, what's going on? I can't access any of my bank accounts. And Mom and Dad are mad at me. What did you do?

To my surprise, Nathan called me a second later. I answered immediately. "Nate, hey. You got my text? Why didn't you answer my calls?"

"Eth, I'm sorry. I've been a little busy running the company," Nathan replied. There was chatter in the background. "Yeah, I cut you off from the family fortune for a bit. Just to give you a more authentic 'average guy' experience."

"But I need access to my account. I have to pay off a loan. My truck broke down just outside Bridgewood."

"Oh no, that's terrible. Fine, fine—I'll call the bank and get you access to the family account again. Happy?"

"Yeah, since it's my money too. How did you even have the right to do that? I don't remember giving you permission to my bank."

"It was in the contract you signed. You gave me total control over the company and all the family accounts. Including yours, little brother."

I frowned. "I did? I don't remember that."

"Well, it was in the contract. You should've read it thoroughly. Anyway, I have to get back to work now."

When I heard giggling in the background, I recognized that voice. "Is that...Anna?"

"What? Oh, yeah. I took her out on a date. To some fancy restaurant in Los Angeles. You gave me the OK."

"Yeah, I did. But I thought you were at work."

"Well, I...I was. But I took a break to call you back and see Anna. Anyway, I have to go. Don't want to be rude to my date."

"Wait! What did you say to Mom and Dad? They were furious at me when I called."

"Oh, just that I think you'll be much happier on vacation for a little while. That's all. Not sure why they'd be so angry at you."

For some reason, I didn't trust Nathan. I knew he had said something worse to Mom and Dad. But why? What was his endgame?

"Okay. I'll let you go now. Talk again soon, Nate."

"Bye, Ethan. And good luck. You'll need it, brother."

The call ended with one final cackle from Anna. What was Nathan's cryptic comment about? And just what exactly was in that contract I signed?

Chapter Seven

I couldn't get over my brother's weird behavior. What had I done to deserve that? As long as he called the bank company and gave me access to the family account again, I could forgive him. Mostly.

I walked down the street, finding Taylor ordering our food at the French fry truck. An elderly couple ran it, handing Taylor two hot dogs. She smiled at them and took the food.

"Thanks, guys," she cheered. "Your food is always amazing!"

The elderly couple thanked her, then Taylor turned around, noticing me. I gestured at the hot dogs. "They're appetizing."

"They're incredible." Taylor handed me a hot dog. "Here you are. Wait, you're not vegetarian or anything, are you?"

"Nope—I'm an omnivore." I bit into the hot dog. "You're right, that is good. Once I get back on my feet, I'll pay you back for everything. For helping me fix my truck, for buying the hot dogs. I promise."

Taylor shook her head, eating her hot dog. "Don't worry about it, Ethan. Everyone needs help sometimes."

Didn't I know it.

"Come on, let's sit on that picnic table over there." Taylor gestured toward a table a few feet away. It had a yellow umbrella over it. "So, how did the phone call go?"

"Oh, uh, my brother told me that he'd help me out," I mumbled as I walked with Taylor to the table, sitting across from her. "He's just busy with work right now."

"I see. What does he do?"

"The same thing as me—a boring corporate job. That's life in the city for you."

Taylor shook her head, finishing her hot dog. "I'm glad that's not me. I like living in a small town—running the inn with my parents, doing my own thing. That's freedom to me."

"Sounds like a nice life. Have you always lived in Bridgewood?"

"Yep, born and raised. I've never known anything else. I was actually supposed to go to New York, but...that didn't work out."

I swallowed the last bite of my hot dog, raising an eyebrow. "Oh, no? What happened? New York is pretty far from here."

Just as she opened her mouth, my phone rang. I pulled it out and noticed the bar was fading and reappearing. I wasn't going to have much time to talk. It was Cheyenne's number I should answer.

"Sorry," I lamented. "I have to take this. Be right back."

She nodded, staying at the picnic table as I rose to my feet. I had to admit—she was beautiful, her dark hair tousled by the wind. Then I scolded myself. Taylor was just a friend. Right?

I walked toward a nearby tree, answering my phone. "Hello? Cheyenne?"

"Ethan, hi," she began. "I need to talk to you."

"What about? Everything okay?"

"Yes and no," Cheyenne whispered. I could hear the sounds of the office in the background. "I'm at work right now. Nathan just got back from lunch. He went on a date with Anna, by the way. Your ex."

I sighed. "Yeah, I know. But I don't care if he dates her. She's not my girlfriend anymore. She can do whatever she wants."

"Right, just thought you should know. I *did* promise to be your spy after all. And you need to hear what Nathan said about you while you've been gone."

"Uh oh. What is it now?"

"He was glad you were gone. Now he can run the company how he wants to. That this is the way it was supposed to be. I think he must've forgotten we were friends or something, because he didn't care who heard him."

"Huh," I replied. "He *has* been acting strange lately. He wouldn't answer my calls, then he said something to my parents that pissed them off. And the final cherry on top? He took away my access to the family bank account. I can't get the Miles fortune anymore."

Cheyenne gasped. "What? Can he even do that?"

"Apparently. It was in the contract he made me sign. I should've read the thing first. Stupid me for trusting my brother, huh?"

"Well, it's too late now. Something weird is going on here, Ethan. I'm worried."

I was too, though I didn't want to admit it and freak Cheyenne out. Or myself.

"Then it's a good thing you're still there," I declared. "It's more important than ever that you become my eyes and ears. And I need a huge favor."

"Anything for you, Ethan. You know you don't have to ask."

"I need you to find that contract. Then text me a picture of it. I have a feeling my brother's up to something."

"Okay, I can do that. Just give me some time. It won't be easy to sneak into his office and find it. He's implemented some new rules since you've been gone. And one of them is to stay out of his office."

"That's fine—take your time, Cheyenne. I don't want you to lose your job. If you get caught, then just forget about it."

"No, I'm going to get that contract for you, Ethan. It's the least I can do. You doing okay otherwise? Did you make it to Bridgewood?"

I nodded, glancing at Taylor. She was gazing at the clouds. "I did. It's a beautiful place. You were right. Had a little trouble with my truck though. Fortunately, the family that owns the Cozybrook Inn is helping me out."

"Aw, that's sweet. The Kennedy family, right? They were nice when I was there."

"That's right, the Kennedy's. And their daughter, Taylor, is incredible. She's saved my butt a few times."

I could sense Cheyenne smiling through the phone. "Oh, I see. Is something brewing there?"

I blushed. "Cheyenne, please. Taylor's been nice to me, but I'm not sure if it'll evolve beyond that. She's got her own problems. And now, so do I."

"Yeah, definitely. I told you...your brother has never rubbed me the right way. Anyway, I'll let you know when I've got that contract."

"Great, thanks. And be careful, Cheyenne. Take care."

"You too, Ethan. Come back in one piece."

I promised I would, hanging up and walking back to Taylor. She glanced up with concern. "Everything all right?"

"Yeah, I'm fine," I reassured her. "A friend just called to

check up on me. The same one who gave me such a good review for your inn."

"That's sweet. When you get back home, tell them we said thank you. You ready to head back to the mechanic now?"

I rubbed my stomach. "Definitely. And that hot dog hit the spot. The next time we go out for lunch, it'll be on me."

Taylor rose to her feet, eyeing me. "The next time, huh?"

I cleared my throat as I tried not to blush. "Yeah, next time. I mean, we'll be seeing a lot of each other now that I'll be working at the inn. Better get used to seeing this old face."

"I could get used to that," Taylor murmured. "Come on —let's see if your truck is ready."

I nodded and followed her, wondering if she was flirting. Or if I was just seeing what I wanted to see. Taylor and I did get along well, plus she was kind and beautiful. And I wanted something good to come out of this trip.

Finding true love would've made all my brother's shenanigans worth it. Almost.

I followed Taylor down the street, heading back to the mechanic. It was a short walk, and we were back in no time. As we entered the junkyard, Mr. Patterson was slamming the hood shut.

"There you are," he grumbled. "Truck's good as new."

"Oh, finally—something good. Thank you, Mr. Patterson."

"Thank me when you pay it off. Until then, you're still on the hook," he snapped. "This inn job better pay it off in full."

"I'm sure it will." I reached into my pocket and pulled out some money. "Here—take this. I brought it with me when I came to Bridgewood. It's not much but it's all I can spare right now."

Mr. Patterson grabbed it out of my hand. "I'll make a

note of how much you still owe. Try not to ruin your truck any more, yeah?"

I hoped I wouldn't, then thanked him again. Taylor patted my truck. "Well, it's good to see her road-worthy again. You heading back to the inn?"

"I am. I should get settled and run the idea of working there past your parents. Just to make sure it's okay."

"Good idea. I'll meet you there. And Ethan? It's good to have you in Bridgewood. You've been a nice distraction."

From what, I wondered? Before I could ask, Taylor was already heading to her truck. She drove off as I was left there scratching my head. I heard Mr. Patterson snickering behind me as he started to work on another beat-up truck.

"What's so funny?"

Mr. Patterson cleared his throat. "You and Taylor. I seen the way you gawk at her, boy. You think you have a chance?"

"Uh, I'm not thinking about that. I'm just trying to focus on my truck and pay off my debt."

Mr. Patterson rolled his eyes. "Uh-huh. Listen, kid—that woman is hard to get. My poor nephew's been trying to win her heart for years. It ain't ever worked."

"You mean Drew, right? The inn's electrician? I met him earlier."

"That's the one. Poor S.O.B. is in love with her, I think. Always giving her the doe eyes." Mr. Patterson shook his head in disgust. "And my nephew's a good boy. So if he can't get her, neither can you. Just sayin'."

For some reason, that bothered me. The way Mr. Patterson spoke about Taylor. And it also hurt to imagine that I couldn't be with her. Like any shred of hope I had of finding the right woman in this town had faded. I pushed those feelings down. Taylor owed me nothing. We were just acquaintances.

"Yes, well...good to know," I muttered. "See you around, Mr. Patterson. And thanks again for fixing up my truck."

He waved me off, returning to work on another truck he was fixing. I headed into the shop one last time to check my bank account. My card still wasn't working—the word ERROR flashed across the screen.

My brother had lied about giving me access. And maybe once Cheyenne sent me a picture of the contract, I'd know more.

With a sigh, I headed to my truck, starting up the engine. I was relieved when I heard the familiar roar with no sign of smoke or damage. I stepped on the pedal, pulling out of the parking lot and heading down the road to the inn. Taylor's truck had already beaten me there.

As I parked it, heading inside, I heard Taylor chatting with her parents at the front desk. I hid behind a potted plant to listen in. Fortunately, they didn't hear the door chime.

"...and he isn't dangerous, is he?" her father demanded. "Or hiding anything? I don't want a repeat of last time."

"Trust me, neither do I," Taylor muttered. "But no, Dad. He's not dangerous. He could've hurt me a million ways by now. He seems sweet—and down on his luck. I think we should let him work here."

"We *do* need the extra help," her mother added. "I agree with Taylor."

Her dad sighed. "All right, all right. He can work and stay here. But if I see anything suspicious, he's gone."

"Oh, I'd be the first to throw him out on his ass," Taylor assured him. "You can count on that."

I didn't know what they were talking about. What had happened last time?

"Good, good. Just be careful, sweetie. I worry about you," her father sniffed. "Anyway, I've got some work to do in my office. You can tell Ethan when he gets here that his room is ready. Then your mother can give him a list of chores."

Taylor nodded, then her father walked off to the end of the hall. His office was sandwiched between the dining area and the storage closet. The inn was quiet for a few moments before Taylor's mother spoke up.

"So, this Ethan..." she began. "He's quite handsome, isn't he?"

Peering around the plant, I saw a hint of a blush on Taylor's cheeks. "Mom, stop. Let's not go down that path again."

"All right, all right." Her mother sifted through paperwork at the front desk. "I know you're still hurting. But you have to open yourself up to love one day, dear. Your soulmate is waiting out there for you. I just know he is."

"I think my soulmate got hit by a bus," Taylor grumbled. "Anyway, I'm heading up to the attic. Tell Ethan that's where he can find me when he gets back."

Her mother nodded, watching her walk off to the staircase. When she vanished, the foyer filling with the sounds of her mother typing on the computer, I walked over to the desk.

"Hi, Mrs. Kennedy," I began. "I'm back. Did Taylor run our deal by you and your husband?"

Her mother nodded, looking up at me. "She did—and we're onboard. Welcome to the Cozybrook Inn, Ethan. Your room's waiting upstairs for you. And I have a list of chores for you to get started on."

"Great, let's see them. I'm eager to pay back Mr. Patterson. I can't stand owing debts."

"You and me both." She reached under the desk, pulling out a piece of paper. "Here you are, Ethan. Cleaning supplies are in the storage closet. And I'd like your help with cooking dinner later if you don't mind."

"You got it, I'll do whatever you need me to. Well, I should get started. Excuse me."

"Of course. Thanks for helping us. Oh, and Taylor's in the attic if you need her. I'm sure she'd be happy to give you a tour of the town or help with your chores." Sharon grinned. "Say, Ethan...you aren't married, are you?"

"Uh, no. Never had much luck with love, actually."

Sharon looked sad. "Oh, I'm so sorry. For what it's worth, neither has my daughter. She just got out of a bad relationship."

I didn't know that about Taylor. I felt bad for her, knowing she didn't deserve that. "Yeah, I did too. Just broke up with my girlfriend yesterday. We...weren't compatible after all."

"A shame. But you never know—maybe you'll find the right person in this town. She could be even closer than you think."

Was Taylor's mother trying to set us up together?

I smiled. "That's the beauty of life, right? Anything can happen. I'm keeping my eyes peeled for someone special."

"Smart idea. Let me know if you need anything. If you're working for us, you're family now. Which means we'll look out for you."

"Thank you, Mrs. Kennedy. I appreciate that."

"Please, call me Sharon," she chuckled. "See you later."

I waved. Her words rang in my ears. *You're family now.* It made me feel all warm and fuzzy on the inside. I didn't even feel like family around my own blood relatives. Even without my money, I already felt a lot more at home around here than back in California. Maybe staying here wouldn't be so bad at all.

Until I looked down at the list and read all the chores I had lined up.

Chapter Eight

I didn't think I'd ever leave my job and become a janitor, but desperate times called for desperate measures.

The first task on the list was to clean the toilets. I grabbed the bucket of cleaning supplies from the storage closet, then made my way around the inn. Each room had its own individual bathroom—including my own. Some were tidier than others. But at least the rooms were empty so I didn't have to ask permission to go in.

I scrubbed the toilets, then wiped down the sink and any part a guest might've touched. The bathrooms were sparkling when I had finished, and it hadn't even taken me long. Then I replaced the bed sheets and made all the beds. I was tired by the end of it but it wasn't over yet.

I had to do the dishes in the small kitchen—which looked like it was still in the eighties, probably the time Taylor's family had opened it—and put them away. For my final task, I just had to empty the garbage and bring it out back to the dumpster. Easy peasy.

But as I picked up the trash bag, I noticed there was a hole in the bottom. Some food scraps, wrappers, and papers fell out. I sighed, bending down to pick them up and noticed something else had fallen out. Drawings—of new fashion. One drawing was of a gorgeous red ballgown. Why would anyone want to throw those out?

I looked in the bottom corner of the page, noticing Taylor had signed her name. Maybe she hadn't meant to throw these out and wanted them back. Just in case she did, I separated them from the rest of the trash. After using the back door to throw the trash bag into the dumpster, I headed up the stairs to reach the attic.

When I opened the attic door an inch, I heard crying. And it sounded like Taylor.

I tiptoed inside, trying to stay quiet so I wouldn't startle her. I noticed she was sitting on the floor next to a mannequin wearing a pretty scarf while sniffling. My heart ached, hating to see her like that. Especially after all she had done for me.

"Taylor?" I asked softly. "Are you okay?"

She jumped, looking up at me. Her eyes were still glistening with tears in the dim light of the attic. "Oh, Ethan—there you are. Yeah. Yeah, I'm fine."

"Are you sure about that?"

She sniffled, rising to her feet and wiping her tears away. "Yeah, I am. Don't worry about it."

"Well, all right. I came looking for you because I found these in the trash. Do they belong to you?"

When I held up the drawings, her eyes widened. "Oh my gosh. You found them!"

She rushed over, taking the drawings from my hand. Taylor looked so happy to see them again.

"So they *do* belong to you," I replied. "Why were they in the trash? Did you accidentally throw them out?"

Taylor shook her head, setting the drawings down on a

side table. I noticed she had other scribblings in a notebook. "No, no...I didn't throw them out. It was Drew."

I frowned. "The electrician guy? And your best friend? Why would he do that?"

Taylor sighed, turning her back. "He thinks my love of fashion is silly. That nothing's ever going to come out of it. That's what we were arguing about in the foyer."

"Oh. It looked pretty tense."

"Yeah, he can get fired up about it. Last week, he saw me drawing some new designs and grabbed them from me. Took them somewhere. I didn't realize he just threw them out in the trash." She turned back to face me. "Seriously, thank you for finding these, Ethan. I'm glad I have them back."

"Of course. They belong to you, after all. Why is Drew so anti-fashion?"

"He thinks it's a waste of time, I guess. He thinks I should be doing more around the inn than being up here all the time."

"I don't see how that's any of his business. What you do in your spare time is your own. And everyone needs a hobby."

Taylor nodded. "Exactly. I just wish Drew would see it that way."

"No offense, but why are you still friends with that guy? He seems like an idiot."

"He's not like that all the time. I think I've painted him in a bad light," Taylor lamented. "He is sweet. Bought me a diamond necklace for my birthday last year. Electricians don't make much so he must've saved for a while. And we've been best friends since diapers, so it's not that easy to turn my back on him."

I felt the same way about my brother. "Yeah, I get that. Still, don't let him discourage you. If you want to draw all day, then that's your right. And I happen to think you're very talented."

Taylor smiled. "Thanks, Ethan. I'm glad to have your support."

"Anytime. What do your parents think about your hobby?"

"They're supportive too. I made my dad a vest for Christmas and my mom a scarf. They both loved them. In fact, they encouraged me to apply to the NYU fashion program a few years ago. To become an actual fashion designer."

"And? Did you get accepted?"

Taylor sighed, gesturing around. "What do you think? I'm still here. No, I didn't get accepted. I never heard back from them."

"Oh, that's too bad. I'm sorry, Taylor. But you don't have to go to school to be a fashion designer. With the Internet, you could do it all on your own."

Taylor shrugged. "I don't know, I'm not good with all that stuff. I'm fine with fashion just being my hobby. It seems I don't have much of a choice."

Taylor didn't know it but technology and marketing were my forte. Maybe in the future—if she'd let me—I could help her market her fashion to the world. My head was already spinning with ideas.

You could take the boy out of the workplace, but you couldn't take the workplace out of the boy.

Taylor cleared her throat. "Anyway, thanks for listening. And for not thinking my fashion is weird."

"Why would I? Although it's not my cup of tea, I know talent when I see it. And you've got something special. Don't forget that."

"I won't." Taylor locked eyes with me. "The more we talk, the gladder I am that you decided to vacation here in

Bridgewood. Come on—let's go see if my parents need help making dinner. I'm starving."

I nodded, following Taylor down the attic stairs and wondering if something was growing between us. Something I knew that Drew fellow wasn't going to like.

After stepping off the attic stairs, standing in the foyer, Sharon came running up to us. "Ah, Ethan—there you are. I noticed you finished all your chores."

I nodded. "I did—followed the list to the letter. I hope I did a good job."

"Are you kidding?" Sharon grinned. "You were perfect! This place looks spotless. Are you sure we can't hire you permanently?"

I chuckled. "While I'd like that, I'm afraid I can only stay for a month. I do have a job waiting for me back in Los Angeles."

If my brother wasn't planning to ruin my entire life. I wondered if he was out there right now, controlling all my money and bragging about it over drinks with Anna.

"Too bad," Sharon replied. "We could use a hard worker like you. I'm very impressed, Ethan."

"I told you Ethan would work out." Taylor smiled. "Anyway, we were just coming to see if you needed help with dinner."

"Yes, please—I won't turn that down. I'm making my famous chicken casserole."

"Yes!" Taylor cried. "That's Dad's favorite too. Ethan, you're going to love it. Come on!"

When Taylor grabbed my arm, dragging me to the kitchen with her mother, I felt those butterflies again. I hadn't felt that way since I was a lovesick teenager. It felt good—like something was finally going right in my life.

When we entered the kitchen, Taylor's father was already in there, cooking the pasta for the casserole. He smiled at us and thanked me for doing such a great job. I helped Taylor and her parents chop up the vegetables and get the casserole ready. When it came out of the oven a little while later, it made the entire inn smell fantastic.

"Mmm." Taylor sniffed the air. "A lot of people come to stay at our inn just to taste Mom's delicious cooking."

"It's part of the reason I married her," Mark joked, kissing his wife's cheek. "I usually fish, then she cooks what I catch. A perfect trade. Anyway, I'll set the table."

As Mark got the plates out of the cupboard, I nodded. "It does smell amazing. I might just have to stay here forever to eat all your food."

"You are too kind," Sharon cooed. "Speaking of guests eating my food, we have a bunch of people checking in tomorrow. So it'll be a busy day. You'll finally get to see what the inn looks like when it's booked, Ethan."

"Loud," Taylor filled in, "but full of love. What's better than that?"

I followed Taylor to the quiet dining hall, sitting next to her as her parents sat across from us. We shared the casserole and chatted over a good meal and drinks. Looking around at them, they seemed like a close-knit family. I never had that with my parents and brother. Money kept us together and little else.

"This is fantastic, Sharon." took another bite. "I'm full but I can't stop eating."

Sharon smiled. "Thank you, Ethan. I'm always happy to cook for such grateful people. There's plenty more if you're hungry later. Pie for dessert too."

"Now you're just spoiling me," I joked. "Hey, Taylor— didn't you say you had a cousin?"

Taylor rolled her eyes, taking another bite. "I did. Madison. She's probably out drinking right now. So much for her helping us out with the inn."

"Madison's going through a tough time right now. She just lost her mother, my sister," Mark explained. "We should go easy on her."

"I'm so sorry for your loss," I whispered. "A death in the family is never easy."

"Thank you—and you're right. My brother thought Madison should come out here for a little while. Clear her head and spend time with family. Escape what happened back home for a bit."

"And to teach her responsibility," Taylor lamented, finishing her meal. "She's nineteen and troubled. Drinking, partying, messing up."

"Let's hope staying here will make her feel a little better," Sharon mumbled. "You'll probably meet her soon, Ethan. She...definitely makes an impression."

"That's for sure," Taylor grumbled.

I got the feeling there was tension between Taylor and her cousin. For some reason, she wasn't that big of a fan of Madison. I remembered Taylor's advice about staying away from Madison and thought maybe she was right. The last thing I wanted to do was make Taylor angry.

"So, I had another question," I began, looking around the table. "Your inn is lovely. Everything from the decorations to the food to how close you all are. Have you ever thought of expanding? As in, opening up inns around the country?"

"We'd love that," Mark answered, sipping his soda, "but we don't have the money. Things are pretty tight around here as it is."

Sharon nodded. "Yes, it isn't cheap running an inn by yourself. We've had to take out some loans to keep the place afloat."

"Oh, I see. What about marketing? I bet a good advertising campaign would get even more people from around the world to visit you. People are desperate to belong, to feel at home even when they're traveling. That could be your selling point."

"We're not good with all that," Taylor lamented. "We wouldn't know where to start."

I beamed. "Lucky for you that you've got an expert in marketing sitting right here. I have a business degree."

"You do?" Mark asked. "That's wonderful. And we certainly wouldn't turn away the help. We just wouldn't be able to pay you much more, I'm afraid."

"Don't worry about it—consider it a freebie for letting me live and work here. You're already paying me enough to afford my truck. Anyway, if you'd like, I can think up a marketing plan for you. Put my degree to use."

"Would you?" Sharon asked with a smile. "That would be lovely. It would be nice to have more guests."

"Absolutely. And Taylor, if you'd like, I could help you market your fashion too. Even open up an online shop to sell them. Sharon, Mark, do you know how talented your daughter is?"

Sharon beamed. "We do. She's made us such lovely clothes."

"And we know she loves it," Mark added. "Nothing brings her as much joy as designing new fashion."

Taylor blushed. "That *is* true. But...I don't know. Opening a shop would be a big step. I don't even think I'm that good."

"You definitely are," I declared. "And people should know about you. Maybe you could even open a shop in the inn, sell some of your fashion here. Yet another marketing idea."

"I like that," Sharon mused. "It would be so nice if your fashion became popular. If it went...oh, what do the kids say...viral?"

"Yes, then NYU would regret not accepting you," Mark added. "I think it's a splendid idea, Ethan."

Taylor shrugged. "I...don't know. I'll think about it."

"You have our vote." Sharon reached out to rub Taylor's arm. "Anyway, for all your hard work today, Ethan, I won't ask you to do the dishes tonight. Mark and I can handle it."

"Are you sure?" I asked. "Because I wouldn't mind."

"Aren't you sweet?" Sharon cooed. "But no, it's okay. Go enjoy your night. And thanks for all your help today. Taylor, you're free too."

"Thanks, Mom," Taylor chirped, rising to her feet. Then she turned to me. "Come on—I want to show you something."

Her parents only smiled at me, especially her mother. Sharon's eyes were twinkling at us. Taylor grabbed my hand, making me feel fireworks again as she led me to the back door. Her parents were busy clearing the table as we left.

When we stepped outside, I noticed the sun was beginning to set. Taylor led me up a tall hill into the forest while still holding onto my hand. Then she paused at the edge of the forest, overlooking a giant cliff. It had a beautiful view of the sunset and the small town below.

"Gorgeous, isn't it?" Taylor let go of my hand to stare at the sunset. "I like to come here a lot. Sometimes to draw or just think."

I nodded, staring out at the town. People were driving home from school and work. "Yeah, it's something special. Way better than the city."

"Definitely." Taylor sat down on the ground, patting the grass beside her. "Wanna watch the sun go down with me?"

I smiled, sitting cross-legged beside Taylor. "I'd like that. Back in LA, I rarely took a moment to just sit down and watch the sunset. I was always too busy. So this is nice."

"And so is the company," Taylor said. "I'm glad you can experience some calm, Ethan. You deserve it."

I was glad too. Something was definitely up with my brother, and I'd have to deal with that at some point. And I had to return home in a month. But for now, I wasn't going to think about that.

I was just going to watch the sunset with a beautiful woman and enjoy the peace and quiet. It was the little moments like that that truly made me feel alive.

Chapter Nine

T aylor and I sat there for a while, watching the sky darken. The sun had completely set over Bridgewood half an hour later. The only lights we could see were the streetlamps overlooking the roads.

"Another day gone," Taylor whispered. "It goes by so fast."

"Feels like my life has just gone by in the blink of an eye."

Taylor turned to me. "Do you ever feel like you're not living up to your true potential? Do you fear you're wasting time?"

I gulped, thinking back to my life in Los Angeles. How devoid it was of excitement and joy. It was all about work, business deals, and money. Not exactly a recipe for happiness.

"I do," I finally answered. "That's partly why I went on this vacation. To find what matters to me."

"I like that. And I hope you find it." Taylor rose to her feet. "Come on, it's getting chilly out here. We should head back to the inn. But thanks for coming with me."

"Of course. And here." I removed my jacket and draped it over her shoulders. "Just so you're not freezing."

She smiled, grabbing onto the jacket for warmth. "Thank you. Bridgewood can get super cold at night."

"No problem. Good thing the blankets at the inn look warm."

"I made those actually," she began, heading down the hill. "Knitted them myself."

I raised an eyebrow. "Really? They were so soft. You're multitalented, then."

She giggled. "Hardly. I just like to keep busy. Everyone needs a hobby. Do you have any?"

"Uh, not really. Still figuring it out."

"Well, you've got time. You're still young." When she reached the back door of the inn, she paused. "I don't know your last name. Do you even have one?"

I snorted. "Yeah, I do. It's..."

I couldn't tell her it was Miles. What if she had heard of my family's company? I was still trying to keep a low profile. But I had to tell her something. For some reason, Marilyn Monroe popped into my head.

"...Monroe," I finally replied. "Ethan Monroe."

"Nice to meet you, Ethan Monroe," she replied. "Let's get inside before we freeze to death out here. Thanks for letting me borrow your jacket, by the way."

When she handed it back, I nodded, taking it from her. She had left a trace of her perfume behind. Lavender and citrus. I tried not to be obvious as I inhaled it and entered the inn behind Taylor. Her parents were gone from the front desk, then I heard a television on in the basement. They must've been relaxing for the night while there was no one to tend to at the inn. The torches on the wall changed colors, lighting up the place.

"Pretty." I gestured around. "This place has some nice interior decorating."

"Wish I could take credit but that's all my mom. But

yeah, I agree. Our guests say they love how pretty and homey it feels."

"I understand why—"

When the door opened behind us, the bell chiming, a breeze blew inside. It made both me and Taylor shiver. When I turned around, I spotted a woman standing there, wearing a bikini and little else. She had dyed blonde hair, dark eyebrows, and red lipstick. She looked to be around nineteen or twenty with a curvy figure.

"Man is it cold out there!" she cried, shivering.

Taylor crossed her arms. "Maybe it's because you're not dressed for it. A bathing suit? At night? Where did you go?"

"The beach," the girl answered, dribbling water onto the carpet as she shut the door. "Did a little skinny-dipping when the sun went down. It was super fun."

Taylor shook her head. "You and I have *very* different definitions of fun."

The girl ignored that, noticing me. She fluffed her hair and smiled. "Well, hello there. You're super handsome. I don't think we've met."

When she held out a hand, I shook it. "Uh, thanks. I'm Ethan. Ethan Monroe."

I tried to remember my last name and keep all my lies straight.

"Cute name," the girl chirped with a wink. "I'm Madison Greer. Taylor's cousin."

"Oh, right. Nice to meet you, Madison. Taylor already told me about you."

"Did she?" Madison glanced at Taylor. "Only good things, I hope."

"When you start doing good things, then I'll start telling people that," Taylor snapped. "You were supposed to do chores today, you know. Dad had a list and everything."

"Oops," Madison scoffed with a shrug. "Chores are

boring anyway. Skinny-dipping was more fun. Hey, Ethan—you should come with me next time. Ever skinny-dipped?"

I cleared my throat. "Uh, no. Can't say that I have."

"Perfect." Madison grinned. "Then I'll be your first time."

"Ethan's too busy for that," Taylor interrupted. "He's working here at the inn now. He'll be in town for a month."

"Only a month? Good news—I am too." Madison's eyes twinkled. "I think I'll tell my dad I'm going to stay a little while longer. That's okay, right cousin?"

When I faced Taylor, I feared she'd burst in anger.

"Are you sure about that?" Taylor demanded. "I wouldn't want Uncle Dave to miss you too much."

"Nah, he'll be fine." Madison for my arm. She tugged me down the empty hallway. "So, tell me about yourself, Ethan. Where are you from? How did you end up in Bridgewood? I only found out about this boring town because my cousin, aunt, and uncle own the inn here. I'm actually from Colorado."

"Ah, I see. I'm from LA."

Madison made a noise of approval in her throat. "Oh, I've always wanted to go to Los Angeles. Maybe try to become an actress or model. It must be fun living in the city of fame and fortune all the time."

I shrugged. "Meh. You start to crave substance after a while. Since being here, I've found out I prefer small towns."

"Boring." Madison feigned a yawn. Then she winked. "But you're so cute that I'll let it slide. So, do you have any plans tonight?"

I glanced back at Taylor, watching us like a hawk.

"Uh, no. I was just planning to head to my room," I answered quickly. "Unpack, read a book, watch some TV. The usual way I spend my evenings."

"Oh, come on—live a little!" Madison cried. "I know

this is a small town but there are some things happening tonight. Apparently, some singles night at the community center."

I turned to Taylor. "Is that true?"

Taylor nodded. "Yeah, the community center hosts a lot of activities. Tonight is the singles night. Speed dating for people to find love."

That piqued my interest. It was the whole reason I had gone on this trip, why I had left everything behind. I found myself curious about the whole thing.

"I've never been to a singles night," I confessed. "I've always found dates through work and parties."

"Really? Well, this is your chance to try it out," Madison declared. "You *are* single, aren't you?"

"I am," I replied. "And looking for someone. The right someone."

Madison's smile widened. "Perfect! Then we should go. It's gotta be much better than doing nothing tonight. Wait for me—I'm just going to change."

Before I could respond, Madison had taken off upstairs, heading to her room. The door shut as I glanced back at Taylor. Her arms were crossed, her eyes glaring at the stairs.

"So, you've met my cousin," she began. "I told you she was a lot to handle."

"Yeah—very forward too."

"Sorry she hit on you. She can be aggressive when it comes to men."

"You're telling me. I like a confident lady, but...not *that* confident."

Taylor giggled. "Well, maybe you'll find what you're looking for at the singles night. There are some good women in Bridgewood."

I was disappointed that Taylor was encouraging me to go. After the time we had spent tonight, was I wrong to think something more could come of it? Maybe I was getting ahead of myself. Again.

"Uh, right," I stammered. "I'll let you know if I have any luck. Are you coming?"

Taylor hesitated. "Nah, I'm pretty much done with love. After my last relationship didn't work out...I don't want to go down that road again."

So Taylor was heartbroken. Maybe that explained her reluctance to date—or get closer to me. Maybe she just wanted to be friends and that was it. It hurt, but she was a good woman. I wanted to keep her in my life in any way possible.

I nodded. "I get that. My last relationship was a train-wreck. Broke up with Anna just a few days ago. She only wanted money and material stuff, not love. And I'm looking for marriage."

Taylor studied me. "So, you're an old romantic. You don't see that much anymore."

"What can I say? All those Disney movies and fairytales ruined me."

"They ruined me too. Not a bad thing to want."

"No, but it *is* hard to find. Though shows like *Love Always Wins* make it look easy."

Taylor's eyes lit up. "You know that show?"

"Of course—it's my favorite guilty pleasure. The only soap opera I watch."

"Me too," she giggled. "I watch it every day in the attic. I'm obsessed, actually."

I grinned. "Same here. Just another thing we have in common, then."

"Absolutely. Seems like we have a lot." Taylor paused. "Anyway, I'm going to head up to the attic and work on some new designs. Have fun tonight."

"Thanks—you too, Taylor. I'll see you tomorrow."

She nodded, heading up the stairs. As she passed, Madison came out of her room, wearing a short, tight red dress. It showed off all her curves. She had touched up her make-up and put on black heels. She passed Taylor in the hallway, giving her a wink. Taylor just rolled her eyes and headed up into the attic.

Madison came down the stairs, smiling at me. "Ah, you waited. Ready to go?"

"I am. We can take my truck—it's parked outside."

"Oh, perfect. I like a man with his own car." She grinned. "Lead the way, handsome."

I didn't say anything to that, opening the door to the inn and walking outside. The sky had grown even darker and shrouded the town in blackness. As I headed into the parking lot, Madison's heels clicking on the gravel behind me, I felt someone watching me. When I looked back, Taylor was peering out the attic window at us. She closed the curtains when she noticed I had seen her.

"My cousin didn't want to come with us?" Madison asked.

I shook my head. "Nah, she was just heading up to the attic to work on her designs."

"Oh, right—her weird fashion obsession." Madison shook her head. "I never got why she loved it so much."

"She's good at it." I unlocked the doors to my truck. "I hope she keeps it up."

Madison studied me for a moment, reaching for the door handle. "You and my cousin...you're not together, are you?"

I coughed to hide a blush. "No, no. We aren't. Just friends."

"All right. Just making sure." Madison hopped into the passenger seat. "I've never seen Taylor with anyone, actually. She's either super private or asexual. Which I don't under-stand. Dating is fun—she should be doing it more."

"I like her approach. To take her time and wait for the right person." I shut my door and turn my key in the ignition. "I'm doing the same thing."

"Really? Good to know." Madison still eyed me. "Anyway, Taylor should've come tonight. Maybe a one-night stand would've loosened her up. She seemed pretty stressed, didn't she?"

I didn't like the way Madison spoke about Taylor. And I didn't want to gossip either, so I just shrugged as I drove down the road. "I hadn't noticed."

"Well, she definitely is. I overheard Aunt Sharon and Uncle Mark talking about some heartbreak Taylor recently went through. Maybe that's related. You know what I think? She just needs to get laid and maybe she'll get over it faster. Then she can move on."

I cleared my throat. "Why don't we listen to the radio?"

"Ooh, the pop station please. That's my favorite!"

I nodded, turning the radio on. At least it stopped Madison from gossiping about Taylor. As Madison drummed her hand to the music, she pointed the way to the community center. It was hard to see through the dark, but the headlights helped to carve a path. It was a large, circular building downtown. Its sign read BRIDGEWOOD COMMUNITY CENTER: YOUR ENTERTAINMENT PALACE. A dozen cars were parked nearby.

"The slogan is super lame," Madison muttered as I pulled into the parking lot. "But it's a small town, after all. Nothing like the big city where I'm from. Something else we have in common."

I nodded, parking the car. "LA is very different from this town. Anyway, we're here now. Shall we head in?"

Madison agreed, stepping out of the car and shutting the door. I didn't know how she could walk in heels that high—especially on gravel. We crossed the parking lot, following the dim street lamps to the front doors of the community center. A note about singles night was posted on the door. It also listed upcoming activities.

I opened the door, gesturing for Madison to enter. She smiled. "What a gentleman. You don't see many of those anymore. Thanks, handsome."

I ignored that comment, following her inside and looking around. The community center was much bigger on the inside. It had conference rooms and different halls for parties and events. It also had a skating rink, an elevator up to the roof, and an indoor pool. A cute little place for families.

"The convention hall for the singles night is this way." Madison pointed at a sign on the wall with an arrow to the left. "Follow me."

I nodded, heading down the hallway with Madison. It seemed she was swaying her hips on purpose in front of me. Looking away, I focused straight ahead as I reached for the door into the convention hall. When we entered, dozens of people were there, chatting and enjoying drinks. An employee at the community center welcomed us inside.

"Are you here for singles night?" he asked.

"We both are, yeah. I take it this is the place?"

"It is—and you're right on time. Enjoy some refreshments and find a place to sit. Are you hoping to find love tonight?"

"I am," I admitted. "What do you think my odds are?"

The employee held up a hand, showing off his wedding ring. "Pretty good, I'd say. I met my husband here last year."

"Congrats," Madison chirped. "That's awesome."

"Thank you. And you two are in luck. We're just about to start."

"Perfect." Madison turned to me with a wink. "I'll see you again soon. Good luck tonight!"

Madison grabbed a soda, then disappeared into the

crowd. She was immediately flirting with all the men in the room. I spotted some beautiful ladies, though looks weren't everything. I had to see if there was someone I had a connection with.

Grabbing a soda, I made my way to an empty table and sat down. I was nervous for some reason. I had been on dates before so what was different now? Maybe the pressure of looking for something serious was getting to me.

Or maybe I just missed Taylor. I found myself thinking about her, wondering if her work was going well in the attic. I hoped she wasn't crying again.

The community center employee cleared his throat, distracting me from my thoughts. "Okay, everyone's seated. Are we all ready to start and get to know each other a little better?"

Everyone in the room nodded. I took deep breaths, trying to calm down.

"Great." The employee beamed. "Feel free to get up and sit at someone's table. Have a conversation, get to know them. See if any sparks fly. Good luck, everyone. On your mark, get set...go!"

Madison got up immediately, speaking with some men at a table across from me. She was making her way around the room. I smiled politely as a red-headed woman walked over, sitting down and chatting with me. She was a cashier at the local grocery store and seemed nice. But I didn't feel a spark.

The next few women were the same—nice enough, though I didn't feel a connection. Not like I had with Taylor. Madison sauntered over to my table a minute later, pulling up a chair.

"Is it okay if I sit here?" she purred.

I nodded. "Sure, go ahead. Anyone here catch your eye?"

"Oh, someone did. But I'm not sure how they feel about me."

"Why not ask them? I don't think you have anything to lose."

"All right." Madison smiled. "I think you're pretty great, Ethan, and I'd love to take you on a date. You're the most interesting person in this town. What do you say?"

I gawked, not expecting Madison to want me. There were other men in the room, some of them much better-looking than I was. As I searched for a response, thinking about Taylor again, my phone buzzed with a text message.

"Sorry," I mumbled to Madison. "Gotta check this."

I pulled my phone out, noticing it was Cheyenne. And what she had texted made me freeze.

CHEYENNE

> Hey, I got my hands on the contract.
> Sending the picture now. I finally found it.
> And Ethan...it's bad.

Chapter Ten

Madison leaned closer, caressing my arm. "Hey, you okay? You look upset."

I forced myself to look away from my phone to glance at her. "Yeah, yeah...I'm fine. Just need to take a moment outside. Be right back."

Madison looked confused, watching me scurry to the back door. I stepped outside into the parking lot as the night air hit my face. It felt good—just what I needed. My heart was pounding, my head spinning with what could be in the contract.

A minute later, my phone buzzed again. It was several pictures from Cheyenne this time. All of the contract. And as I quickly read through the images, realizing what I had signed, I felt sick enough to throw up.

My phone rang. Numb, I picked it up. "Hello?"

"It's me," Cheyenne answered. "Did you have a chance to read the contract?"

"I did. And...I'm speechless. I can't believe what I signed."

Cheyenne sighed. "I know. I'm so sorry, Ethan."

Silence filled the phone as I pondered the contract.

Without knowing it, my brother had written up a contract where I passed along the company to him indefinitely. Not for a month. I also gave him access to the family fortune, bank accounts, and everything else. I was just a nobody now and he was the new CEO.

In short, he had screwed me over. And I had fallen for it.

"I should've read through that damn contract," I muttered, pacing. "I shouldn't have just blindly signed it, I should've read it carefully first. God, what was I thinking? Maybe I deserve this."

"No, you don't. Your brother played you," Cheyenne raged. "Knowing how much you wanted true love, he tricked you into signing the contract. You trusted him and he exploited that."

"Yeah, but I should've known. My brother was always jealous. And I knew he was angry when my father passed the company to me. I can't even imagine what Dad will say when he learns the son he didn't want in charge is now leading his company for good."

"Maybe he can get your brother to change the contract. Sign it all back to you."

I sighed. "I don't think it'll be that easy, Cheyenne. My brother plays for keeps. He was always a menace. And now, he's won. I'm out of the company."

"Don't say that. There has to be a way to beat him at his own game. A legal way to prove you were duped into signing the contract."

I rubbed my temples. "I don't know—I'll need to think about it. As of right now, I've got no money and I'm trapped in a small town. I should get used to living here."

"Well, despite everything that's going on, I hope your time in Bridgewood is nice. And that you figure out a way to get the company back. Nathan isn't a great boss. He's been ordering people around, making them feel inferior. People already miss you. And I do too."

"Sounds like my brother. I'm so sorry you have to deal with this, Cheyenne."

"And I'm sorry he took advantage of you. I just hope he doesn't find out I took pictures of the contract. I had to bribe the security guard to turn off the cameras, then sneak into his office. Wasn't easy."

"I know. I'll find some way to make it up to you, Cheyenne. I promise."

"Don't worry about that right now. Just focus on surviving out there in Bridgewood. Do you need me to loan you some money to get back?"

"No, I actually found a job. At the inn. The Kennedy family has treated me well. For the time being, I think I'm okay. I'm going to stick with my original plan to stay here for a month. After that...I don't know what I'll do about my brother, but I need to figure it out."

"Okay. Good luck, Ethan. I'm rooting for you. Now, I'm about to go out with my fiancée but let me know if you need anything, okay? I'm here for you. Even hundreds of miles away."

I thanked her, then let her go to enjoy her evening. I took a few minutes to catch my breath and stare out at Bridgewood. The town was nice—much cozier than Los Angeles. And if I couldn't get my company back and expose my brother, I might just have to stay forever. It didn't seem like there was much for me back in LA.

I pulled out my smartphone, calling my parents. They didn't answer. Whatever Nathan had said to them about me enraged them. They had never stopped talking to me before. I scoffed, wondering how long it took Nate to plan all this. He had everything covered—he knew how to ruin my professional *and* personal life.

If I wasn't so angry, I would almost be impressed. In a fit of rage, I texted my brother.

ME

I saw the contract I wrote. I know you lied to me and made me sign away the company. You know tricking someone into signing a contract is a crime, right?

My brother took only seconds to respond.

Prove it. And I don't regret a thing. You had this coming

. That only made me angrier. But I didn't want to give my brother the satisfaction of pissing me off so I stopped texting him, putting my smartphone back into my pocket. I didn't want to waste time arguing. I needed a plan—and a good one —to get my money and company back. And it would have to be my own since it didn't seem like my parents were going to help.

For now, all I could do was get back to singles night. I pushed open the back door and entered the convention hall. People were still mingling, getting to know each other. Madison was sipping champagne near a back wall. When she saw me enter, she smiled, slinking over with a sway of her hips.

"Hey, handsome. You're back," she purred. "I missed you. Everything okay?"

I cleared my throat. "Yeah, I'm fine. Just some family drama."

"Been there. Hope everything's all right. So...have you given what I said earlier some thought?"

I blinked. "Sorry, I got caught up in family drama. What did you say to me earlier?"

"That I like you. And want to go on a date sometime. What do you think?"

Madison was very beautiful—and any guy would've been crazy to turn her down—but I didn't feel a spark with her, not like I felt with Taylor. There must've been a reason she had told me to stay away from Madison.

As I opened my mouth to respond, to find some way to gently turn her down, the door to the convention hall opened. And the most beautiful girl walked inside. Taylor. My jaw nearly dropped when I realized it was her.

She was unrecognizable from her regular clothes. She wore high heels, a red dress that flowed to the ground, and had put her dark hair up in a bun. Her lips were the same color as her gown and her eyelids a smoky black.

She was like a model, a girl straight out of my dreams.

"Taylor," I blurted out loud. "She's here."

"She is?" Madison asked, looking over her shoulder. Then she rolled her eyes. "Why would she come to singles night? I didn't think she was into dating anymore."

Before I could stop myself, my feet were pulling me toward the door. I heard Madison's heels following closely behind. As I approached the doors, Taylor was chatting with the employee who was welcoming her to the singles night.

"...and you can take a seat wherever you'd like," the employee continued. "I hope you find someone special tonight."

Taylor nodded, noticing me. Then she smiled. "Hi, Ethan. Madison."

Madison only rolled her eyes. "Why are you here?"

Taylor sighed. "I didn't want to come, actually. But my mom gets emails from the community center and learned about the singles night. She convinced me to come. To get all dressed up too."

"You look gorgeous," I blurted out before I could stop myself. "That dress is...wow."

Taylor smiled, tucking a loose strand of dark hair behind her ear. "Thanks, Ethan. It's an original. I just finished sewing it last week."

"You made it yourself?" I inspected the dress. "That's incredible. You did a great job."

"Thank you. So, have you two met anyone interesting tonight?"

"I thought I had." Madison turned to me. "I'm just waiting to hear if he feels the same way."

"Oh." Taylor realized Madison was talking about me. "Well...good luck with that. I promised my mom I'd mingle so I should get to it. See you later."

As Taylor walked away, blending in with the crowd, she began speaking with some of the local men. A pang of jealousy rippled through my stomach. I didn't like seeing her with anyone else.

But she wasn't mine. I had no choice but to let her go.

Madison cleared her throat. "Hey, Ethan—do you want to get out of here? I know a great bar just outside the city."

"Uh, actually, I'm not feeling too well," I stammered. "I think I'm going to call it a night. Need me to drive you back to the inn?"

"Don't bother," Madison huffed. "I can take care of myself."

Madison stormed out of the conference hall, clearly upset I wasn't falling prey to her charms. I hoped she'd make it home all right. I glanced toward Taylor, noticing her chatting with some handsome man in the crowd. I just shook my head and walked toward the exit.

As I left the building, I looked up toward the sky,

noticing how beautiful the stars were. You could see each sparkling dot so clearly. We didn't have that back in Los Angeles—there was too much light pollution. I didn't want to waste a perfectly good, starry night so I headed back inside the building and rode the elevator to the roof.

As I stepped off, I leaned against the railing, looking up. I counted the stars in the sky and wondered what I would do about my brother. If there was anything that could be done.

I never thought when we were playing as kids that he would be the one to betray me, his own flesh and blood. But that was Nathan—in all his glory.

When I heard the door to the roof open behind me, I glanced over, wondering who it could be. I feared it was Madison coming back. But it was Taylor instead. She smoothed down her dress, then walked over to me.

"Hey," she began. "I saw you slip away. Everything all right?"

I nodded, leaning against the railing. "Yeah, just got tired of the crowds. And Madison was coming on a little strong."

Taylor shook her head. "That girl will flirt with anything that has a pulse. Are you going to take her up on her offer?"

"Nah, she's not my type. Did you meet anyone at the singles night? I saw you chatting with some guys."

"The men were nice enough, but no one caught my eye." Taylor shrugged, glancing up. "Wow...the stars are beautiful."

I nodded. "That they are. If you had to choose, which do you think is more beautiful—a starry night or a sunset?"

"Oh, man. That's a tough one." Taylor paused to think. "Hmm...probably stars. There's just something magical about them."

"Agreed. I could watch them all night." I cleared my throat. "I'm glad you came—there's something I need to ask you."

Taylor turned to me. "Oh? What's that?"

"I might have to stay in Bridgewood a little longer than a month. Not sure how long yet, but some things happened back home that I can't get into. You think your parents will hire me on for a while?"

"Are you kidding? Of course they would. My mother was still talking about how good of a job you did. You'll always be welcome at the Cozybrook Inn."

I sighed in relief. It was good to know that even if my parents never talked to me again and my brother took over every aspect of my life, I had something for me here. Maybe that fresh start that I wanted.

I just didn't think I'd get it so quickly.

"Good, that takes a weight off my shoulders." I sighed. "Thanks, Taylor."

"Of course. Is everything all right? Back home, I mean?"

I hesitated, not knowing what to say. "Right now, things are kind of a disaster. Family drama. I don't want to get into it."

"I understand. Well, whatever's happening, I hope it gets resolved soon. Not that I don't like having you here, though. You're a good man, Ethan. The town is lucky to have you."

Hearing Taylor say that made me feel like a million bucks. I wasn't sure I deserved it—considering I was lying about my background—but it was nice to hear.

"Thanks. I think you're pretty great too." She smiled at me. "If you don't mind me asking, why are you so opposed to love? Madison told me you weren't planning to date again."

Taylor was quiet for a few moments. I feared I had upset her.

"Sorry," I stammered. "You don't need to answer that if you don't want to—"

"No, it's all right," she interrupted. "The last guy I was interested in was from out of town, like you. Even broke down on the side of the road. We got along well, and things escalated quickly."

"Oh. Did he not feel the same way? I can't imagine a man not liking you back."

Taylor looked flattered. "Thanks—and yeah, he did. But he was only using me. He had...other goals in mind. Then he left town, and I never heard from him again. And he kinda tried to screw over my family's inn. But I don't want to talk about that. Since then, I haven't been searching for love. Even my boyfriend before him wasn't great."

"I'm sorry. It can be tough to find the right person. Like looking for a needle in a haystack."

"You're telling me." Taylor shook her head. "He was rich and thought he was better than everyone because of it. Since then, I just can't stand rich people. The world would be a better place if they all died off."

Taylor hated rich people? I cleared my throat, fearing what she would think when she found out who I was. Not like I was rich anymore. My lovely brother had made sure of that.

"Right. Well, trust me—any man who leaves you is clearly stupid. You're better off without that loser."

"That's what my parents keep telling me. I hope they're right." Taylor turned to me. "What about you? Have you been any luckier in love?"

"Nah, not really. You might think this is silly, but...this whole vacation was for me to find love. I wasn't having much luck in LA so I thought a change of scenery would be nice. I'm just...I'm tired of fake love. I want something real."

"I completely understand that." Taylor glanced back toward the sky, then gasped. "Look—a shooting star! You have to make a wish. But don't tell me what it is or it won't come true."

I nodded, closing my eyes. "All right. Let me think..."

It took me a second, but I finally decided on something to wish for. It wasn't love, or to reconcile with my parents or stop my brother. It was something simpler than that.

I wish to be happy.

When I opened my eyes, Taylor had moved even closer, staring at me. "Well, I made a wish. Hope it comes true. Did you wish?"

"I did," Taylor whispered. "And I might be able to make it come true right now."

"Really? Can you give me a hint?"

Instead of speaking, Taylor leaned closer, placing her lips against mine. They were soft and tasted like cherries. And as we kissed on the roof, the shooting star still exploding across the sky, I couldn't even remember my problems back in LA.

Chapter Eleven

I didn't know how long Taylor and I stood there kissing under the shooting star, but somehow, it didn't feel long enough.

She pulled away first, breathless. Her cheeks were flushed. "Wow, that was..."

Electrifying. Exhilarating. Passionate. Everything a first kiss should be, especially if it was going to turn into something else. Something more.

"Perfect," I filled in.

She nodded. "Absolutely. The truth is, I've had a crush on you since we met. I just didn't know if you felt the same. And...I was afraid, given my history."

I reached for her hand. "I know. I am too. But the way I feel around you...I've never felt this way around anyone. I'm glad I came to Bridgewood."

Even if my life was falling apart back home.

Taylor smiled. "I am too. Not to ruin the moment, but I'm starting to get cold. Maybe we should head back to the inn."

"Of course. I'm pretty tired." I gestured toward the roof door. "Ladies first."

She smiled, heading back inside the community center. We walked downstairs before heading out of the building. Taylor had taken her own truck to get there so I took mine and followed her back to the inn. When we arrived, a taxi was pulling away, then Madison was entering through the inn's front doors.

I hoped she wouldn't be upset I had chosen her cousin over her. Madison struck me as a girl who had never been told "no" a day in her life.

After parking around the back, I met up with Taylor, following her inside. We were both still giddy from the kiss. As we entered the inn, Madison was standing there, removing her shoes. When she saw how happy we looked—the kiss probably written all over our faces—she sneered.

"Have a good time tonight?" she asked.

I nodded. "I sure did. One of the best nights of my life, in fact."

"Same here." Taylor winked at me. "Goodnight, Ethan. See you tomorrow."

"Goodnight, Taylor. And again...that dress looks fantastic. You should be very proud of yourself."

I thought Madison might burst out of jealousy. Her eyes narrowed, then she crossed her arms. "Taylor, can I talk to you? Alone?"

Taylor nodded. "Sure. What about?"

"Oh, just inn stuff." Madison smiled sweetly at me. "You go ahead and get your rest, Ethan. See you tomorrow."

I glanced between Taylor and Madison, wondering what was going on, but didn't push it. I just nodded and headed upstairs to my room. As I walked to my door, I heard harsh whispers coming from downstairs. I leaned over the handrail to try to overhear but couldn't make out a word.

When I heard footsteps, I rushed inside my room, shutting the door but keeping it open an inch. I saw Taylor storm through the crevice and head up to her attic. She slammed the door, then Madison walked upstairs with a smirk. She didn't notice my door slightly open as she headed to her room.

What was the matter with Taylor? I knew I had to find out.

I quickly changed into something more casual, then left my room and headed up the attic stairs. I could hear Taylor's parents snoring in their room down the hall. Other than that, the attic was quiet—and empty. After I had walked up the stairs, I opened the attic door an inch.

"Taylor?" I whispered. "Are you in there? Everything all right?"

She walked over to the door, still in her dress and looking upset. "Ethan, it's you. Yeah, I'm fine. Just tired. Goodnight."

Before I could say anything else, she shut the door in my face. I wondered why she was acting so strange. She couldn't stop grinning at me earlier. Now, she seemed upset. Had Madison told her something?

I shook my head, walking downstairs on the way to my room. I decided all that drama could wait until tomorrow. Right now, I needed some sleep after a stressful day.

It seemed my brother wasn't the only one playing a sinister little game.

After brushing my teeth and changing into my pajamas, I fell fast asleep. The bed was soft, the blanket warm. The inn wasn't the worst place to end up stranded. At this rate, it was looking like my permanent home.

After getting dressed in jeans and a t-shirt the next morning, I headed downstairs, walking into the kitchen. I smelled the heavenly aroma of pancakes cooking. Taylor's parents stood nearby, making pancakes on the stove. Taylor and Madison were sitting at the dining room table but weren't speaking.

"Ah, Ethan—good morning," Sharon chirped. "I made some coffee. You can have a cup if you'd like. The pancakes will be ready soon so take a seat."

"Perfect, thank you." I reached for a clean mug, filling it with coffee and milk. I walked toward the table and sat next to Taylor. She barely looked my way. Madison was staring at us, a devious smirk on her face.

"Hey," I began, clearing my throat. "Did you have a good sleep?"

"I know I did." Madison sounded a little too cheery.

Taylor cleared her throat. "Ethan, can I talk to you outside? It won't take long."

"I always have time to talk to you." I set down my coffee cup. "Lead the way."

Madison just watched us go with a smirk, making me wonder if she knew what was going on. I followed Taylor to the back door. She stepped outside onto the deck where a dozen chairs and tables were set up for the guests. It led into a nearby forest with a trickling ravine. Squirrels, rabbits, and other animals were running through the bushes while birds squawked in the trees.

"What a nice day," I murmured, closing my eyes. "Feel that sunshine—"

"Last night was a mistake," Taylor blurted out, making me open my eyes. "Coming to singles night, kissing you. All of it."

I frowned. "I...don't understand. Why the sudden change of heart? You looked so happy last night. I was too."

Taylor shrugged. "I just...I thought about it and my track record with love isn't great. I'd rather not go down that road again. You're a great man, Ethan, but I'm not ready."

"Are you sure?" I crossed my arms. "Because I heard you and Madison whispering last night when I went to bed. Did she say something to you? Something that changed your mind? Because you can't listen to her. She's just jealous and trying to get under your skin."

Taylor avoided my eyes. "It...was nothing. Now, excuse me. I need to help my parents set the table."

As Taylor turned, heading inside, I grabbed her arm. "Wait. Look me in the eyes and tell me that kiss meant nothing to you. If you can do that, then I won't bring it up again."

Taylor sighed. "Ethan..."

"You can't do it, can you? I knew it. What are you so afraid of, Taylor? What did your last partner do to you?"

Taylor took a deep breath, then turned around. Her eyes locked onto mine. "That kiss meant nothing, Ethan. I want us to just be friends. Okay? Okay."

I flinched. Did Taylor mean that?

As I searched her eyes for answers, she headed through the back door, vanishing inside the kitchen. I stayed out on the patio for a second to think about everything. Last night, I thought I had lost my job and old life but had gained Taylor.

Now, I had nothing at all. What had happened?

I shouldn't have been surprised. With the way my week was going, I should've known this was bound to fall apart too.

With a sigh, I entered through the back door, shutting it behind me. Taylor was helping her parents set the table as they placed the pancakes, sausages, and orange juice down. Madison was still smirking.

"Ethan, you're back." Madison patted the seat beside her. "You can sit with me. Saved you a seat."

Taylor didn't speak. She clearly didn't want me to sit next to her.

"Uh, okay." I sat next to Madison. "The food looks amazing. Thank you."

"Of course." Mark reached for a pancake. "My wife is the best. After this, I'll give you your chore list, Ethan."

"And in an hour, we'll have some guests arriving. There'll be more people joining us at mealtime." Sharon added ketchup to her sausage. "And we have something special for you, Ethan."

I glanced up from my plate. "Oh?"

Mark handed me an envelope across the table. "Here—your month's salary in advance. We wanted to help you pay off that car loan faster. I know Mr. Patterson isn't the nicest to deal with so it's best to get it over with quickly."

"Wow. Thank you." I took the envelope. "This should pay off most of it, then I'll try to figure out the rest. Are you sure you can afford this?"

"Things might be a little tight, but we'll manage." Sharon reached for her husband's hand. "We always have. Even during the worst recessions, we've always found a way to keep the inn going."

I felt like I owed them something for being so nice to me, so I cleared my throat. "Well, I appreciate it. I want to help you out with marketing. I have an idea...if Taylor is onboard."

For once, Taylor finally looked up. "What is it?"

"Well, you love fashion, and the inn needs money to keep going. So why not combine the two? A charity fundraiser at the community center. Proceeds from your fashion sales will go to benefit your inn. And people will finally see your talent. I think it's a win-win."

Taylor hesitated. "Oh, I don't know—"

"What a wonderful idea!" Sharon cried. "Taylor, you should do it. How quickly could you make outfits?"

"Well, I already have a lot ready. Just give me a few more days to add some finishing touches." Taylor turned to me. "I hope you know what you're doing."

All my successful business ideas and parties were on the

tip of my tongue, but I kept silent. "Trust me, I do. May as well put my marketing degree to good use."

"You have a marketing degree? That's so awesome," Madison gushed, leaning toward me. "You'll have to tell me more sometime."

Now it was Taylor's turn to roll her eyes.

"Uh, there's nothing much to tell. It's boring, actually." I tried to change the subject. "So, what's everyone watching on TV lately?"

As we ate breakfast, we chatted about pop culture and things that needed to get done around the inn. I helped Taylor and her parents wash the dishes. She still gave me the cold shoulder. As Madison sat at the table, reading the latest magazine, I was dying to know what she told Taylor. But first things first.

"Do I still have time before the guests arrive? I'd like to get the money to Mr. Patterson now."

"Of course, there's plenty of time." Mark wiped his hands. "Then when you come back, I'll give you the chores and we'll prepare for the guests arrival."

"Sounds good. I won't be long."

"Could I come with you?" Madison piped up. "I haven't seen Mr. Patterson in a while. Just wanted to say hi."

Taylor narrowed her eyes. "Why? You never liked Drew's uncle. You always thought he was weird and rude."

"Yeah, well..." Madison shrugged. "I changed my mind. What do you say, Ethan?"

"Uh, okay." I reached into my pocket for my keys. "Let's be quick."

Taylor just shook her head but said nothing as I headed for the exit. Madison followed close behind, walking with me to my car. She looked giddy about something. As we hopped in, she turned to me.

"We should do something fun today," she giggled. "Let's

go out to eat. Or dancing. There's a great club a few towns over."

I started the engine, shaking my head. "Sorry, can't. Didn't you hear your aunt and uncle? We've got guests coming and I need to do some chores."

"Raincheck, then." Madison put her feet on the dash. "Maybe tonight."

I ignored that, turning to her. "Madison, I need to ask you something."

She looked eager. "Yeah?"

"It's about Taylor. She's been weird with me ever since we got back last night."

Madison rolled her eyes. "Oh, her. Who cares? Taylor's usually in a bad mood. Has been ever since her last relationship didn't work out."

"Right. Well, I was just wondering, did you say anything to her? Maybe after I went to bed?"

"Maybe I did, maybe I didn't. Give me some incentive to tell you."

I sighed. "Like what?"

"Go on a date with me," she answered without hesitation. "Just one date. And I promise I'll tell you what I told Taylor."

I didn't want to, but I didn't see any other choice. I had to know what Madison told her. Then maybe I could make it right.

"Fine, one date. Now what did you tell Taylor?"

Madison shook her head, holding out her hand. "Nuh-uh. Pinky promise first."

I scowled and locked my pinky with hers. "Fine, there. Now will you tell me?"

"Okay, fine. I saw how close you two were getting. I just quickly reminded her that her past relationships hadn't worked out. And now she was miserable. I asked her if she wanted to go through that again. She must've realized I was right."

I tightened my grip on the steering wheel. What right did Madison have to meddle between me and Taylor?

"Why did you do that?" I demanded. "I was starting to like Taylor, you know. And I think she feels the same way about me."

"Because trust me—it won't work out. Taylor's super boring anyway. I think you and I could have something special, don't you think?"

I sighed. "Madison...look, I think you're great. But I do have feelings for Taylor. So I'm sorry, but I'm not interested in you."

Madison's face contorted. "Not interested? Why not?"

"I just don't feel a spark between us, that's all. It's nothing personal. And I'd appreciate it if you'd stop butting in between me and Taylor. If you cared about me, you'd let me be with her instead."

Madison shook her head. "How dare you! Do you know how lucky any guy would be to get with someone like me?"

Uh-oh. I had unleashed an angry, jealous beast.

"I do, and I wish you the best in finding him. But it's not me. Now, if you wouldn't mind, I'd like you to get out of my truck. I need to get to Mr. Patterson's before the guests arrive."

Madison scowled, opening her door. "I always get what I want, Mr. LA."

She stepped out, slamming the door behind her. She stomped over to the inn and entered through the doors. Once she was gone, I sighed, leaning on the steering wheel. I just couldn't catch a break.

I pulled out of the parking lot, heading into town toward the mechanic's shop. When I arrived, entering the building,

Mr. Patterson was talking with Drew at the front desk. Just another person I didn't want to see.

I cleared my throat as I approached. "Mr. Patterson? I have something for you."

Both men turned around, scowling at me. What a warm welcome.

"What is it, boy?" Mr. Patterson demanded.

"I've got some money for you. To pay off my truck." I handed over the envelope. "The Kennedys surprised me with an early salary this morning. That should cover most of it. And I promise, I'll get the rest to you soon enough."

Mr. Patterson tore the envelope out of my hands, looking inside. "Hmm, so you're right. This'll do for now. I better have the rest soon, boy."

"You will. Anyway, I have to get going. See you around."

I left the shop, feeling their eyes on the back of my head. As I crossed the parking lot, heading to my truck, I heard footsteps behind me. When I turned around, it was Drew— and he was following me.

"Hey, outsider," he began. "Wait up. I need to talk to you."

"Sorry, can't. Have to get back to work at the inn."

"It's about Taylor," Drew began. "I saw you kissing her last night. I told you to stay away from her, didn't I? I meant it."

How did Drew even know about that? I hadn't seen him at the singles night. Was he stalking Taylor?

"Or what?"

"Just wait and see," Drew spat. "Finish your business and get out of Bridgewood, outsider. We don't want you here. And I won't let you get in the way of me and Taylor."

I scoffed. "You and Taylor? She told me you're just friends. Doesn't seem like there's anything between you two. Especially not when she was kissing me."

His jaw clenched. "I'm warning you—"

"Look, I know you're upset she only sees you as a friend, but you've gotta let it go. Stop being so controlling and obsessive and let her live her life. Before she ends up hating you forever."

As I turned around, thinking the conversation was over, Drew lunged at me from behind.

Chapter Twelve

I hadn't gotten into a fistfight since second grade when Timmy Rosen called my mother a llama. Private school was wild and I had to defend my mother's honor. I never thought I'd get into another fight until I found Drew on top of me, punching and kicking.

"What the hell is wrong with you?" I demanded, trying to push him off. "Get off me!"

"Stay away from Taylor!" he screamed in my ear, still landing punches. One hit my lip, and I felt it start to bleed. "She isn't yours!"

I mustered up all the strength I had, lifting a leg to kick Drew in the stomach. He cried out and fell back. I stood up, catching my breath and preparing for another round. If he wanted a fight, I'd give him one.

"Taylor doesn't belong to you. She can be with whoever she wants," I spat. "Now, are you going to stop or do I have to kick your ass?"

Drew growled, rising to his feet. He was swaying a bit but still wanted to fight as he lifted his fists. Just as I prepared to fight him again, the door to the mechanic shop opened. Mr. Patterson poked his head out.

"What the hell is all that racket?" he demanded. "You two fighting out here?"

"He started it." I pointed at Drew. "I was only trying to get to my truck."

Mr. Patterson rushed over, standing in between us. "I don't give a rat's ass who started it! Knock it off—both of you. Or I'll get the cops involved."

Drew backed down, though he seethed. "This isn't over, outsider. Not by a long shot."

Before I could respond, Drew stomped off to his truck, getting in and driving away. I shook my head. Was he that much in love with Taylor that he had to fight me over her? It seemed so childish.

"You oughta get outta here too, boy," Mr. Patterson grumbled. "And get that lip cleaned up. Looks nasty."

I lifted a hand to my lip, feeling blood. "Yeah, yeah—I'm going. Just tell your nephew to stay away from me. I don't want trouble. And maybe he should stay away from Taylor too. It's a little creepy how obsessed he is with her."

Mr. Patterson sighed. "That boy...he's been in love with that girl ever since he was a kid. I told him love only ends in heartbreak, but that dumbass wouldn't listen to me. And look where it's gotten him—single and alone, getting into fistfights. What an idiot."

As Mr. Patterson walked back to his shop, muttering about his nephew, I turned and headed back to my truck. I needed to get back to the inn for another day of work and to clean up my lip. I hoped the guests and the Kennedys wouldn't be too concerned about my busted face.

I arrived at the inn about ten minutes later, parking around the back and walking through the front doors. Mr. and Mrs. Kennedy were going over paperwork at the front desk. I didn't see Taylor or Madison anywhere.

Sharon looked up, smiling at me. "Ah, there you are. Did you pay off—oh my gosh, your face. What happened?"

Mark noticed too, gasping. Taylor walked into the foyer while carrying cleaning supplies and saw my face. She looked upset, setting the box of supplies down.

"Ethan, you're back," she began. "What happened to your lip?"

"Oh, I, uh...fell down," I mumbled. "Do you have a first aid kit around here? Something I can clean up my lip with?"

"We do. I'll show you to it," Taylor answered. "Come on, follow me."

I heard Sharon and Mark muttering about my lip as I followed Taylor up the stairs. Madison was in her room, blasting pop music. Taylor only shook her head as we passed. She walked toward a hallway closet, pulling out a first aid kit.

"You've got some scratches on your arm too." She pointed at me. I looked down and realized she was right. "Come on—let's head to your room. You can sit on the bed while I patch you up."

"Thanks." I gestured for her to follow. "My room is right this way."

She nodded, waiting for me to unlock the door with my key. I entered the room and sat on the bed. She closed the door, bringing the first aid kit over with her and setting it down on the sheets. The room was quiet for a minute as she got the bandages ready.

"How did this happen?" she asked, applying a bandage to my arm. "You fell down?"

I didn't want to tell her about Drew. I feared it would upset her, finding out the truth about her best friend. But I did still want her to be careful around that guy.

"Yeah, I did. I can be pretty clumsy sometimes," I explained watching her apply the bandage. "Thanks."

"Of course," she replied, reaching into the box to grab a face cloth. "Here, let me fix up that lip."

She wiped away the blood with the face cloth, leaning closer to me. I inhaled her intoxicating lavender perfume and thought about our kiss. It was so perfect, so right. How could she regret it?

"There," she whispered softly, still inches away from me. "All better."

I swallowed hard. "Thanks. How do I look?"

"Still pretty rough. But handsome as always."

"Thank you, I try."

She giggled. "I bet. Well, I hope you feel better. But just tell me one thing."

"Shoot."

Taylor rose to her feet, picking up the first aid kit. "You didn't fall down, did you? What happened?"

I sighed. "You sure you want to know? You might not like it."

"Try me."

"All right." I cleared my throat. "It was Drew."

She frowned. "Drew Patterson? My best friend, Drew?"

"That's the one. He told me to stay away from you—that he saw us kiss last night. We exchanged some words and the next thing I knew, he was on top of me, punching and kicking. His uncle had to break it up."

Taylor was quiet for a moment, shocked. "Wow, I...can't believe that. I've never seen Drew do anything aggressive."

"There's a lot you don't know about him, Taylor. That guy's hated me since our first meeting."

"Why? You've never done anything to him."

I rose to my feet. "Sure I have. I kissed you—the girl he's in love with. You *do* know he's in love with you, don't you?"

Taylor sighed. "I know. It's been obvious since first grade. I don't feel the same way and I know it hurts him, but you can't force feelings where there aren't any. I thought he was cool about it."

"Yeah, real cool," I replied sarcastically, pointing at my bandaged arm. "He thinks you're his. And it's almost...obsession. You should be careful around him."

She shook her head. "Drew would never hurt me. But I'll talk to him. Tell him to stay out of my dating life and that he needs to leave you alone."

"Thank you, I'd appreciate that. Drew is one more problem I don't need."

"Of course. Well, I'll be downstairs, getting ready for the guests. They should be here soon. Did you pay off some of your debt to Mr. Patterson?"

"I did—only have a little bit more to go. Didn't expect to get into a fistfight while I was there. But hey, life comes at you fast."

The corners of Taylor's mouth turned upward. "That it does. Anyway, meet us downstairs when you're ready. Check-in time is always busy."

As she turned, I reached for her arm. "Wait. One more thing."

She turned around. "Oh? What is it?"

"I know what Madison told you. I made her tell me. That she pointed out how your relationships never work out?"

Taylor sighed. "So she told you. Yes, she did. And she's right. My love life has been a trainwreck."

"So has mine, but that isn't stopping me. Madison has a crush on me, so she'll say whatever she can to get you to back off. Don't give her the satisfaction." I stepped closer. "I know that kiss meant something to you. Because it meant something to me. Don't you think we have something between us?"

"Of course I do," Taylor whispered. "And I haven't felt this way about anyone in a long time."

"Then why fight it?"

"Because...because love never works out for me. Not after the last time. And I don't want to get heartbroken again. It hurts too much."

"Who claimed I was going to break your heart? That's the last thing I want, Taylor. Trust me, I'm sick of bad relationships too. I want my happily ever after. I want something real, and I think we have it between us. It's growing. And it'd be a shame to stop it before it turns into something great."

Taylor shook her head. "I don't know, Ethan..."

"Just one date. Come on, that's all I'm asking. And if you're still afraid, then we can end it. No harm done."

She sighed. "All right—one date. I'll let you know when I'm ready. Right now, I'm busy working on my fashion for the fundraiser."

"Right. I'm sure whatever you come up with will be amazing. And I'm not just saying that—you're talented."

Taylor smiled. "Thanks, Ethan. Here's hoping the auction will be good for both my fashion *and* the inn. See you downstairs."

As I nodded, she turned, opening my door. But then she paused.

"Is something wrong?"

"Even if things don't work out between us..." She turned around, considering me. "I think you're an incredible man, Ethan, and you deserve someone special. Remember that."

I fell silent as she headed downstairs. But I thought I had found my someone special. I thought it was Taylor. If Drew and Madison could back off, maybe it would happen.

Shaking my head, I left my room, locking the door behind me. As I walked down the hall, the music inside Madison's room stopped and she flung open her door. She smiled wide when she saw me.

"Ethan, there you are," she giggled. Then she noticed my arm and frowned. "What happened to you?"

"Just an accident. I'll be fine," I lied. "Excuse me, I have to get downstairs."

"Wait a second, handsome," she purred, grabbing my arm. "Did you forget about our little deal? You owe me a date."

Talk about a deal with the devil. I almost recoiled.

"Right now? I have to get to work. We've got guests checking in today."

"Then as soon as you're done work. We can go shopping," Madison said, her eyes lighting up. "It'll be fun. I'm going to get my hair and nails done for tonight. See you then!"

She rushed downstairs, leaving the inn for the salon. I could only shake my head. I didn't want to go out with Madison—or have Taylor think I was into her cousin—but a deal was a deal. I learned in business school that you had to honor every deal and contract.

Even if it was the worst deal ever, like my brother's.

I headed downstairs, walking to the front desk to greet Sharon and Mark. Taylor had gone up to the attic to continue working on her fashion. Just as I asked her parents if they needed help, the doors to the inn opened. Our first guests under my watch.

It was pretty exciting. Maybe the whole inn job was growing on me.

A young woman—maybe in her early twenties—with dark hair, ripped jeans, and a plain t-shirt entered, dragging a suitcase and carrying a backpack. She was holding the hand of a two-year-old boy, blond and wearing overalls.

"Welcome to the Cozybrook Inn," Sharon chirped. "Here to check in?"

The woman nodded. "Yes, I am. Sophie Brewster. This is my son, Jacob."

"Ah, here you are." Sharon looked it up on their computer. "Your room is upstairs. Our employee, Ethan, will show you to your room."

"This way, ma'am," I began, pointing at the stairs. "Follow me. What brings you to the inn?"

I thought making small talk might make the guests feel more comfortable. The whole theme of the inn seemed to be family—a kind of warm welcome and closeness you couldn't get just anywhere. I certainly didn't get this kind of service staying at five-star hotels around the world.

"Just wanted to take my son out." Sophie followed me. The boy scanned the place and sucked his thumb. "We don't get to go on vacation that much."

"Ah, I see. Well, we hope you'll have a good time here." I led her up to her room. "Here's your key. If you need anything, at any time, let us know."

"Thank you. I'll let you know."

I nodded as she entered her room, putting her suitcases down. Her son was pointing around the room and making cooing noises. The woman pulled out her phone, looking disappointed when she saw no notifications. I figured it wasn't my business and headed downstairs.

One guest down. Not to sound cocky, but I was getting pretty good at this.

When I headed back to the front desk, Sharon was still there, checking in another guest. Mark had walked away to mop the floors. He passed me a list of chores as I walked by.

"Nice work with the first guest." He smiled. "You're a natural. When they're checked in, can you get started on your chores?"

"Of course, no problem."

"You're the best, Ethan. Don't let anyone tell you otherwise!"

I smiled, heading to the front desk when I froze in my tracks. Sharon was greeting another guest—and I recognized her. She was Victoria Dunlap, the wealthy business owner of Dunlap Development Properties in Los Angeles. The Miles Marketing Company had worked with her on a few occasions. I had seen her at many parties, usually chit-chatting about work. We weren't friends but she would definitely recognize me.

And I didn't want to blow my cover. I finally had another chance with Taylor, and I couldn't risk her finding out who I was, knowing how much she hated rich people. She'd never talk to me again if she knew I was a millionaire's son. I debated faking sick and running out the back door but then Sharon spotted me.

"Ah, there he is. Our best employee," Sharon joked. "Ethan, here's another guest. Ms. Dunlap. Can you show her to her room?"

Victoria looked over, noticing me. Her eyebrows raised. "Say, you look familiar. Have we met?"

Phew—she wasn't entirely sure who I was. Maybe that was a good thing.

"Uh, no. I don't think so," I lied, gesturing at her bags. "May I take your suitcases upstairs?"

"Yes, please," Victoria replied. "I have my key. Lead the way."

I nodded, taking her suitcases as Victoria followed. Sharon got back to working on her computer. I didn't speak as I brought Victoria up to her room—one right next to Sophie's. Her son babbled inside.

"Well, here you are." I set the suitcases down. "I hope you enjoy your stay at the inn."

"Thank you. I've heard good things about it. I wanted to

try it out—get away from my hectic life in LA." She paused. "Are you sure we haven't met before? Have you ever been to California?"

"No, ma'am. I've lived here my whole life," I lied again. "Let me know if you need anything. And I hope you enjoy your time at the inn."

She nodded, looking skeptical as she entered her room and shut the door. I took a deep breath. What would I do if Victoria recognized me? What if she remembered where she knew me from and told Taylor who I was?

Then I'd have a whole other problem on my hands. Was life ever going to give me a break?

By the way things were going, I was leaning toward no.

Chapter Thirteen

Leaving the guests to unpack, I headed downstairs, noticing more people coming in. One was an old lady with white hair and a green dress. She carried her purse on one arm, an urn in the other with the picture of a white-haired man taped to the front.

"I'm Katherine. Katherine Cabot," the woman told Sharon. "You can call me Kathy. I rented a room a few weeks ago."

"Yes, of course. Here's your key." Sharon leaned over the desk. She noticed the urn and frowned. "Was that your husband?"

Katherine paused, looking down at the urn. "He was. My Chester. He passed away last month."

"Oh, I'm so sorry. Please, let us know if we can do anything for you. Here, I'll give you a discount on your room."

Katherine sniffled. "That's kind of you—thanks. I decided to come to Bridgewood when I saw an ad for it online. I wanted to scatter his ashes somewhere."

"There are lots of great places here. Beaches, cliffs, and more," Sharon gushed, typing on the computer. "There, you've got a discount now. Enjoy your stay at the Cozybrook Inn. Our employee over there, Ethan, will get you set up."

The woman nodded, dragging her suitcase and urn over to me. "Hello, young man. You must be Ethan."

"I am. And I heard what you told Sharon at the front desk," I whispered. "I'm so sorry for your loss."

"Thank you. It's been a difficult adjustment." Katherine sighed. "Anyway, I'd like to get to my room now. I need to unpack."

"Right this way, please."

I led Katherine up the stairs, passing Mark who was mopping the floor. After I showed her to her room, dragging her suitcases for her, she set the urn down on the bedside table and turned to me.

"This room is lovely," she began. "The whole inn is. I can see why it has such rave reviews online."

"I know—a friend of mine stayed here and loved it too. That's how I learned about it. Didn't expect to start working here but it's been wonderful."

"That's good to hear." Katherine paused. "This may be quite forward, young man...but do you have someone special in your life?"

My mind immediately went to Taylor, though I wasn't quite sure what we were. I struggled for an answer. "I, um...I don't know. Maybe. Why do you ask?"

Katherine caressed the urn. "It's just...I miss my Chester so much. He gave me sixty years of marriage. And I want others to have that too. I've been telling everyone I meet—if you find someone special, hold onto them. Make sure you tell them you love them every day. Because you never know when they'll be gone."

I glanced at the urn, nodding. "That's good advice. Thank you, Mrs. Cabot. I'll remember that."

"You're welcome, young man. Take care."

I left the room, quietly shutting the door behind me as Katherine began to unpack. I thought about her words. To tell people you love them, to hold onto someone special. I was trying to hold onto Taylor—even if she wasn't making it easy.

When I walked down the stairs, Sharon was checking in three different people at once. She looked busy. I walked over, wanting to help. It was the least I could do.

"Ethan, you're back," Sharon began. "How are the guests?"

"Good so far. I showed them all to their rooms." I glanced around the foyer. "Are these the other guests?"

"Yes—that's all for today. This is Abigail McKinney."

Sharon pointed at a girl in an oversized sweater standing in line with a pink suitcase. She looked around Madison's age.

"Hey," she spoke. "Nice to meet you. I heard a lot about the Cozybrook Inn online."

Sharon smiled. "We're pleased to hear that. Ethan, escort Ms. McKinney to her room, please. I'll get the others checked in."

I nodded, gesturing for Abigail to follow me. When she did, I led her up the staircase, then took her to a vacant room. She used her key to unlock it and stepped inside while looking around.

"Cozy," she murmured, setting her suitcase down. "Now I get how it got its name."

"Yeah, it's a great place. Say, you look a little young to be traveling."

"I am—just graduated high school. This is my grad trip to myself. Saw this town online and thought, why not?"

I smiled. "That's nice, I hope you enjoy it. Say, aren't you hot in that big sweater? I find it warm in here. I think the Kennedys are trying to make me sweat."

The girl looked uncomfortable, tugging her sweater

down a little more over her body. "Uh, no—I'm fine, thanks. I like wearing sweaters."

"Okay then. Enjoy your stay here. And let me know if you need anything."

She nodded, beginning to unpack as I left the room. When I did, I bumped into Taylor. Her grin was infectious.

"You're in a good mood. What's up?"

"I finished my clothes for the fundraiser," she squealed, tugging my hand. "I know you're busy, but you have to see. Come, come, come!"

She tugged on my hand, dragging me up the stairs as I chuckled. The butterflies were dancing around my stomach again. Taylor led me into the attic, showing off the clothes on the nearby mannequins.

"I've been working on this stuff for years," she began. "It's a good thing I was so prepared. And this piece might just be my favorite. I think it'll sell like hotcakes."

Taylor led me to a mannequin, pointing at a blue and purple dress. It was gorgeous—something a Victorian lady might wear, but still chic and modern at the same time. I would've paid good money to see Taylor wear it.

"You're right." I inspected the dress. "It's beautiful. Once people see it, they'll know how much of a talented fashion designer you are."

Taylor smiled. "Thanks, Ethan. If it weren't for you, well...I wouldn't have the courage to do this at all. Now all we need to do is book a hall at the community center. If we can on such short notice."

"Leave that to me." I patted my smartphone. "I can be pretty persuasive."

"Okay, great. Let me know when we're good to go. In the meantime, I won't keep you—I know you're busy. Just thought I should show you."

"I'm glad you did. Thanks for letting me see it all beforehand." I reached for my smartphone. "People will be jealous I got to witness the Taylor Kennedy originals first. Just remember me when you're famous, okay?"

Taylor snorted. "I doubt I'll get *that* big but I admire your faith in me. Just need to put a few finishing touches on these outfits and then I'll be ready."

"Great—I'm eager for the world to see your work. And for the inn to make more money. I'll call the convention hall right now and see what they've got available."

Taylor thanked me, turning back to her mannequins as I headed toward the door. Her voice stopped me a second later.

"Hey, Ethan?" she began. "Maybe you can explain something strange I overheard."

I turned around, glancing at her. "Oh? What's that?"

"I heard you tell one of the guests you've never been to LA. Why did you lie to her?"

Suddenly, the attic was suffocatingly hot. I tugged at my collar and searched for an answer.

"Sorry," Taylor spoke. "I didn't mean to eavesdrop or anything. Had to use the bathroom and heard you chatting."

"Oh, that? She kept insisting she knew me from somewhere. And I've never met her before. To get her to stop, I told her I'd never been to her hometown of LA. That was it."

Thank goodness I was a pro at thinking on my feet. It was a side effect of working in the business industry where anything could happen—and appearances were everything. Fortunately, Taylor seemed to buy it.

"Ah, that makes sense." Taylor measured some fabric. "We get some strange guests from time to time. I think you handled it pretty well."

"Thanks—I'm just doing my best."

"You're better than you think you are," Taylor assured me. "Sorry, didn't mean to accuse you of anything. I was just curious."

"Nah, it's understandable."

She nodded. "Okay. Ever since my last relationship...well, I've had some trust issues. I might need some reassurance from time to time."

I smiled. "I can do that. Plenty of reassurance, coming up. Anyway, I gotta get back to work. Good luck with your fashionista-ing."

She giggled, thanking me as I headed down the stairs. My face felt hot. All these lies were going to catch up to me one day—I just knew it. And I hoped Taylor wouldn't get hurt.

Pushing that aside for now, I found the number online for the community center and called. It rang a few times before a secretary finally answered.

"Hello, Bridgewood Community Center," she began. "What can I do for you?"

"Hi there. I was wondering if it would be possible to rent a convention hall? I'm hosting a fundraiser for the Cozybrook Inn."

"Oh, I'm so sorry—all our convention halls are booked up. Demand is high, I'm afraid. Between arts and crafts shows and hockey games, there are lots of people who want to book our services."

"Well, that's disappointing. Any chance I can get a table at that arts and crafts show? That would work."

"I'm sorry—all the tables are booked. Is there anything else I can do for you?"

I sighed. "No, thanks. Have a great day."

I hung up, wondering what we were going to do. That community center was the largest around—it would attract a ton of people to promote the inn and Taylor's fashion. Now that dream was slipping away. We could've held it somewhere else but what if no one showed up? This had to be a success.

I wanted to see Taylor happy—and I wasn't about to give up. I already had a plan in mind.

I called Cheyenne, hearing the phone ring. She finally picked up. "Hello, Ethan? Is that you?"

"It's me. Don't worry—everything's fine. My brother find out it was you who leaked the contract yet?"

"No, though he *is* suspicious. The security guard has kept his mouth shut."

I nodded. "That's good, keep me updated. Anything going on around there that I should know about?"

"Not really—it's been business as usual. Your brother's had a few dealings with some companies, including Oliver Vaughn."

I shook my head. I had brokered the deal between us—we were going to promote his hotels and get a percentage of the profits. Now my brother was getting all the credit for it. That made my blood boil.

"And, of course, he's still badmouthing you," Cheyenne continued. "Everyone thinks you almost destroyed the company. Your parents included."

I rolled my eyes. "Of course they do—my brother has gone to great lengths to ruin my reputation. Anyway, in the meantime, I need a small favor."

"Of course, name it."

"Can you call the community center here in Bridgewood and book a convention hall ASAP? On behalf of the company? I tried, but they're all booked up. If you say you work for the Miles Marketing Company, one of the richest companies in the States, they might make room for us."

Cheyenne paused. "A community center? Why? What are you doing over there, Ethan?"

"Oh, just a little of this and that. I'm doing my best to help the inn I'm staying at keep afloat. And we need that convention hall."

Cheyenne sighed. "All right—it's a little unusual, but I'll

see what I can do. I'll let you know. And be safe over there, Ethan."

I promised I would, hanging up. I walked down the stairs, finding Sharon still checking guests in. I hoped I hadn't been gone too long. A man in his early twenties stood nearby, talking on the phone in Korean as he clutched a suitcase. He was dressed casually in a hoodie, jeans, and sneakers. It looked like a tense phone call.

I waited for him to finish, ending the call with a sigh before I stepped forward. "Hi, there. Staying at the inn?"

He nodded as he put his phone away. "I am. Are you the one who's showing me to my room?"

"Of course—right this way. Is everything all right? I couldn't help but overhear your phone call."

He looked sad, grabbing his suitcase and following me up the stairs. "Yes, we're fine. Just some problems with my parents. They're very old and sick."

"Oh, I'm sorry to hear that. Anything we can do?"

"Send them a million dollars?" he joked. "My parents need money. I've been sending them some ever since I moved to the US for school, but I'm worried about them. Sometimes I think I should move back to South Korea and take care of them. But it's always been my dream to become an engineer in the States."

I frowned, stopping at a vacant room. "Sorry, that's a tough situation. I hope it works out for you. Well, this is your room. Let me know if you need anything."

"Thank you. My name's Eric Cho by the way. I'm staying in New York, but a friend told me this place is lovely. And I needed a little getaway."

I smiled. "Yeah, that's a popular opinion. Enjoy your time here."

He thanked me again, entering his room and putting his clothes away. As I headed down the stairs, there was only one person left—a shady-looking woman standing near the door, her hoodie covering her dark hair. She wore track pants, sneakers, and carried camo suitcases. I'd guess she was in her twenties.

Sharon looked up, smiling. "Ah, there's our newest employee. Ethan, meet Breanna Fallon. Ethan will show you to your room, Ms. Fallon. And that's it for the guests."

Only a handful? The inn deserved a lot more. Hopefully —with the fundraiser and my marketing advice—I could get them a lot more guests. And in turn, a lot more money.

Then maybe something good will have come out of this disaster.

"Hello there." I turned to the woman. "Follow me, Ms. Fallon. I'll show you to your room."

The woman nodded, dragging her suitcase with her. She didn't speak as I led her upstairs to a vacant room. Once I opened the door, she entered, glancing around.

"I hope the room's to your liking. Let us know if you need anything else."

"Will do," she unzipped her suitcase. "Thanks."

As she pulled out some clothes and toiletries, setting them up, I noticed a pocketknife in one of the compartments. She certainly looked like a woman who could take care of herself. Not wanting to anger her, I remained silent and closed the door as I left. The guests were the least of my concerns these days.

When my phone rang, I pulled it out of my pocket, noticing it was Cheyenne. I rushed to the hallway bathroom to accept the call so nobody would overhear. Anxiously, I pressed the answer button and held it up to my ear. "Hello? Cheyenne?"

"It's me. And I think you're going to like this," she began. "I got you your conference hall. Once I name-dropped the Miles company, they practically did whatever I wanted."

I sighed in relief. "Thank you—the Kennedys will be glad to hear it. They need this fundraiser."

"You've gotten close to them, haven't you? Sounds like it."

I nodded. "I have—they're good people. If I can help them in any way, I will. I mean, they gave me a job and a place to sleep. Without them, I'd be homeless, jobless, and hungry. And my brother would be laughing all the way to the bank. So I pretty much owe them everything."

"Yeah, I understand. Well, just be careful. I don't know how familiar people over there are with your company, but someone's bound to recognize you soon. And if you're still trying to keep your identity a secret, then you should watch it."

Cheyenne was right—I had to play it safe. I had come too close to Victoria almost finding out who I was.

"Yeah, I hear you. I'll try not to rely on the company name too much. For my sake *and* yours. Don't want my brother to find out what's going on. Thanks for everything, Cheyenne."

"You got it, Ethan. Talk soon."

As I hung up, leaving the bathroom, I noticed a black limousine pulling up outside. I found it strange—no one around here drove that kind of vehicle. As I watched from the window, wondering who it could be, a familiar face got out of the backseat.

Diana. My ex-girlfriend.

A million things ran through my mind but the most common one was, "What the hell is she doing here?"

Chapter Fourteen

My heart was pounding. I had to find out what Diana wanted—and get her to leave. I couldn't risk her ruining everything I had tried to build here. It was bad enough Victoria already had suspicions about me.

I sprinted down the stairs, passing the front desk. Sharon looked up from her paperwork. "Ah, Ethan, all done with the guests? I need you to—"

"In a second!" I called out, opening the front doors and stepping outside.

As I walked down the steps of the inn, Diana was approaching the doors. She stuck out in this town like a sore thumb—with an expensive jacket, high-heeled boots, a designer purse, and a diamond necklace. Everything about her screamed money.

She lowered her sunglasses. "Ethan, is that you? You look different."

"You're just not used to seeing me out of a suit. What are you doing here, Diana?"

"I came to find you," she replied, and I noticed her chauffeur waiting near the limo behind us. "I heard what happened on the news. How you lost everything, even access to your family's fortune."

I shrugged. "Yeah, well...that's the business world. Sometimes you strike a good deal, other times, you get a bad one."

"True enough. And now your brother's taken over the company. I spoke to him—he told me you went to some small town to find love. Had to look up Bridgewood on a map. Are you seriously out here on some kind of love quest?"

I shrugged. "So what if I am? You know LA—how everyone can be so fake. Is it wrong I want something real?"

"Always the hopeless romantic." Diana sighed. "But back to your brother for a second. Are you sure him taking over the company is such a good idea? He always struck me as the irresponsible type."

"You're right about that," I grumbled. "But I have no choice now. The company's in his name. So, you came all this way just to check up on me?"

"Maybe I did. Would that be so wrong?"

I crossed my arms. "I know you, Diana. I know you must be up to something. You proved that when you went through my files. What are you *really* here for?"

She smiled. "All right, you caught me. I've come with a proposal. I want us to get married."

My jaw dropped. "You...what?"

"Don't get it twisted, Ethan. It's not out of love. It's a marriage of convenience."

"Well, when you put it like that, how could I not marry you? Sounds like the healthiest marriage ever."

Diana rolled her eyes. "Stop being a smartass and listen for a moment. Marrying me would be good for you—you'd have access to money and power again. You need that if you want to get back on your feet. And together, with the knowledge you have of your company's dealings, we could finally crush the Miles Marketing Company for good."

I sneered. "That's what you've always wanted, right? Why you dated me? So you could destroy us and make your company more powerful?"

Diana blinked. "Well, of course. Why else would I date you?"

"Look, I'm flattered by the offer. And right now, things between my brother and I aren't great. I *would* love to see him lose it all."

"Then say yes," Diana encouraged. "We'll sign the marriage license right now. You can fly back to LA with me and get out of this silly little, small town. And then we can start plotting to ruin your former company."

I thought about it, but I just couldn't. I didn't want to marry Diana—didn't want to go back down that road. She was a two-faced snake. And as much as I hated my brother, I couldn't destroy the family company. Dad had worked so hard to build it up and I didn't want him to see it come tumbling down. Especially in his condition.

"No deal," I finally answered. "I like this town—I want to stay. I've already got a job and a place to sleep here. If I never go back to LA, I won't be sad about it."

Diana shook her head. "Pitiful. You have changed, Ethan. And not for the better."

"No—this is who I always was. I always wanted love and never felt right running my father's company. Maybe my brother did me a favor by taking over."

In some twisted way, maybe all this was meant to happen. I was still mad at my brother for playing me though.

Diana sighed. "Keep telling yourself that. Trust me—you'll miss all the money and power soon enough. You have my number if you change your mind. Goodbye, Ethan. Enjoy your new life in poverty."

Diana turned, heading back to her limo. Her chauffeur opened the back door for her, and she vanished inside behind black tinted windows. I sighed in relief as the limo pulled away, disappearing down the street. She was gone—hopefully for good.

I opened the doors to the inn, entering the foyer. Sharon looked up from her desk. "My, what was all that about?"

"So sorry, Sharon. Didn't mean to be rude. But I saw someone outside. A black limo."

Her eyes widened. "The last time a black limo was here, it belonged to Taylor's boyfriend. Which, unfortunately, didn't last too long. Who was it?"

"Uh, it was nothing. Just someone who was lost." I stepped closer. "Taylor's been quiet about her last relationship. What happened? And why does she hate rich people so much?"

Just as Sharon opened her mouth to tell me, I heard someone approaching from the stairs. It was Taylor. She was still happy. I hoped she would stay that way.

"I think the clothes are finished now. My hands hurt from all that sewing, but it was worth it. So, did you get the convention hall rented?"

I nodded. "Yep—for tomorrow afternoon. The fundraiser's been given the green light."

"Oh, that's wonderful!" Sharon cried. "I'll get to work on baking some goodies. More of an incentive for people to donate to us. Thank you for setting it all up, Ethan. Usually, the community center is booked months in advance. How did you do it?"

I shrugged, smiling. "I have my ways. And it was no problem. Now, I should go see what chores Mark has for me."

"I'll come with you," Taylor offered. "I've got some free time."

"While you do that, I'll get started on the desserts. And I'd like to have a little welcoming party for our guests," Sharon chimed in. "I'm going to set up some drinks and sandwiches in the dining hall. In an hour, please call all the guests downstairs."

"Will do." I watched Sharon walk to the kitchen. Then I turned to Taylor. "Ready to get started?"

Her eyes sparkled. "With you? Of course. Lead the way."

That gave me the butterflies in my stomach again. I led Taylor to Mark down the hall, asking for the chore sheet. He was still mopping the floors as he handed it over. We decided to split the chores—with me cleaning the bathrooms and Taylor doing the laundry. We finished in record time. The inn was spotless.

"Well, those chores just flew by," I remarked. "We make a good team."

Taylor nodded. "We sure do. Come on—let's go get the guests. Mom should be ready by now."

I followed Taylor upstairs, knocking on the doors of all the guests to tell them there was a welcoming party in the dining hall. Sophie was trying to get her son to stop crying, Katherine was muttering about her lost husband, and Abigail had put another sweater on. I wondered what she was trying to cover up. Eric looked worried about his parents, Breanna was barely talking to anyone, and Victoria was still trying to place where she knew me from.

That last one was getting on my nerves.

We led them into the dining hall, encouraging them to take some of the drinks and snacks Sharon had placed on the tables. She had done a great job—offering juice, coffee, tea, and water, then making egg and cucumber sandwiches for everyone. Her food was always amazing.

Mark joined us a minute later, kissing his wife's cheek and taking a sandwich. Then they started mingling with everyone and getting to know their guests. I chatted with Sophie and her son, making silly faces at him. He thought it was the funniest thing ever.

"Too cute," Taylor cooed. "You're great with kids. Do you have experience? Maybe nieces or nephews?"

I shook my head. "No, not yet. My family's pretty small."

"Well, I'd never be able to tell. You're a natural."

"I try." I poked Jacob's stomach and made him giggle. "I'd love to be a father someday."

"It's hard." Sophie patted her son's head. "But worth it."

"If you don't mind me asking...are you raising him on your own? With no partner or parents to help?"

Sophie sighed, nodding. Her son played with the string on her pants as we spoke. "Yeah, that's right. My parents disowned me for having a child out of wedlock. They text me every day to let me know how disappointed they are. In fact, they texted me something nasty when I got here. And the baby's father disappeared when I told him I was pregnant. It's been...challenging, to say the least."

"I'm so sorry," Taylor cried. "That's awful. But you seem to be doing a great job."

"Thank you—I'm trying. Money is tight but I wanted to take him somewhere. Give him some good memories of his childhood."

I smiled. "I think he'll look back fondly on this trip. Whatever happens, you two are lucky to have each other."

"Very true." Sophie stared at her son. "Maybe we've got all we need."

As I continued to play with Jacob, making him giggle, I heard Abigail approaching Sharon. She looked shy, gesturing at the food.

"Um, how many calories are in this?" she asked. "The sandwiches? I'm...kind of on a diet."

Sharon blinked. "A diet? But why, dear? You don't need to be."

Abigail looked uncomfortable, pulling her sweater down over her body. She always did that when people spoke to her.

"Yeah, well...there's nothing wrong with trying to watch your weight. And I don't want to eat too much, especially before dinner."

"I see. I believe the egg sandwich is about 230 calories. Not too much."

"Right." Abigail broke a sandwich in half. "I'll just have a little then. I'll be in my room if anyone needs me."

As she walked away, leaving the party, I found it strange. Why was Abigail so obsessed with calories?

Victoria walked over, clearing her throat. "Sorry to interrupt," she began. "But I think I know who you are."

I gulped. "You...you do?"

She nodded. "You look just like the son of that business owner. Even have the same name as him. Ethan M—"

"Well, I'm sorry, but I have no idea who you're talking about," I interrupted. "I must just have one of those boring faces that looks like someone else. I mean, if I was a business owner's son, would I be here?"

"Hmm." Victoria studied me. "I guess you have a point. And I heard he lost all his money anyway. Poor guy."

"Good." Taylor sipped her tea. "I think rich people shouldn't exist. They hoard all their money, getting rich off other people's ideas. They should lose it all."

Victoria looked offended. "Is that so?"

I chuckled nervously. "Taylor doesn't mean that—she's just blowing off steam. Come on, I think we have some more chores to do."

Taylor looked confused as I pulled her arm, leading her into the hallway. She gave me a funny look when we were out of earshot of the welcoming party. "What was all that about?" Taylor wondered.

"Victoria's incredibly rich, you know. And powerful back in LA. You don't want to offend her and lose her business, do you? Or have her give the inn a bad review online?"

Taylor sighed. "I guess not. We need the business. But what's up with her thinking you're some businessman's son?"

"I don't know. She must be confused," I lied. "So, what do you want to do now?"

Taylor checked her watch. "I think I'm going to head to the store to pick up a few things. Some groceries and toiletries we need. Do you want to come along for the ride?"

As tempting as it was to spend more time with Taylor, I remembered my date with Madison. The one against my will. I wanted to get it over with so I could get her off my back for good.

"Uh, I can't. I think I'm going to rest and just take it easy," I replied. "I'll see you later tonight."

Taylor nodded, grabbing her keys and leaving the inn. I sighed in relief when she didn't ask questions. I headed up to my room for a little while, getting ready for my date. Madison returned an hour later to knock on my door.

"You in there, handsome?" she called. "It's me. The hottest girl you've ever gone on a date with."

I rolled my eyes, opening the door. "Hey, Madison. Ready to head out?"

I noticed she had gotten her hair done—now it was wavy instead of straight—and her nails were perfectly manicured. She was wearing another tight dress, this one sparkly and purple with black heels.

She smiled, reaching for my hand. "I am. Come on!"

She dragged me down the stairs, making me hope no one would see us. But the Kennedys and the guests were still mingling in the dining hall. If Taylor saw us together, I would've been mortified. I didn't want her to get the wrong idea.

She dragged me out to my truck, then I unlocked the doors. "Can I ask a favor?"

Madison smiled, batting her eyelashes. "Of course, handsome. Anything for you."

"Can you not tell Taylor about this?"

"Trying to keep me as your dirty little secret, huh?" Madison smirked. "All right, I'll keep it quiet. You afraid she won't like you anymore if she knows?"

"Uh, no," I lied, getting into my truck. "I'm just a private person. Anyway, you wanted to head to the mall?"

Madison nodded, pointing the way as I drove. I took us to the Bridgewood Mall which was busy this time of day. We parked underground, then took the stairs up into the mall. It wasn't like the shopping places back in LA, but it was pretty big for a small town.

"Come on, let's window shop and see if anything catches my eye." Madison dragged me past some stores. "Ooh, new shoes!"

For the next hour, Madison shopped, giving me her bags to hold. She was maxing out her credit cards for the latest fashion. I just rolled my eyes, glad she wasn't asking me to pay. My money was tight these days.

As she tried on a sparkly black gown in a store—skintight as always—she turned away from the mirror, glancing at me. I was sitting on the bench and waiting for all this torture to be over.

"So, what do you think?" she asked. "Super sexy?"

"Uh, sure," I lied. "You should get it."

She beamed. "See, that's why I like you, Ethan. You always know what to say."

I just rolled my eyes, waiting for her to change out of the dress and pay for it. Once she was done, she grabbed my free hand, dragging me toward the food court. My other hand was nearly breaking with all the bags she had me carrying.

"Let's get some dinner before heading back to the inn."

She scanned the food court. "Ooh, they have sushi. Come on, I'm starving."

Madison dragged me toward the line, ordering a sushi platter for us to share. And then she made me pay for it. I obliged, wanting to get our date over with quickly. We sat in the food court as Madison rambled on.

"This place isn't a five-star restaurant, but it'll do." She dipped her roll into soy sauce. "Maybe you can take me to this nice place just outside Bridgewood one day. And then we can go skinny-dipping after..."

I was barely listening, just nodding along and eating to remain polite. I didn't see Taylor anywhere, which was a good sign. But I did see someone familiar in the crowd.

Drew.

And when he noticed us, he pulled out his smartphone, snapping a picture of me and Madison eating together.

Chapter Fifteen

I rose to my feet, pushing through the crowd of people. Drew noticed me chasing him and took off toward the doors. As soon as I stepped outside, Drew dove into his truck, vanishing down the street. With that incriminating photo of me and Madison on a date.

I sighed, hoping if Taylor saw it, she'd understand. Or at least hear me out. But how did Drew even know we were there? He didn't seem like the kind of guy to visit a mall. And he wasn't even carrying any bags.

I turned around, heading back to our table. Madison looked pissed when I sat down. "What the hell was that? Where did you run off to?"

"Sorry." I rubbed my stomach. "Guess I'm not feeling too well. Can we wrap this up?"

Madison sighed. "Fine. Despite your little Houdini routine, I had a good time. We should head to a fancy restaurant for our second date."

There wasn't going to be a second date. And even though Madison had coerced me into coming here, I still wanted to let her down easy.

"Madison, look—I don't know how much clearer I can

be," I cried exasperatedly. "I'm not interested in you. I like Taylor and I want to give things a shot between me and her. You're a great girl, though. You'll find someone amazing."

"Oh no, don't give me that speech. That 'it's not you, it's me', bullshit," Madison spat. "What does Taylor have that I don't, huh? Is it the fashion thing? Because I'm clearly more attractive than her."

I was trying to stay calm but the more I spoke to Madison, the more infuriated I became. I needed to shut it down. "It's got nothing to do with that. There's just a spark between me and Taylor—that's all. And no offense, but I don't feel it with you. So leave me alone. No more meddling, no more dates. Please."

Madison shook her head. "You're an idiot, Ethan. Now grab my bags and drive me back to the inn. We're done here."

Finally. With glee, I picked up Madison's shopping bags and threw out our scraps. I led her to the parking lot where I drove us back to the inn. She stepped out, grabbing all the shopping bags from the back of my truck.

"You'll regret blowing your chance with me!" she spat.

She slammed my door, heading inside the inn with a huff. I only shook my head and turned off the ignition. As I got out, I realized Madison would've fit in great with all the other women I had met in Los Angeles.

But not Taylor—she was different. And that was why I liked her.

I entered the inn, hearing Madison slam her door upstairs. I hoped that would be the end of her harassment. As I walked past the front desk, I found Sharon there, typing at her computer. The welcoming party in the dining hall must've ended.

"Ethan, you're back," Sharon cried. "Madison looked upset. There must be something in the water. Taylor came back and stormed off to her room."

"Really?" I gulped. "I'll go check on her."

Sharon nodded, returning to her work as I headed toward the staircase. I took it up to the attic and knocked on the door to Taylor's room. I couldn't hear anything inside the attic.

"Taylor?" I called. "Are you in there?"

I heard footsteps, then the door opened. And Taylor didn't look happy. "Ethan, there you are. Back from your date?"

My face fell. Of course Drew had told her—he didn't want us together either. He and Madison had more in common than they realized.

"Let me guess," I lamented. "Drew sent you the picture of me and Madison at the mall?"

"That's right," Taylor cried. "You could've at least told me you were interested in my cousin."

"I'm not!" I cried, leaning on the doorframe. "Okay, look —I know the picture probably looked bad, but you've got it all wrong."

Taylor raised an eyebrow. "So, you weren't on a date with my cousin?"

I hesitated. "Well, uh...I guess I was. But it's not what you think. I only went out with her as a deal. I demanded to know what she told you. She said she'd tell me—for a price. The price was a date. And now, I feel like I need a shower."

"Hmm. That does sound like something my cousin would do." Taylor sighed. "Why didn't you just tell me? Why did I have to find out from a text by Drew? Who was pretty smug about it, by the way."

I rolled my eyes. "Of course he was. I didn't want to hurt your feelings—that was all. And I made it clear to Madison that I'm not interested in her like that. That there's someone else I'm into."

"Oh?" A smile tugged at Taylor's lips. "And who would that be?"

The mood had turned playful between us again—something I liked. I hated fighting with Taylor.

"You know her," I played along. "Dark hair, beautiful, an interest in fashion. We have a great connection too."

"Yeah, I agree." Taylor sighed. "All right—I believe you, Ethan."

I sighed in relief. "So you aren't mad at me anymore?"

"No, I'm not. As long as you don't go out with Madison again."

"Believe me, I didn't even want to go out with her in the first place," I groaned. "She took me shopping and damn near bought the whole mall. Not exactly an enjoyable first date."

Taylor snorted. "Oh, no? What would you prefer for a first date?"

I shrugged. "I don't know—something we both like. Something fun."

"Well, there *is* a mini carnival in town. It opens tonight, actually."

"Good timing. If you're still up for a date, we should go. A little celebration before the fundraiser tomorrow."

Taylor nodded. "Sounds good. In the meantime, you should probably stay away from Madison. Her wrath can be scary—especially when she doesn't get what she wants."

"Yeah, you're telling me. I'll be careful. And you should do the same around Drew. I'm telling you—I think that guy is stalking me. He's clearly trying to get between us, just like Madison. I've avoided calling the cops because I know Drew's important to you, but it's still worrying."

"I agree. And thanks for not calling the police on him yet. Hopefully he'll leave you alone. In the meantime, let's not give them what they want," Taylor declared. "No more secrets between us. Deal?"

I swallowed, knowing the biggest secret of all—my past—

was one I couldn't tell Taylor. But it was too late to turn back now.

"Deal," I finally responded. "No more secrets."

"Good. Dinner's soon if you wanted to rest before then, by the way. Mom asked the guests what they liked, and they decided on shepherd's pie."

My stomach growled at the thought. "Mmm, my favorite. I had sushi with Madison but that sounds much better. Looking forward to it. See you later, Taylor."

She nodded, closing her door and getting back to work on designing new outfits. With my chores done and nowhere else to go, I headed downstairs to get to my room. But I paused when I heard voices. It was coming from Madison's room—and they were low and hushed.

"I'm trying my best, but it's not easy," she continued. "Uh-huh, okay, I understand..."

I shook my head, not even wanting to know what she was up to. Returning to my room, I took a shower and shaved before I heard a knock. I opened it—fearing it was Madison —but found Mrs. Cabot standing there, holding her urn.

"Hello, Mrs. Cabot," I began. "Is there something I can do for you?"

"I need to ask a favor," she replied, gesturing at the urn. "I want to scatter my husband's ashes, but...I don't want to go alone. And since you remind me so much of him..."

"You want me to accompany you?" I filled in. "Because I can do that."

Her eyes lit up. "Would you? Oh, thank you, young man. I'd appreciate that."

"It's no problem. Do you know where you want to scatter the ashes?"

She nodded. "The beach looks lovely—and it's not too far from here. Could you take me?"

"Of course—follow me to my truck. I'm sure your

husband is very thankful you came all this way to scatter his ashes."

Mrs. Cabot smiled sadly. "Thank you—I hope so."

I led Mrs. Cabot past the rooms where Madison had finished her strange phone call. Then we headed downstairs, walking out to the parking lot. I helped Mrs. Cabot into the passenger seat with her urn before starting my truck. I used the GPS on my phone to guide the way to the beach.

When we arrived, it was mostly empty except for a few teenagers playing in the water. It was a beautiful place— clean, blue water, shiny sand, and some rocks to sit on and watch the waves. I helped Mrs. Cabot out of my truck before we approached the edge of the shore. I stood nearby just in case she needed my support.

Just as she opened the urn, she paused. "I...don't think I can do it."

I frowned. "Why not?"

She turned to me, her eyes glistening. "I don't want to say goodbye. I don't want to let him go. This urn...it's all I have left of my Chester."

I placed a hand on her shoulder. "That's not true, Mrs. Cabot. You always have Chester—he goes everywhere you do. You can't see him, but his love is all around you. Forever and always."

She blinked back tears. "Do you mean that?"

"I do. You don't have to be afraid—this is what he would've wanted. Come on, I'll do it with you. Are you ready?"

She took a deep breath, turning the urn over. "I'm ready. Goodbye, Chester."

I tipped the urn with her, letting the ashes fall out into the water. They floated away and disappeared. All she had left was the empty urn and her husband's picture. We stood in silence for a few minutes, just watching the waves together.

"Well, I guess that's it." Mrs. Cabot sighed. "Chester's been laid to rest."

"You did well," I told her. "I'm proud of you. And Chester would be too."

She sniffled. "Thank you. But I wish I had died with him."

"Don't say that, Mrs. Cabot. You still have so much to live for. Trust me."

She turned to me, shaking her head. "No, you don't understand. With Chester gone, I've lost his salary. I never had a job—I was a stay-at-home wife. And because of that, I risk losing our house. Losing everything. My bills are late."

"I'm so sorry," I whispered. "I wish there was something I could do for you."

My father's money could've saved her, but I didn't have access to it anymore. And I didn't think my brother would help out a total stranger. There was nothing I could do.

"Yes, me too," she sniffled. "This will probably be my last trip. I...don't know where I'll end up when I lose my house."

"You don't have any family? Any friends back home?"

"None. We lived a quiet life, and I couldn't have children." Mrs. Cabot turned silent. "Anyway, I'd like to go back to the inn now. I need some rest before dinner."

I nodded, guiding her to my truck in the parking lot. The ride was quiet. *That poor woman,* I thought as I took us back to the inn. *If it wasn't bad enough to lose her husband, now she was going to lose her house.*

"Thanks for coming with me, young man. And for the encouraging words." Mrs. Cabot reached for the door handle. "Despite everything...the love Chester and I had for each other keeps me going. And I hope you experience that one day."

"I hope so too," I murmured. "You're welcome, Mrs. Cabot. Rest easy now."

After getting out of the truck, I took Mrs. Cabot inside, leading her back to her room. She looked very tired and needed rest. I did the same—heading back to my room and napping before the chime of a bell woke me up. When I opened my door, Sharon and Mark were walking down the hall, ringing bells.

"Dinner, everyone!" Sharon called. "Come and get it while it's still hot."

That brought everyone downstairs. I left my room, following the crowd of guests to the dining hall. Sharon had plated the shepherd's pie and set it out on the table. Taylor saved me a seat, then I sat next to her and started asking questions about the carnival. Madison sat far away from us but kept glaring over.

"This looks amazing," Abigail exclaimed, sitting at the table. "But how many calories are in it? And fat?"

Sharon smiled as she took her seat, passing out napkins. "I already looked it up for you, dear. It has 420 calories and fourteen grams of fat. Go on—try it. It's delicious."

Abigail inspected the plate, then frowned. "It *does* look good...but I'm not that hungry. Mostly tired. I think I'm just going to head back to my room."

"Are you sure?" Mark asked. "Because it's better when it's fresh."

Abigail nodded, rising to her feet. "Yeah, I'm sure. But thanks for cooking for me."

"Okay, dear." Sharon sighed. "There will be leftovers later if you want some."

Abigail thanked her, then headed up the stairs. The rest of the guests joined us, and we chit-chatted across the table. Mrs. Cabot still looked a little sad with dark bags under her eyes. But that was understandable with everything she was going through.

I cleared my throat. "So, me and Taylor are heading to the carnival tonight. Is anyone else interested?"

"Oh, that's right—the annual carnival." Mark smiled. "It's always such a fun time. Yes, Sharon and I will be there."

"And you all should come too." Taylor gestured at the table. "It's a yearly tradition in Bridgewood. You should get out and explore what the town has to offer while you're here."

Some of the guests were skeptical, but they decided to check it out. After dinner, I helped Taylor and her parents wash the dishes. The guests headed to their rooms before the carnival. Madison gave me an icy glare, then disappeared upstairs. I just shook my head and finished drying off the dishes.

Taylor checked her watch. "The carnival's starting soon —it's almost dark. I'll meet you by the truck, Ethan. Just need to change."

I nodded. "Okay, see you soon."

She scurried away, heading up to the attic. Sharon and Mark were just watching us with a smile. I turned to them, wondering what they were grinning about.

"What is it?" I asked. "Food on my face?"

"No, nothing like that." Sharon smiled. "It's just...you make Taylor so happy. We can tell by those big smiles of hers. And she makes you happy too."

I nodded. "She sure does."

"We think you look very cute together, that's all," Sharon continued. "And we hope it works out."

"Yes, for sure," Mark added. "Taylor deserves a happily ever after. She's been through enough."

I still didn't know exactly what she had been through, but judging by the way her parents spoke about it, it didn't sound good. Before I could respond, I heard footsteps approaching.

When I turned around, my jaw dropped. Taylor was wearing a gorgeous golden dress that went to her knees. She was going to stand out for sure in the crowd. She paired it with boots and a ruby necklace, letting her hair down, wild and free.

And it was at that moment I realized I was falling in love with her.

"You look...amazing," I blurted out. "Like some kind of golden goddess."

Taylor giggled. "I wouldn't go that far, but thanks. This is one of my more recent dresses. I'll be showing it off at the fundraiser tomorrow."

"It's amazing, dear," Sharon gushed. She and Mark watched us with pride. "Have a good time at the carnival, you two. You deserve it."

"We will." I held out an arm. "Are you ready?"

"Absolutely." Taylor locked her arm with mine. "Now let's go win every prize at that carnival and have a damn good time."

Chapter Sixteen

I escorted Taylor out to my truck, opening the door for her like a gentleman. Then I drove us downtown where the carnival was in full swing. It had several booths to play games, a dining area where a man was cooking hot dogs, and a mini Ferris wheel. The city had strung lights around to make it look magical.

"So, this is a yearly tradition?" I parked on the road.

Taylor nodded, reaching for her door. "Yep—my parents used to take me here as a kid. I went last year, but...it was with my ex. I wasn't planning to ever go again."

"Well, I'm glad I could convince you to come out. It looks fun." I smiled. "Come on—let's see what we can win."

We walked into the carnival area, our arms locked. People were playing carnival games and had brought their children. Little kids ran around us, giggling and playing tag. I spotted a massive teddy bear sitting on a vendor's table. It was the grand prize in a ring toss game.

"Look at that." I pointed at the bear. "That thing is monstrous. Bigger than my head. I want to win that for you."

"Are you sure?" Taylor asked, turning to me. "That ring toss game is hard. I tried to win last year but couldn't do it."

I rolled up my sleeves, realizing this was my chance to be a hero. "Oh, I'm ready. Come on."

We patiently waited in line, watching an elderly man try to win the bear for his six-year-old grandson. He kept missing the rings. When he had no more left, he sighed, turning to his grandson.

"Sorry, Charlie. Grandpa tried his best."

"Better luck next time," the vendor taunted, popping his gum. "Next!"

The little boy was still staring at the bear as his grandfather grabbed his arm, leading him away. I knew I had to win this thing. For Taylor's sake *and* to rub it in the carnival worker's face.

"You here for the ring toss?" the vendor asked, gesturing at me.

I nodded. "That's right. How much?"

"Five dollars for a game," the vendor answered, glancing at the rings. "You get three rings. Three chances to get it around this cup. You win, you get the giant bear."

"Don't mind if I do." I took the rings. "Okay, let's do this."

The first ring I threw didn't even come close to the cup. I could hear the worker snickering. Feeling embarrassed, I flung the ring again, watching it bounce off a cup and fall on the ground. The giggles from the employee were starting to get on my nerves.

"Only one shot left," the employee warned. "Too bad you aren't going to make it."

Taylor shook her head, whispering to me. "That guy is awful. Don't worry about it, Ethan—I don't want that bear anyway."

But I hadn't given up hope yet. "Oh, no—I'm winning that thing. Now it's personal."

Taylor held her breath as I threw the ring again, silently

praying it would land on the cup. I closed my eyes and couldn't bear to watch. When I heard a clink, I opened them, realizing the ring had fallen around the cup. Even the carnival worker looked surprised.

"You did it," he said, blinking. "Huh. No one's ever won before."

"First time for everything." I grinned. "One bear, please."

The employee rolled his eyes, handing me the bear. He replaced the prize with another toy as I handed the bear to Taylor.

"Here you are, my lady," I began in my British medieval knight voice. "One bear for the fair maiden."

Taylor giggled, taking the bear. She had to use two hands to carry it. "Thank you, Ethan. But if you don't mind...I'd like to give the bear to that little boy."

She pointed at the boy with his grandfather, still staring back at the bear from a distance. His grandfather was playing —and losing—another game at a nearby tent. I sighed, realizing Taylor was right.

"Yeah, I get it," I agreed. "That little boy is clearly in love with it."

Taylor smiled. "Thanks, Ethan. Come on—let's go make his day."

We walked over to the boy, his grandfather losing at a mini fishing game. Taylor handed the bear to the child. "Hey, we saw you eyeing this bear for a while. I wanted you to have it."

"Me?" the boy cried, staring at the bear.

The grandpa turned around. "Oh, someone finally won that darn thing. Are you sure you want to give it to my grandson? That's very nice of you but you won it fair and square."

"We insist." I smiled. "Go on—it's yours now. Hope you enjoy it."

Taylor handed it over, then the boy took it. He immediately cuddled the bear and smiled. Just by the look on his face, we knew we had done the right thing.

"Thank you." The grandfather said, watching watched his grandson with a smile. "You've made his night."

"It was our pleasure," Taylor chirped. "Enjoy the bear and have a good evening."

We waved goodbye, then started walking around the carnival grounds. The boy was still hugging the giant teddy bear like he had won the lottery. I thought it was sweet. But that was Taylor—she was a kind person.

And it was one of the reasons I loved her.

"It was kind of you to give that boy the bear." I walked side-by-side with Taylor. "His whole face lit up."

Taylor shrugged. "It was nothing. Life can be hard and miserable sometimes. Kindness is the only way we'll get through it."

"Agreed. You showed me a lot of kindness when I first got here. I don't think I would've survived Bridgewood if not for you."

She shook her head. "You would've been fine—trust me. But it was my pleasure."

"Kind, beautiful, *and* humble," I flirted. "You're just the whole package, aren't you?"

Taylor grinned. "You're one to talk. I can't believe a man like you is single."

"Yeah." I sighed. "Sometimes it takes a while to find the right person. Sometimes you have to visit a small town and have your truck break down before your dream woman comes to save you. Like a knight in shining armor."

She smiled. I didn't know how she did it—that just by gazing into my eyes, she could stop time around us. It was like no one else was at the carnival.

But the moment faded when I spotted Drew in the

crowd. He pushed through the people, tapping on Taylor's shoulder. And just like that, the magic was gone.

"Oh, Drew—you're here." Taylor didn't sound too excited. "Come to enjoy some carnival games?"

Drew glanced at me. "Something like that. How's that lip healing, outsider?"

"Just fine," I snapped. "Taylor patched me up and I'm feeling better than ever."

Drew's fists balled at that. If he wanted me and Taylor to spend less time together, he was failing.

"This has got to stop," Taylor scolded, glancing between us. "All the fighting. Drew, you can't beat people up on the street."

"Hey, he started it!" Drew cried.

"What?" I sneered. "That's so not true. You tackled me first, buddy—not the other way around!"

"I don't care who started it!" Taylor cried. "I just want it to end. You don't need to be best friends, but you *do* need to be civil. And stay away from each other. Got it?"

"Fine," I grumbled. "Minding my own business is what I was trying to do anyway."

"Yeah, right," Drew muttered. Then he glanced at Taylor, his eyes softening. "Can we talk for a minute? In private? I have something I want to tell you."

Taylor hesitated. "Can it wait? I'm kinda in the middle of something here."

Drew glanced at me. "You came to the carnival with *him*?"

"She did." I stepped closer. "And she doesn't want to talk to you right now. So go away."

Taylor fell silent, facing the ground. There was an awkward pause as Drew glanced between us before stepping back.

"Fine," he grumbled. "But we still need to talk at some point. See you later."

He walked off, blending in with the crowd. I was just glad that was over.

"You okay?" I asked Taylor.

She nodded, turning to me. "Yeah, I'm fine. It's just... Drew's gotten a lot more demanding since you came to town. Always wanting to talk to me, getting mad when I'm too busy. It's like he changed overnight."

Maybe because he realized me and Taylor were falling for each other. But I didn't admit it.

"I'm sorry," I replied. "That must hurt, considering you grew up together."

Taylor nodded. "Definitely. Anyway, let's go do something fun."

"Sounds perfect." I locked my arm with hers. "I saw a cotton candy machine near the entrance. In the mood for some sticky candy that'll get stuck in your teeth?"

Taylor giggled. "Definitely."

We walked toward the cotton candy vendor, buying two bushels. I got the blue one and Taylor got the pink cotton candy. As we ate it, our mouths turned colors, making us look funny.

"You look like the Blue Man Group," Taylor joked. "Your mouth's totally blue."

"And yours is as pink as a unicorn," I joked back. "We probably look very silly."

"Oh, for sure." Taylor smiled. "But it's fun being silly with you."

And there it was again—that look that could stop time. Whenever we stared at each other, I never wanted it to end.

"So, what do you want to do now?" Taylor asked.

I gestured at the Ferris wheel. "Only one thing left. You ever been on a Ferris wheel before?"

"Yeah, a long time ago," Taylor whimpered. "I'm...actually afraid of heights."

"Well, we don't have to go on it if you don't want to."

Taylor took a deep breath. "No, it's okay. I want to ride the Ferris wheel with you."

"All right. Don't worry—I'll keep you safe."

Taylor sighed in relief at that, grabbing onto my arm. We pushed through the crowd to head to the long line standing in front of the Ferris wheel. As we waited, I noticed the guests from the inn had arrived. Mrs. Cabot pushed over to us first.

"Hello, young man," she said. "Thanks again for helping me scatter my husband's ashes on the beach. I still miss him, but...I feel like his soul is at peace now."

"It definitely is," I replied, patting her shoulder. "You're welcome, Mrs. Cabot. Let me know if you need anything else."

"That was sweet of you." Taylor glanced at me. "I'm glad you were able to find some peace, Mrs. Cabot."

"Thank you, dear. It's been a tough few months." Mrs. Cabot glanced around, watching people lining up for rides and playing games. "My, I haven't been to a carnival in decades. Not since my husband and I went in the seventies."

"Sounds like you had a great time," I replied. "Would you like to ride the Ferris wheel with us?"

Mrs. Cabot glanced between us, shaking her head. "No, that's all right. You kids go and have a good time. I'm going to check out the food. See you at the inn."

We said goodbye, watching as she hobbled over to the food vendor. Taylor was smiling at me when I looked back.

"What? Do I have cotton candy on my face?"

Taylor smiled. "No. I just... I think that was a kind thing to do for Mrs. Cabot. You can tell she needed that."

"It was no problem. Mrs. Cabot is a nice lady—I wanted to help."

Taylor was still smiling at me as we moved forward, the line getting closer to the front. We were so close to getting onto the Ferris wheel. I noticed Sophie and her son, Jacob, in the crowd while playing some games. At least it looked like they were having a good time.

I didn't see Abigail, Victoria, or Eric anywhere in the crowd. Maybe they didn't have time to come to the carnival. The only other guest who had arrived was Breanna—and it looked like she was in trouble. A middle-aged man was yelling at her while a cop stood nearby.

"Uh oh." I gestured at Breanna. "Looks like our guest's in trouble."

"Come on, let's figure out what's going on," Taylor replied. "We can get back in line after."

I nodded, stepping out of line with Taylor as we approached Breanna. When we stepped a little closer, we could finally hear what the man was saying. The cop was busy writing it down in his notepad.

"...and I'm telling you, she stole my wallet!" the man cried. "We bumped into each other, then I checked my pocket, and it was gone."

"I didn't steal your stupid wallet," Breanna spat. "Sure, I bumped into you, but it was an accident."

"Excuse me, what's going on?" I interrupted.

"This dude thinks I stole from him," Breanna explained. "But I didn't. I swear!"

The cop looked Breanna up and down, then rolled his eyes. "Uh-huh, sure. Where did you put his wallet?"

"I didn't take it!" Breanna replied.

"Do you have any proof Breanna took your wallet, sir?" Taylor crossed her arms.

The man huffed. "Well...not exactly. But I think bumping into me was more than a coincidence. I want this girl jailed—"

The employee from the cotton candy booth walked over, clearing their throat. "Sorry to interrupt, but sir, you left your wallet at my booth. You put it down to get your cotton candy."

Both the man and the cop looked surprised. Breanna had been telling the truth.

"Oh." The man took the wallet from the vendor. "Well, um...thank you for returning it. I'll just be going now."

"Um, excuse me?" Breanna demanded. "Aren't you going to apologize for accusing me?"

"You probably would've stolen it, given the chance," the man sneered. "I've seen your type before."

"Her type?" I asked.

"Yeah—young people with tattoos, up to no good," the man continued. "They're angry they never amounted to anything, so they take it out on the world around them. If not me, she'll steal from some other poor S.O.B. Trust me."

The cop nodded. "Stay out of trouble, miss. I'll be keeping an eye on you."

Breanna just shook her head, watching as the cop and the angry man walked away. I felt bad for her. She hadn't done anything wrong, but she had gotten blamed for it anyway. Where was the justice?

"You all right?" I asked Breanna. "That was pretty rude of those guys to accuse you of something with no proof."

Breanna sighed. "Yeah, yeah—I'm fine. Just a normal day in my life. People see my tattoos and hoodie, and act like I'm a beast or something."

"Well, we want you to know we don't see you like that," Taylor declared. "And we hope you have a good time at the carnival."

"Thanks. I just wanted to have some fun and look what happened." Breanna rolled her eyes. "But maybe it's my fault. I...don't have the cleanest background."

"What do you mean?"

She sighed. "Promise you won't tell anyone?"

Taylor nodded. "Of course. We promise."

"Well, when I was a kid, I got into some stupid stuff. Gangs and drugs. I wanted to impress a friend of mine." Breanna sighed. "Spent some time in juvey for a while. I just got out last year."

I gasped. "I didn't know that. I'm sorry all that happened to you."

"Yeah, me too. But I'm trying to do better. I came to Bridgewood to get away for a new start. It's not working too well."

"Well, it's admirable that you're trying," I comforted her. "Don't give up. You can change, Breanna—and you deserve better. Don't forget that."

I saw a small smile tugging at her lips. "Yeah...I guess so. Thanks, guys. See you around."

She walked away, heading to the food vendor to grab a hot dog. We watched her go in silence before Taylor spoke.

"Poor girl," she lamented. "She's made some mistakes and trying to do better, but wherever she goes, some asshole's accusing her of something. But it was nice of you to console her."

"I tried. I hope everything works out for her. In the meantime, we should keep an eye on Breanna. Just to make sure no one else messes with her."

"Good idea. Now, what do you say we get back to the Ferris wheel?"

"I'd say you read my mind." I wrapped my arm around Taylor's. "Let's go."

As we lined up at the Ferris wheel, I spotted Drew and Madison whispering near a booth.

And whatever they were talking about, it looked like they were up to no good.

Chapter Seventeen

I pointed at Drew and Madison, nudging Taylor. "Look —Bridgewood's hottest new couple."

Taylor glanced over at them. "Huh. Didn't know they were friends."

"Me either. Looks pretty intense." I shook my head, turning back to the Ferris wheel. "Whatever's going on, I don't want to get involved."

"Yeah, good idea. Maybe they'll go on a date."

And leave me and Taylor alone forever? That sounded great to me. I was already rooting for their relationship.

As the line moved, we stepped forward, buying two tickets to the Ferris wheel. The employee opened the gate and let us sit down. We waited until other people were seated before the ride started slowly. Taylor closed her eyes, not daring to look down. I placed my hand on hers.

"It's all right," I whispered. "I got you."

She nodded, her eyes still tightly closed. "Okay. I believe you, Ethan."

"Why are you so scared of heights, anyway? Did something happen?"

She still had her eyes firmly shut. "Yeah. When I was ten, I traveled to Disneyland with my parents. One of the few family trips they could afford. Anyway, I ended up getting stuck on one of their rollercoaster rides. Not fun."

"I bet. I'm so sorry."

"Thanks." She finally opened her eyes, looking around. "Hey, this isn't so bad. And you can see all of Bridgewood from up here."

"You sure can." I watched Taylor gaze out at the town. The Ferris wheel brought us up to the top and turned slowly. "Beautiful, isn't it?"

"Very." She turned to me. "Thanks for convincing me to come on the Ferris wheel, Ethan. I'm having a great time."

"Me too. I'd say that was a pretty awesome first date."

Taylor's eyes twinkled. "The best."

When she laid her head on my shoulder, I felt butterflies again. It felt so natural to be with Taylor—so right. And come hell or high water, no matter what Drew, Madison, or my brother did to us, I was going to fight for it.

The Ferris wheel took us to the bottom, then stopped. The employee opened the gate and helped us stand up. As we walked away, more people stepping up to ride, I turned to Taylor.

"So, how was that? Your first Ferris wheel ride?"

"It was amazing." She smiled. "The company was too."

"Well, that's good to hear. And if I'm not being too forward...I'd like us to have a second date. If that's okay with you."

She nodded. "I'd love that. We'll plan something after the fundraiser tomorrow. I want to get that over with. Then maybe we can catch a movie or something or go out to eat. I promise I won't take you shopping and force you to carry my bags."

I snorted. "That's appreciated, thanks. Hey, I see a photo

booth over there. Come on—let's get a picture. So we don't forget tonight."

Taylor agreed, grabbing my hand. We walked hand-in-hand through the circus grounds, and I felt like I had won the lottery with her on my arm. I took her to the photo booth, opening the curtain and letting her jump in first. I joined a second later and placed a five-dollar bill in the money slot.

"Okay, say cheese," I called, turning to the camera. "Three, two...one!"

When the light went off, we both smiled. For the next shot, we did a super serious *Blue Steel* impression. We couldn't stop giggling at that. As the timer counted down, I turned to Taylor.

"Okay, last picture," I promised. "What face should we make? Silly, serious, happy?"

"I have an idea," she whispered. "Close your eyes."

When I closed my eyes, hearing the picture click, I felt Taylor's lips on mine. This kiss was different from our first—it was hungrier, more urgent. I felt blood rushing to every part of my body and hoped she wouldn't see my boner poking through my pants.

When she pulled away, breathless, I opened my eyes. "That was...damn, I'm not even going to sugarcoat it. It was the best kiss of my life."

Taylor smiled. "Yeah, mine too. I hope I didn't come on too strong."

"Nah, it was perfect." I reached for her hand. "Come on —let's check out the photos."

We stepped out of the booth, the sheets of photos printing in a box on the side. It spat out two sheets of pictures. I took one, handing her the other and smiled at the photos. We made a good couple—and staring at the kissing photo was enough to make heat rise through my body again.

"A nice memento of the evening," she beamed. "I'll keep it safe in the attic. Right beside my bed and workstation."

I smiled, placing mine in my wallet. "I'll keep it there—so I can see your adorable face every day."

She giggled. "That's cute. So, what do you want to do now?"

I shrugged, glancing around. "I think we've done everything. It's a pretty small carnival. Want me to drive you back to the inn?"

"That would be great, yeah. Before Drew tries to get me to talk to him again. I don't know what he wants."

But I had a feeling. He hated us together—he wanted to stop what was growing between us. And I was afraid he'd find a way to do it, especially with Madison's help. I was quickly growing tired of both of them.

As we headed to the parking lot, we spotted Sharon and Mark showing up at the carnival, hand-in-hand. They smiled at us and paid for two tickets before vanishing inside the circus grounds.

"I guess Mom and Dad decided to come after all." Taylor hopped into the passenger seat of my truck. "I hope they have fun. They've been married for...sheesh, thirty years. Their anniversary is coming up soon."

"That's incredible," I gushed, getting into the truck and starting the ignition. "What do you think their secret is?"

Taylor paused. "Probably friendship. And respect. They're always hanging out—doing things together. They must be the glue that keeps them going strong."

"Good to know. I'll try to learn from their example."

Taylor sighed as I pulled away. "I'm trying too. If it weren't for them...I think I would've completely given up on love a long time ago. But Mom and Dad's encouragement keeps me going."

"I'm glad. They do make a cute couple."

"The cutest." Taylor paused. "Hey, Mom told me a limo pulled up to the inn earlier. What was that all about?"

"Oh, uh," I stammered, my hands gripping the wheel. "It was nothing. Someone at the wrong address."

"I see. But still, a limo? No one around here has that kind of cash. They must've been rich."

I stopped at a red light, the glow illuminating the car. "Yeah, must've been."

Taylor scoffed. "I wish the rich would die off."

I gulped, stepping on the gas when the light turned green. "That's a bit harsh."

"Okay, maybe. But they're so selfish. Hoarding all their money. Living in luxury while us normal people suffer. It's just not right."

"Agreed." I stole a glance at Taylor. "You're passionate about this. About hating rich people. Did something happen between you and a rich person or something?"

Taylor turned silent. Once again, I feared I had upset her.

"Sorry, I'm prying," I stammered. "Don't answer that—"

"No, it's okay." She took a deep breath. "It's time I told you what happened. And how it's related to my last heartbreak. Let's get back to the inn—I'll tell you over a cup of tea."

I nodded, continuing to drive back to the inn. I wondered what she was going to tell me. What had happened that made her hate the rich so much?

I pulled into the parking lot of the inn ten minutes later, then opened Taylor's door for her and led her inside. The guests who had stayed behind were still in their rooms except for Eric. He was pacing in the hallway, talking on the phone in Korean again.

When he hung up, I nodded at him. "Everything okay?"

He looked sad. "My parents are struggling. I might have to move back home to take care of them. I can't afford a caretaker and they need my help—as much as I've loved living in the States."

Taylor frowned. "I'm so sorry, Eric. That's a tough situation."

He nodded. "Very, very tough. At least I'll have some memories of this place when I head home. Anyway, I should get to my room. Don't let me keep you two."

He walked away, heading to the stairs and disappearing into his room. I shook my head and gestured for Taylor to follow. We entered the empty dining hall, turning the light on.

"What kind of tea would you like?" Taylor asked. "We've got a whole bunch. Green, black, orange pekoe. I can even put in some fresh honey from the garden. Dad's the one in charge of maintaining the beehive out there. No way am I going near those angry bees. Can't afford getting stung and ruining my sewing hands."

I chuckled. "Just green is fine—no honey, thanks. You guys do it all at the inn, huh? Cooking, gardening, beekeeping?"

Taylor sighed, turning the kettle on. She put two green tea bags in separate mugs with the logo of the inn. "We sure do. And unfortunately, last year, someone saw profit in that."

I frowned, sitting down at a nearby table. "Huh? What are you talking about?"

She turned around. "Have you ever heard of a man named Oliver Vaughn?"

My breath caught in my throat. Of course I had—every businessperson worth their salt in Los Angeles knew about him. He was a very, very wealthy investor who was trying to expand and start his own hotel chain. One that would rival the Hilton hotels. We had just established a deal in my office before my conniving brother took the company out from under me.

A deal I wasn't sure would turn out with him in charge.

"Uh, no," I lied. "Who's that?"

"Right—you probably wouldn't. He's big in the business world. Anyway, he's some rich dude from Los Angeles. Owns a company out there. He came to Bridgewood last year. He was passing through when his limo broke down on the side of the road."

Uh oh. I knew where this was going.

When the kettle started boiling, Taylor poured the tea into the mugs. "And of course, me and my dad just happened to be driving by and stumbled across him. Helped him get back on the road. He decided to stay here for the night and was immediately impressed by our inn."

"How impressed?"

Taylor brought the teas over to the table, sitting across from me. "Obsessed, more like. He started taking notes and asking lots of questions. I just thought he was interested. Turns out, he was planning to steal our ideas and put them in his new hotel chain. He could tell how much people loved staying here. I think he was trying to steal that coziness for his own gain."

That sounded a lot like the businesspeople I knew. "Go on."

"I don't know where he is now. But before he left, he thanked us for showing him around. Like a fool, I told him all our secrets, everything that makes the inn special. Even showed him my fashion." She sighed. "Now he's probably planning to implement those ideas into his hotel. He'll get rich and famous off our creativity, off ideas that belonged to the inn first. It just isn't fair."

"No, it isn't." I reached across the table, placing my hand over Taylor's. "I'm so sorry. He had no right to barge in here and steal your ideas. Have you tried suing? Or telling people online?"

Taylor scoffed. "We don't have the money for a lawyer. And who would believe us, anyway? We're just a small little inn. We can't compete with someone like Oliver Vaughn. His hotel will be big and beautiful—with some of our ideas thrown in, like our cooking and fashion—and there's nothing we can do about it."

That made my blood boil. Just like my brother had done to me, Oliver Vaughn had stolen from Taylor. We had a lot more in common than she knew.

"Well, that sucks," I sighed. "I wish I could help you."

"You have." She caressed my hand. "Just for listening. Thank you, Ethan. Now you see why I hate rich people."

I swallowed hard. "Yeah, I do. And it's understandable. But...how does this relate to your last heartbreak?"

Taylor took a sip of her tea, looking embarrassed. "Well... Oliver didn't just scope out our inn and steal our ideas. He also helped himself to something else."

"Such as?"

"Me." Taylor avoided my gaze. "He charmed me enough to get me into bed. He was the first man I gave my virginity to. I thought...I thought we had something special. He had me believe that."

My eyes widened. "Oh, wow. I had no idea."

She sighed. "Yeah. He told me he loved me—that he was going to give us money so the inn would never need to worry about paying its bills again. He even talked about expanding, about helping us grow. Little did I know at the time that he was planning his own hotel chain and saying all that to get a tour of the place. He just wanted to know all our secrets— what made our inn so likeable to guests."

"He sounds like a selfish prick. But Taylor, you can't blame yourself," I urged. "You didn't know what he was up to, what he had planned. Anyone would've fallen for it."

She shook her head. "No, I should've been smarter. I'm

not Madison—I don't jump into bed with men I've just met. It was so...unlike me. But I took a chance and got hurt. And then I nearly gave up on love entirely. Mom and Dad spent so many nights watching me cry, telling me it would be okay. But Oliver was long gone and the pain was still there."

I felt so terrible for Taylor. I wanted to do something to help her—something to ease her heartbreak. And destroying Oliver Vaughn was high on my list. If I still had access to my company, I would've ended our contract and warned the world about him. But I didn't.

"Again, I'm sorry," I whispered. "And I never want you to feel that way. Used or taken advantage of. So if I do anything that makes you uncomfortable, tell me. I won't get mad."

Taylor gave me a small smile. "Thanks, Ethan. You don't know how much that means to me. You know...I wish I had met you long before Oliver. Because if I had, he wouldn't have stood a chance."

"I wish that too."

She took a deep breath, finishing her tea. "Well, there it is —you've heard my story. You can think less of me now."

"Think less of you? Are you kidding?" I scoffed. "I still think you're the most beautiful, intelligent, and creative person I've ever met. And it's Oliver's loss, not yours. You've got nothing to be sorry for—only he does."

"You mean that?" Taylor gazed into my eyes.

"A thousand percent. And hey, let's not waste our breath on that loser anymore. He doesn't deserve it. Why don't we go watch some movies in my room? Just relax together?"

Taylor set her tea down, grinning. "You don't know how perfect that sounds. I vote for *The Princess Bride*. That movie's awesome."

"Agreed. You've got good taste in movies," I complimented her. "Go on ahead—I'll wash up these dishes."

Taylor thanked me, heading to my room upstairs and

waiting outside my door. I quickly washed our mugs of tea before my phone buzzed. Pulling it out, it had only one bar but the text had gone through anyway. It was from Cheyenne.

CHEYENNE

Bad news. Nathan knows what I did for you. I just got fired from the Miles Marketing Company.

Chapter Eighteen

Cheyenne had gotten fired. All for helping me.

I felt so guilty for being the reason she had lost her job. And madder at my brother—if that was even possible. I called her, then she answered on the second ring.

"Hey," she sniffed. "You got my text, huh?"

I nodded. "I did. I'm so sorry, Cheyenne. I shouldn't have gotten you involved in this mess."

"No, it's all right. You needed help. And I couldn't turn my back on a friend in need. I don't regret a thing."

I was glad she wasn't blaming me at least. "Well, thank you. As always, I'm grateful to have you in my life. What are you going to do now?"

She sighed. "I'm not sure. Start looking for a new job, obviously. My girlfriend's upset. Without my company salary coming in, we may need to postpone the wedding. I just can't afford it without that job."

Now I felt guilty. Cheyenne's life had been turned upside down too—not just mine. Did my brother even care about all the harm he had caused?

"Oh, wow. Shit," I stammered. "I'm sorry. Tell Alicia I'm sorry too."

"I will. For now, I'm just going to take it easy. And keep searching LinkedIn for any available jobs."

"Good idea. So, what did my brother say to you? How did you find out?"

"The security guard told Nathan—got a nice little paycheck out of being a snitch. He knows I'm the one who broke into his office and sent you the contract. He dragged me into his office, lecturing me about loyalty and being a team player."

I sneered. "He's one to talk. And then he just fired you?"

"Yep—claimed I wasn't company material and that I should pack up my desk. He found a new replacement for me pretty quick. Guess who it is?"

"I don't know. Who?"

"Anna. Your ex-girlfriend," Cheyenne answered, much to my surprise. "She was waiting as soon as I walked out of your brother's office. Then she immediately sat at my desk. My desk, Ethan. That bitch is sitting in my chair!"

"God, that makes my blood boil. Anna and my brother must be working together then. Joke's on him—she doesn't love anything but money. He'll find that out the hard way."

"Good. And I hope it hurts," Cheyenne cried. "Anyway, I'm going to spend some time with my fiancée and try to forget about all this drama. Just wanted to update you. I can't be your spy anymore, sorry."

"That's all right, Cheyenne. Your well-being is more important to me than spying on my brother. Take care, okay? And remember I'm here to talk anytime you need me."

At last, I could hear Cheyenne smiling through the phone. "Okay, Ethan. Take it easy over there in Bridgewood."

I promised I would, hanging up and putting the mugs away. When I walked up the stairs, Taylor was still waiting outside my door, her eyebrow raised. "Heard you talking to someone. What's going on?"

"A friend from back home called. Cheyenne," I explained, unlocking my door. "We worked at the same company together."

"Oh." Taylor sounded suspicious as she entered my room. "Was she a friend or...something more?"

"Just a friend." I flicked on my light switch. "I think of her more like a little sister than anything. Besides, she's getting married. To a woman. So I'm not her type."

"Ah, got it." Taylor seemed to visibly relax when she heard there was no competition for my heart. "So...where do you want to watch the movie?"

I turned the TV on. "Uh, well, I was thinking...maybe the bed? If you're comfortable with that?"

Taylor glanced at my queen-sized bed, thinking it over. I hoped I hadn't come on too strong. The last thing I wanted to do was remind her of her ex-boyfriend. Who I still couldn't believe I had met.

It was a small world after all.

"Unless you're not," I stammered. "I could go down-stairs, get one of the chairs from the dining hall—"

"No, it's all right." Taylor sat down on my bed. "So soft. You want any snacks before we start the movie?"

"Nah, I'm still full from dinner and all that cotton candy. You?"

"I'm good too. But just to warn you, I *love* The Princess Bride. So if you hear me mumbling the words under my breath, you'll know why."

I chuckled. "Got it. All right, let me just put it on..."

I started the movie on the TV, then got into bed next to Taylor. She seemed a little uncomfortable at first so I didn't touch her. I got under the blankets, my eyes glued to the screen as Taylor moved around and got comfortable. I felt my eyes getting heavy as the movie played.

True to her word, Taylor mumbled. I thought it was cute. She must've seen this movie a hundred times. I was just glad to have her near me—even if we weren't touching. Just having her in the room made me feel a thousand times better.

When I felt my eyes closing, I didn't resist. The next thing I knew, I was waking up to sunlight through the curtains and something sleeping on my shoulder. When I opened my eyes, looking down, it was Taylor. And she looked so precious when she slept.

Her mouth was open slightly, a little drool coming out of the corner of her lips. She was taking slow breaths with her eyes closed. She was a beautiful sight even in the morning, her brown hair tousled over her face. I wanted to hold her forever —to keep her safe from the whole world.

I stayed like that for a while, just watching her sleep. The room was quiet and the TV must've shut itself off last night. I could hear the birds chirping through the window, making me wish I could stay in bed with Taylor all day. I would be the happiest man alive.

After ten minutes, her gentle snoring stopped. Then her eyes fluttered open. She glanced around before meeting my gaze.

"Hi," she murmured.

"Hello, sleeping beauty," I joked. "Did you have a good sleep?"

"I did." Taylor yawned, sitting up and stretching. "You make a good pillow. What time is it?"

I glanced toward the clock, realizing it was a little after seven. "7 a.m. Probably a good time to get downstairs and help your parents with breakfast."

"Definitely. But I had a great time last night. At the carnival, watching the movie. I think I just have a great time with you no matter where we go."

I smiled. "Yeah, I feel the same. So, today's the big day. The fundraiser. Are you ready?"

Taylor rose to her feet, taking a deep breath. "I think so. I mean, I've worked hard on my fashion for years. If I'm not ready now, then when?"

"Good point. Sometimes you just have to take a leap of faith. For what it's worth, I think people are going to love you."

"Aw, thanks." Taylor smiled. "You've always been my biggest cheerleader. Since day one. Which I appreciate, by the way. And that you didn't judge me after I told you about Oliver last night."

I shrugged. "Nothing to judge. And it doesn't change the way I see you at all. Now, shall we get breakfast?"

"We shall." Taylor walked to my door. "Here's hoping Mom's cooking bacon. I'm craving something salty."

When Taylor opened the door, Madison was standing in the hallway, probably spying on us. She was standing a little too close to the door for my liking. We didn't speak, pushing past her. She narrowed her eyes when we walked out of my room and headed downstairs.

When we walked into the dining hall, the guests were there, eating the breakfast that the Kennedys had made. Taylor was in luck—Sharon had fried bacon and eggs and left them out for us. As usual, Abigail was asking about the calorie and fat content.

"I'm just trying to watch my weight, that's all." Abigail sat down. "It would be helpful if I had your nutritional facts."

"Oh my God, stop being so annoying," Breanna grumbled, taking a slice of bacon. "Just eat the damn breakfast or don't."

"No, it's all right," Sharon added. "I can find the nutritional facts—"

But Abigail was clearly upset at Breanna's words. She rose to her feet, then stormed off upstairs.

"I don't think you should've spoken like that," Sophie cautioned, feeding her son bacon bits. "She was hurt."

Breanna shrugged. "Well, it was getting on my nerves. Sorry not sorry."

"Someone should really go check on her." Mark glanced at the staircase. "Make sure she's okay."

"I'll do it," I offered. "I've spoken to Abigail a bit before. I'll see if she needs anything."

"And I'll get us both a plate in the meantime," Taylor added. "Good luck."

I nodded, walking out of the dining hall as Madison was coming in. Things were awkward between us now. But I reminded myself that it wasn't my fault—she had chosen to make it weird ever since I turned her down. Why couldn't she just accept that I wanted Taylor instead?

Keeping my head down, I passed her and headed upstairs. The guest rooms were empty except for Abigail. I knocked on her door, pressing an ear against the wood. I didn't hear anything.

"Abigail?" I called. "It's me, Ethan. I wanted to check on you. Can I come in?"

No response. The door was open a bit so I pushed it open, finding her room empty. It wasn't until I checked the bathroom that I found Abigail. She was standing on the scale next to the toilet, weighing herself. She sighed when she saw the number.

"Not good enough," she grumbled. "Almost there..."

I cleared my throat. "Abigail?"

She jumped, stepping off the scale. "Ethan? What are you doing in my room?"

"I'm sorry—I didn't mean to barge in. But your door was half-open, and I wanted to check on you."

Abigail glanced at the door. "Oh, I probably forgot to lock it. You wanted to check on me? Why?"

"Well, Breanna's words were a bit harsh. And then you stormed off without any breakfast. Are you sure you're okay? Do you want me to get you some food?"

The mention of food made her nose crinkle. "I...no, thanks. I'm not hungry anyway."

"Are you sure? I've barely seen you eat since getting here—"

"I'm fine!" she yelled. "Why can't you people just leave me alone?"

My eyes widened, fearing I had upset her. The last thing I wanted to do was anger a guest. I knew how important reviews were for the inn. So I just nodded, turning toward her door.

"Okay, I'm sorry. I'll leave you be."

But as I opened her door, she sighed, rushing after me. "Wait! I'm sorry, that was rude of me. I didn't mean it."

"It's all right, Abigail. You don't have to explain."

"No. Maybe...maybe I should. Maybe it would feel better to talk about." Abigail sat down on her bed, sighing. "The truth is...ever since I was a little girl, I've been struggling with an eating disorder."

Suddenly, everything made sense. Asking about calories, being uncomfortable around food, barely eating. And weighing herself when I walked in.

"I was treated for it but it's come back. Even stronger," Abigail continued, looking down. "There's just this little voice in the back of my head that tells me I should hate my body. That I'm not good enough."

"I'm so sorry, Abigail. But that voice is wrong." I sat next to her. "You *are* good enough. And your body is special. I know there's a lot of pressure on girls and women from the media to be skinny, but it's all just bullshit. There's nothing wrong with your body. And I hope you can learn to love yourself one day."

Abigail looked up, giving me a small smile. "Thanks, Ethan. Maybe one day. For now...it's going to be a struggle."

"Yeah, I know. Is there anything I can do for you?"

"No, but thanks for asking. This is something I have to overcome myself."

I rose to my feet. "All right—but if you need anything, don't hesitate to ask. Now, would it be okay if I asked you to come down and have some breakfast? Just a little. We'd love to have you with us."

Abigail thought about it for a moment, then nodded. "I guess I can. Okay, let's head back downstairs."

That felt like progress. I let her go first, following her to the dining hall. Taylor and the others looked up with smiles as we sat down. Breanna focused on her plate. I was relieved to see Abigail reaching for some bacon and fruit. At least she wouldn't be starving.

"So, has everyone heard about the fundraiser? It's for our inn." Sharon glanced around the table. "You're all welcome to come. It's happening this afternoon at the community center. My daughter, Taylor, will be showing off her fashion creations."

"And she's talented," I added. Taylor blushed.

"I think I'll go," Abigail piped up. "I like fashion."

"Yes, same here," Sophie chimed in. "I'll bring Jacob too. Who knows—maybe he'll grow up to be a fashion designer."

"Not my thing." Breanna finished her plate. "But good luck."

"Thank you." Taylor turned to Eric and Victoria. "How about you two?"

"Can't." Eric sighed, staring down at his plate. "I have to

take a call with a new caretaker for my parents. This one is cheaper, though I'm worried about their qualifications."

"Good luck with that," I replied. "Sounds like a tough position."

Eric nodded, staying quiet. Then Victoria piped up. "I might come to the community center. I love fashion too— I'm always looking for new dresses to wear to board meetings."

I could tell Taylor didn't like that she was so rich and powerful, gritting her teeth. "Well, thanks for your support. Mrs. Cabot?"

"Hmm? Oh, yes, I'll be there," Mrs. Cabot confirmed, finishing her breakfast. "I could use a new scarf. My late husband got me one but I'm too afraid to wear it. Don't want it to fade."

"Perfect, I'll have scarves available. Mom, Dad—need my help washing the dishes?"

"Yes, please." Mark rose to his feet. "And Ethan, I have another chore sheet for you before we take a break for the fundraiser."

"My favorite," I joked. "Let me see what you have for me today."

Mark pulled a sheet out of his pocket, handing it to me. It had the usual chores—mop the floors, scrub the toilets, then dust the rooms. I also had to get up on the roof and clean the leaves out of the gutters. That last one wasn't my favorite, but I did it anyway.

After taking a shower and changing into some fresh clothes, it was almost noon. Sharon had baked some focaccia for us to enjoy. After eating, Sharon and Mark put the BE BACK SOON sign on the inn's front door, then we all headed out to the parking lot. Mrs. Cabot, Victoria, Sophie and her son, and Abigail all rode in Sharon and Mark's van while I took Taylor.

She came down the stairs, her arms full of new fashion. I helped her bring more down and load her designs into the back of my truck. Once we were ready, I drove to the community center, noticing how nervous Taylor looked. She was gripping the seat pretty hard.

"Hey, you all right?" I pulled into the community center's parking lot. "Just breathe, Taylor."

She took a deep breath. "Yeah, I'll be okay. Just worried people won't like my designs. What if they hate it?"

"Impossible." I turned off the ignition. "But even if they do, will it stop you from making fashion?"

"No, of course not." Taylor firmly shook her head. "I love creating new designs. I'd never stop."

"Then there's your answer. Either way, it doesn't matter. You love your fashion. That's the most important thing."

"Yeah, I think you're right." A smile tugged at Taylor's lips. "Has anyone ever told you that you have a way with words? You just seem to always know the right thing to say."

It came with a marketing degree, I wanted to tell her. Being charismatic got you more business deals. But I just smiled instead. "Thanks. Now, come on—I'll help you carry everything inside."

Taylor got out of the truck, giving me half her designs. We carried them in and greeted the employees who showed us the way to the convention hall I had booked. Taylor looked around, amazed.

"I still can't believe you got approved for the convention hall," she gushed. "Usually this place is overbooked."

"We received a call from the secretary at the Miles Marketing Company, actually," the nearby employee explained. "They insisted we book this room for Ms. Taylor Kennedy."

Little by little, my lies unraveled.

Chapter Nineteen

Taylor frowned, pausing in the hallway with her clothes on her arms. "The...who? Why would they want to book a conference hall for me?"

"The Miles Marketing Company. They're big in Los Angeles." The employee shrugged. "And I have no idea why, Ms. Kennedy. But they pushed."

While Taylor was still trying to figure it out, I gestured at the door to the hall. "Eh, why look a gift horse in the mouth? Come on, we need to set up."

The employee led us to the empty convention hall, unlocking the double doors for us. Other events were going on down the hallway. Our room was small, but it would do for the fundraiser.

"Okay, let's spread the mannequins around." Taylor scanned the room. "Maybe one over there and one here. Let people see what I have to offer."

I nodded, doing as Taylor asked. We assembled mannequins around the room and placed her clothes on them for sale. Her parents and some of the guests showed up a few minutes later, helping us set up. Madison waited by the doors with her arms crossed.

"Who invited her?" I mumbled to Taylor.

"I think my mom did." Taylor sighed. "And she's up to no good. Let's just hope Madison doesn't try anything. She always hated it when the spotlight wasn't on her."

I watched Madison, looking angry as she glanced around the room. But my attention was distracted when some people began to pour in. They marveled at Taylor's fashion, running their hands along the fabric. It looked like they liked it.

When Drew walked in next, I almost groaned. Why couldn't that guy just leave us alone?

"Hey, Taylor." Drew walked over to her. "Nice clothes."

"Oh, thanks." She smiled apprehensively. "Ethan's the one who suggested this fundraiser, actually. The money will go to benefit the inn."

Drew glared at me, his jaw clenching. "Is that so?"

I nodded. "That's right. Why not promote the inn and Taylor's fashion at the same time? Kill two birds with one stone."

Drew turned to Taylor. "Right. Well, I came to show my support. I'd like to purchase a dress or something."

"Really?" Taylor asked, raised an eyebrow. "You always called it was a waste of time. That I was better off working around the inn."

He shrugged. "Yeah, well, I had a change of heart. Realized how talented you are. Now, are you going to let me buy something or not?"

"Okay, sure." Taylor led Drew to a nearby mannequin. It had a blue sequin dress on it. "This one is so pretty..."

As she showed him around, I rolled my eyes. There was no way Drew was interested in Taylor's fashion. He just wanted to be here to spy on us—to get between us as always. And Madison was peering over, making me wonder if she was trying to do the same.

"Here you are." Taylor handed the blue dress to Drew. "That'll be sixty dollars."

"For one dress?" Drew roared. "Are you kidding?"

"Well, it takes a lot of time and effort to make a dress like that. The materials can be expensive. I think it's definitely worth the money."

"I do too," I cut in. "In fact, Taylor should probably be asking more for it."

Drew was staring at the dress. "I don't know. Seems a bit steep to me."

I crossed my arms. "Are you saying something that Taylor worked hard on isn't worth the money?"

"I'm not saying that at all," Drew spat, reaching into his pocket. He pulled out three twenty-dollar bills and handed them to Taylor. "Here—for the dress. Anything I can do to support you."

Taylor took the money, smiling. "Thank you, Drew. That's kind."

He ignored me as he kept his eyes on Taylor. "You're welcome. Now, can we talk in private? I have something I need to say to you."

"You can just say it here, Drew. What's going on?"

Drew turned back, glaring at me. "I don't want to say it in front of him. Please, Taylor. Just five minutes of your time."

"Drew, I'm busy right now." Taylor glanced around the room. "Look at how many people are here. I should convince them to buy my stuff."

Drew sneered. "You never have time for me anymore, Taylor. It's like we're not even friends these days. Do decades of friendship mean nothing to you?"

Some people looked over at Drew's raised voice. Taylor was embarrassed, leaning closer to him. "Keep your voice down, will you? I don't want to argue in public. Of course I still value our friendship. I've just been busy these days, Drew. I don't see what the big idea is."

Drew shook his head. "You never do. Whatever, Taylor. I'm outta here."

With the dress in his hands, he headed to the exit doors, not even looking back. I wasn't sad to see him go. Madison watched him leave, muttering as he passed. He grumbled something back before vanishing down the hall.

Taylor sighed. "Well, that didn't go over too well."

"At least you got him to buy something," I reminded her. "Why does he want to talk to you in private so badly?"

Taylor shrugged. "I don't know, but I wish he'd read the room. I'm not ignoring him—I'm just busy. Now, I'm going to go mingle with some people over there. Can you stand here and give people the prices if they're interested in any of these pieces?"

"Of course—go mingle and have fun. Let me know what else you need me to do."

Taylor thanked me, disappearing into the crowd. I stood near a row of mannequins that had Taylor's scarves, mittens, and hats on them. People began to saunter over and browse her fashion. Victoria was one of them, picking up a purple scarf with glitter.

"This is beautiful!" Victoria exclaimed. "It'll definitely make me stand out in LA. Not many people wear scarves—it's too warm. I'll take it."

"Perfect, let me just check the price tag." I inspected the scarf. "Ah, only thirty dollars. Let me tell you, that's a steal—"

Madison sauntered over. "For that thing? I wouldn't pay a dollar for that. I saw something similar in a Goodwill bin for fifty cents."

"Really?" Victoria questioned. "Hmm."

"She's joking," I whispered. "It's definitely worth the

money. Go ahead—try it on. I just need to speak with my associate for a second."

Victoria nodded, wrapping the scarf around her neck and looking in the nearby mirror. I grabbed Madison's arm and led her away from the crowd. She was smirking the whole time.

"What is wrong with you?" I demanded. "Are you trying to ruin Taylor's career?"

"Oh, please. She doesn't have a career," Madison spat. "She's a nobody from a small town. No one cares about her fashion."

"That's not true. Lots of people care." I glanced around the hall. "Look at how many showed up. And more importantly, I care. Taylor's talented."

"Do you mean that or are you just saying that because you want to sleep with her?" Madison wrinkled her nose. "Her clothes are nothing to write home about."

I shook my head. "Your jealousy's obvious, Madison, and it's pathetic. Don't ruin this for Taylor. If you can't be civil, just go back to the inn."

I turned around, not even giving her a chance to respond. I didn't need to see Madison's face to know that comment probably pissed her off. Heading back to Victoria, I smiled.

"The scarf looks great on you," I said. "So, what do you say? Still interested?"

"Yes, definitely." Victoria reached into her wallet. "Here you go. And please tell Taylor how gorgeous her clothes are."

Victoria handed me the money, then pushed her way to the exit. I was happy for Taylor—another sale. I walked through the crowd, heading to her where she was selling a top hat to an elderly man. He placed it on his head of grey hair and handed her the money before leaving.

"Made you another sale." I handed Taylor the thirty dollars. "Victoria showed up and bought a scarf."

Taylor's eyes lit up. "Did she? That's so nice. Here, I have an envelope for the money."

She pulled an envelope out of her pocket, making my eyes widen. It was thick—there were a lot of bills inside.

"So, I guess the fundraiser is going well?"

Taylor giggled. "Definitely. Mom and Dad are going to be so happy. And people are going to be wearing my fashion around town. So it's a win-win for everyone."

I smiled. "I'm so glad it all worked out—"

When we heard a thud, we looked toward the exit. Madison was standing there, knocking over mannequins. On purpose. What the hell was that girl up to now?

Taylor ran over, most likely wondering the same thing. "Hey, stop! What are you doing?"

Madison crossed her arms. "No one cares about your stupid fashion, Taylor. When are you going to get it through your thick head? You're a nobody from a small town. Do you think you have a chance at being some famous fashion designer?"

Taylor struggled to find the words. "Well, I...I don't know. But today was a success, I'm sure of that. And this little tantrum of yours isn't helping."

"Yes, what is the meaning of this?" Sharon demanded as she and Mark ran over. "Do I need to call your father and ask him to come get you?"

"Call whoever you want, I don't care," Madison shot back, acting like a spoiled teenager. "I'm leaving anyway."

She left the convention hall, slamming the door behind her. I shook my head and rushed to help Taylor pick up the mannequins and fix the clothes. People were murmuring about Madison's behavior as Sharon and Mark walked over to us.

"I'm so sorry, sweetheart," Mark told Taylor. "Madison's behavior was inexcusable. We'll have a chat with her."

"Don't bother." Taylor smoothed out the wrinkles on a mannequin's dress. "That girl will never change. Let's just get back to the fundraiser and be glad nothing was ruined."

Her parents nodded, though I could tell Madison's behavior was bothering them. If Madison wanted to cause a scene, she had done it. People would definitely be talking about her outburst now whenever the fundraiser came up. Fortunately, the townspeople returned to browsing the mannequins and hadn't fled in horror.

As Sharon and Mark walked away, chatting with some people they recognized in the crowd, Taylor shook her head. "See, what did I tell you? Madison's trouble. Best to stay away from her."

"No need to tell me twice. That girl always finds a way to make everything about her."

"Naturally." Taylor rolled her eyes. "Something's been bothering me all afternoon."

"Oh? What's wrong?"

Taylor pulled her smartphone out of her pocket. "This Miles Marketing Company. Why would a company I don't even know want to rent a room for me? Why go to all the trouble?"

"Uh, I don't know." I shrugged. "Maybe your inn caught their attention or something."

"Maybe. I'm going to look them up online—"

"No!" I cried. When Taylor stared at me, I tried to calm down. "It's just...why look into it? It all worked out for the best. Maybe we shouldn't spoil the mystery."

"I have to know. Or it'll bother me." Taylor typed in the company's name. "Ooh, they have an official website."

I held my breath as she clicked on the link. This was it—she was going to see my face and name on the page and realize I had lied about my past. That I came from money. Taylor was never going to look at me the same way again.

Then she frowned. "Huh. I don't recognize this guy. Do you?"

When Taylor showed me the website, my heart was pounding. But it wasn't the same website I had remembered. My brother had changed it—removed every scrap of my face and name. It only featured himself and what the company had to offer.

Phew. Saved by my brother's narcissism.

"Uh, no," I lied. "No clue."

"They're based in LA. Strange, I've never been there. How does this Nathan Miles guy know me? Why pull some strings to rent a hall in a community center for me? I mean, I know their company does marketing and stuff, but I didn't hire their services."

"No idea. Maybe you've got a doppelganger living in LA, and he's mistaken her for you."

"Very funny." Taylor put her phone away, scanning the crowd. "I guess I'll never know. Anyway, better get back to it. I can't believe the turn-out..."

As Taylor rambled on about how excited she was that people were paying attention to her fashion now, I was sighing in relief. How many times had Taylor come close to the truth about me? Too many. And I was getting sick of dodging bullets.

Maybe I needed to tell her. Maybe I needed to confess that I was Nathan's brother who once had control of the company before he screwed me over, then I came to this small town to find love. But what if Taylor couldn't forgive me for lying to her? What if she saw me as just another Oliver Vaughn?

That was what I was terrified of.

Pushing it out of my mind for now, I helped Taylor promote her fashion. I used some of the tips and tricks I had picked up in business school to convince the townspeople to buy her clothes. Once most of it was gone, the envelope even heavier with money, Sharon and Mark urged Taylor to make a speech.

She cleared her throat, standing in front of everyone. "Thank you all for coming to my first fundraiser. It was to benefit the Cozybrook Inn, the place my parents own. And we made a lot of money today that'll help it continue to stay open. It's a time tough to be a business owner, so we appreciate all the support. Thank you so much!"

People began cheering, holding up Taylor's clothes. I knew they'd love their fashion—even if she hadn't believed it.

Taylor glanced at me in the crowd. "And I wanted to thank a special someone for their help. Ethan, you were a pleasant surprise. I'm so glad you came to Bridgewood and encouraged me to put my fashion out there. I owe it all to you."

I shook my head. "Oh, stop it—you'll make me blush."

Everyone laughed, then finished their shopping. Taylor and her parents were busy counting their money as people left the hall. I walked over, eager to see how much we had raised.

"8,000?" Sharon asked, her eyes wide. "My goodness. That could pay our rent for months!"

Mark nodded. "And it's all thanks to Taylor, our talented fashionista. And Ethan for giving her the courage to do this."

"I'm just glad it went well." Taylor beamed. "You guys deserve it."

"Thank you, sweetie, but it was your fashion. You deserve some too." Sharon split the money. "Here—you'll take half and we'll take the other. Buy yourself something nice or save it. Whatever you want."

Taylor glanced down at the money. "Are you sure?"

Mark nodded. "Positive. You earned it, sweetheart."

Taylor took the money, holding it in her hands. "Wow.

This is more money than I've ever seen in my life...but I think I know what I want to do with it."

"What?" I asked. "Book a ticket to the Dominican Republic and enjoy the beach?"

"Ha, no." Taylor shook her head. "I want you to have this, Ethan. Pay off your truck and save some of it."

My eyes widened. "Taylor, that's very generous. But I can't accept it. That's your money, fair and square. I don't want a dime from you."

"But...what about your truck? You need this money as much as I do."

I shrugged. "Keep it. I'll find a way to pay it off."

Taylor smiled. "You're too good to me, Ethan. Thank you. Now, what do you say we go out and celebrate our success? I've got a place in mind and some money to blow."

"I say I like that idea." I grinned. "Lead the way."

Chapter Twenty

I rode with Taylor, driving and following her instructions to a little tavern while her parents followed in their van. Mike's Tavern was a small bar on the edge of town. There were drinks, pool, and live music on the stage. It was a rock band playing instrumental music. It wasn't too crowded, the perfect place to celebrate Taylor's achievement.

After we parked around the back, we entered, following Taylor to a table. Her parents walked in after us and took their seats. A waitress came over, carrying a notepad and a serving tray.

"Hey there," she chirped. "What can I get you?"

"A bottle of champagne, please," Taylor replied with a smile. "We're celebrating tonight."

"Coming right up." The waitress headed toward the bar.

I glanced around. "This is a nice place. Not like the bars back where I'm from, but I like it."

"I bet everything is big and glamorous in Los Angeles," Sharon swooned, turning to Taylor. "Imagine doing a fashion sale there, dear? You might catch the attention of a famous fashion designer."

Taylor sighed, playing with the edge of the table. "That

was the hope when I applied to NYU's fashion program. But that didn't work out."

Mark frowned. "So sorry, sweetie."

"But it wasn't the end," I added. "Look at how far you've come. Besides, you don't need NYU. They need you."

Taylor gave me a small smile. "Maybe you're right. Hey, there's our drinks."

The waitress returned, carrying a large bottle of champagne and four glasses. She placed them on the table and took our food order. We were still full from dinner, though we ordered some onion rings as an appetizer.

After the waitress walked away, Taylor lifted her glass. "To new beginnings. And Ethan, for making the wise decision to come to Bridgewood."

"No—to you, Taylor." I lifted my glass. "Today's success was all you. You deserve the best."

"Hear, hear!" Mark cried.

Taylor smiled at me as we sipped our champagne, toasting to her. We chatted for a bit about her fashion and the chores that needed to be done tomorrow at the inn before a different song was played by the band. Taylor rose to her feet, her eyes wide.

"I love this song!" she cried. "Ethan, we have to dance together. What do you say?"

I nodded, rising to my feet. "Sounds perfect. Though I'm not much of a dancer."

"Don't worry—just follow my lead." Taylor winked, grabbing my hand. "They taught us how to line dance in school, so I've got some idea. Mom, Dad? You want to join us?"

Sharon and Mark were grinning at us. No doubt they thought we made a cute couple. They shook their heads, gesturing at the champagne bottle.

"You go ahead, dear," Sharon encouraged her. "We're just going to sip our champagne."

Taylor nodded, dragging my hand to the dance floor. I didn't know how she was able to give me butterflies every time. We were only inches away from the band, listening to them play an instrumental version of "Kiss You All Over" by Exile. When Taylor started swaying to the beat, I copied her.

"Hey, nice moves!" she hollered over the music. "You're a natural."

I snorted. "Hardly, but thanks for the encouragement. You have a great taste in music!"

"I know!" Taylor yelled back with a wink.

When dancing with Taylor—spinning her around and shaking our hips like Elvis—I forgot all my troubles. I barely remembered my brother's name. She was the only person in the world who could make me feel like that.

When the song ended, changing to "Kiss Me" by Sixpence None the Richer, I was out of breath. "Well, that was fun. You're an amazing dancer."

"I try," Taylor hesitated. "Hey...do you want to... maybe..."

"Slow dance?"

She nodded, giggling. "Yeah. Guess I got a little nervous there to ask you."

Adorable.

"I'd like that." I offered my hand. "But I want to do it right. My lady, may I have this dance?"

"You may," she said with a grin, taking my outstretched hand.

She put her hands around my shoulders, then I placed mine on her waist. She didn't seem to mind the contact. We slow danced to the song, looking anywhere but each other's eyes for the first minute. Then we slowly became more confident and met each other's gaze.

"You have pretty eyes," I blurted out without thinking.

She smiled. "Thanks. Yours are pretty amazing too."

I cleared my throat as we continued to slow dance. "So, was your fashion sale everything you thought it would be?"

"Definitely." She beamed. "I never thought I'd get this far. Seriously—thanks again, Ethan. Without your support, I wouldn't have had the courage to do it."

"No problem. Sometimes people just need a little push in the right direction."

"Definitely. It's still bothering me why that company from LA would rent out the hall for little old me though. Do you have any idea?"

"Uh, no," I stammered. "Just glad it all worked out for the best. So, what's next for the fashion designer of the year?"

Taylor giggled. "Cute title, but hardly. And I don't know. Doesn't seem like there's much opportunity in this town."

"Oh, I beg to differ. If I learned anything in business school, it's that sometimes, you have to make your own opportunities. And your own luck. You know what I think you should do next?"

She stared up at me, her hands so gentle and soft around my shoulders. "What?"

"A fashion show." I smiled. "Right here in town. Maybe in a public space. Like a park or something."

As much as I wished I could've rented another hall for Taylor at the community center, I had lost my ties to the company completely with Cheyenne gone. Maybe Nathan knew that and planned to fire her all along.

"A fashion show?" Taylor paused. "That would take a lot of work. And I'd need models."

"I'd be willing to don one of those suits you made," I replied. "And I'd help find you people to model the clothes. And make a little stage. I'm pretty good with a hammer."

A slow smile spread across Taylor's face. "All right—

you've convinced me. I've always wanted to put on a fashion show."

"Well, now's your chance. And I have no doubt people will show up thanks to the success of the sale."

"Good point." Taylor squealed. "Oh, I'm so excited! This is going to be amazing. When we get back to the inn, I'll get started on some new clothes right away. I'm thinking floral for this time of year..."

As Taylor talked about her fashion, her eyes lighting up, I was mesmerized by her. She spoke about it with such passion, such love. I only hoped she'd talk about me like that one day.

When the door opened, I turned my head, looking to see who had entered. And to my disappointment, it was Drew. He scanned the tavern before his eyes landed on Taylor. And then he started coming our way.

"Uh oh," I muttered. "Look who just arrived."

"Drew? I'm surprised to see him again." Taylor pulled back from me. I missed her touch already. "He was pretty upset at the community center. I wonder what he wants."

Trouble, most likely. I wished I still had my money so I could've paid him to leave us alone. I didn't like the way he acted around Taylor—and how negative he was about her fashion.

"Hey, Taylor," he began awkwardly. "There you are."

"Drew, hi," Taylor replied while looking uncomfortable. "What are you doing here?"

"I wanted to apologize for my behavior at the community center. That wasn't cool—especially to do to you. So...I'm sorry."

Taylor nodded. "Thanks, Drew. I appreciate that."

"Yeah, of course. Figured it was the right thing to do." He noticed me for a second, then turned back to Taylor. "So...a tavern. This isn't your kind of place. Did Ethan convince you to come here?"

"No, actually. I asked him to come here," Taylor corrected him. "We're celebrating the success of the fundraiser. And planning a fashion show."

"Seriously?" Drew cocked an eyebrow. "Like those famous fashion shows in Paris or whatever? You think you can pull it off?"

Taylor looked a bit disappointed by that comment so I stepped in. "I think Taylor can do anything she puts her mind to. I'm going to help—and it'll be a success. I just know it."

"You're going to help, huh?" Drew sneered. "Haven't you done enough?"

"Excuse me?" I spat.

Drew shook his head. "You come to town, then start poking your nose in where it doesn't belong—"

"Guys, stop," Taylor scolded, getting between us. "That's enough."

"Agreed." I turned my back to Drew. "Now, if you don't mind, me and Taylor were dancing. So please, get off the dance floor."

"Oh, I'm not going anywhere," Drew snarled. "Thought I'd come and join the party too."

I turned back around, raising an eyebrow. "You left the community center way before Taylor suggested we come here. How did you know to find us at the tavern? You just said this isn't Taylor's usual place."

Drew stammered, searching for an answer. "I...was driving by and saw Taylor's parents' van outside. I decided to come in and apologize. That's it."

I crossed my arms. "I find that hard to believe. You're always showing up wherever we go. You know what I think? That you're stalking Taylor. And by extension, me. That's how you knew I was at the mall."

"That's ridiculous!" Drew cried, turning to Taylor. "You can't believe this crap, do you?"

Taylor paused. "I mean...Ethan does have a point. You do seem to show up wherever I go. I thought it was a coincidence before but now...I just don't know."

Drew glared at me. "I knew this would happen. I knew you'd twist Taylor's mind and turn her against me!"

"I think you've done that all on your own, buddy. Here's a tip," I began. "You want to win a girl over? Insulting her dreams and stalking her isn't the way to do it. Just saying. Now, if you wouldn't mind, we were kinda in the middle of something."

Drew's jaw clenched, then I saw his fists ball. He was going to hit me. But this time—unlike the mechanic shop—I was ready. When he lunged out, intending to punch me, I ducked. Then I kicked him in the groin.

He cried out, falling to the floor. Taylor gasped and put her hands over her mouth. Other people in the tavern noticed —including Taylor's parents—and murmured, looking over in shock. Even the band stopped playing. As Drew held his groin, trying to recover, his phone fell out of his pocket. And I noticed the screen was unlocked and on something interesting.

It was one of those Find Your iPhone apps—and he was tracking Taylor's phone. Suddenly, it all began to make sense. I reached down and snatched the iPhone before he could grab it off the floor.

"Look at this." I tossed the phone to Taylor. "Seems he's been stalking you after all."

Taylor studied the app, her face twisting in anger. "Drew, what the hell is this? You've been tracking my smartphone?"

Drew slowly rose to his feet, his eyes wide. "Taylor, I can explain—"

"No! I don't want to hear it." Taylor threw the smartphone at Drew. "I tried to give you the benefit of the doubt since we've been friends since kindergarten. But you've been nothing but rude when it's come to my fashion. And you've gotten even worse since Ethan moved to town! Between constantly picking a fight and tracking my smartphone, this is the final straw. I never want to see you again. Leave me and Ethan alone, Drew—for good."

He looked like he was about to cry. I started to feel bad for him but then I paused, remembering what an awful person he had been to Taylor. He deserved this.

"Wait, Taylor," Drew pleaded. "Let's talk this out—"

"No. Just leave, Drew," Taylor cried, turning her back on him. "I don't want to hear it."

I thought Drew might try to plead some more but then he turned quiet. He glared at me, putting his smartphone back in his pocket. "You've screwed me over for the last time, outsider. This isn't over."

He stormed to the door, vanishing outside. Everything turned quiet in the tavern for a few moments. Taylor looked mortified, noticing everyone's gaze on her.

"Let's get out of here," she whispered to me. "I want to head back to the inn."

I nodded. "All right—let's go. I'll just tell your parents."

Taylor headed to the door, waiting for me there. People were still gossiping about the fight.

"No fighting in my bar!" the bartender called, wiping down a glass. "If you're going to get violent, you gotta leave."

"We were just heading out," I explained, walking over to Taylor's parents. "Are you two going to stay? Taylor wants me to drive her home."

"For a little while," Sharon replied. "What was all that about? With Drew?"

"Yes, it was nasty," Mark added. "He tried to punch you."

"Wouldn't be the first time." I shrugged. "He's been pretty negative to Taylor for a while. Then we found out he's been tracking her phone and stalking her."

"What?" Sharon asked, wide-eyed. "How can he do that?"

I shrugged. "He must've linked her phone to his when she wasn't looking. Anyway, Taylor's done with him. She told him to take a hike."

"Good," Mark replied. "Sheesh, I can't believe Drew would do this. We've known that boy since he was a toddler."

"People change, I suppose." Sharon shook her head in disgust. "Is Taylor okay?"

"I think she will be. I'll drive her home now. See you two later—and have fun."

They thanked me, returning to their drinks. Taylor was still waiting for me at the door. We left the tavern wordlessly as I led her to my truck and hopped in. Fortunately, Drew had vanished. But I was ready to kick him in the groin again if he tried anything else.

"Hey, you okay?" I glanced at Taylor in the passenger seat as I started the ignition.

"I just lost my oldest friend," Taylor sniffled. "So no, I'm not okay. But I'm glad you were there for support. I had a great time with you, despite Drew butting in."

I gave her a small smile. "I did too. Come on—let's head home. We can watch movies until you fall asleep."

"Sounds like a plan." As I pulled out of the tavern's parking lot, she spoke again. "You've treated me better than my childhood friend. For that, I wanted to thank you."

"Of course. It's the least I can do. You saved me—got me off the streets. I won't forget that."

"It was no problem. And this whole time, you had a bad feeling about Drew. I should've listened. Instead, I thought he was harmless."

"Hey, it's not your fault." I stole a glance at her. "Anyone would have a hard time throwing away an old friendship like that. This is Drew's fault—not yours. He's the one who became creepy and obsessive."

"Yeah." Taylor stared out the window. "I just hope that's the end of it."

I did too—for both our sakes. But I had a feeling it wasn't.

When we arrived back at the inn, most of the guests had returned and headed to their rooms. I heard light snoring as me and Taylor entered through the doors. She turned to me, gesturing upstairs.

"I'll meet you in your room in a few minutes. Just want to change into something cozier."

"Okay, see you soon."

We both headed up the stairs, going in separate directions. I headed to my room, unlocked the door, and looked for something for us to watch. Something funny that would take her mind off Drew. As I searched through the comedies, I heard a knock on my door.

I walked over, opening it. And my jaw dropped.

Taylor was standing there in a silky red nightgown—looking like a dream.

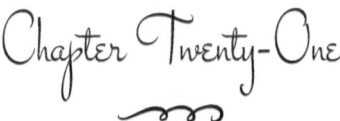

Chapter Twenty-One

I stumbled over my words just like any man standing in front of a gorgeous, half-naked woman would. "You, uh...that's quite the outfit."

Taylor looked down. "I just wanted something more comfortable, that's all. Do you have a problem with it?"

Hell no.

"Of course not." I paused. "It's just...you've never been like this before. So forward. What's going on?"

Taylor shut my door, walking toward my bed and sitting down. "I like you, Ethan. And I want to see where this can go. I think I'm ready to take things to the next level."

Any man probably would've jumped for joy at that moment. But I knew nothing could happen between us—at least, not tonight. And my secret was part of it.

"Don't get me wrong, I like you. I think you're gorgeous, funny, smart, and so talented." I sat next to her. "But...I don't think we should do anything tonight. Except watch a movie and cuddle."

Taylor furrowed her eyebrow. "What? Why?"

"Because you're tipsy from all that champagne. And still upset about Drew. Right?"

Taylor sighed. "Yeah, I guess I am. But that doesn't mean I don't want you."

"I know. But if we're going to have sex, I want you to be fully sober for it. And with a clear head. Do you understand?"

Taylor rose to her feet, looking embarrassed. A red blush covered her cheeks. "Yes, I think I do. I'm sorry, Ethan. Didn't mean to make you uncomfortable."

"Oh, no. Not at all." I stood up. "And I want you too. But only when we're both completely into it. Your time with Oliver Vaughn wasn't great, and I don't want you to have any regrets between us."

"I understand." Taylor looked toward the door, clearing her throat. "Anyway, I, uh, should probably get back to the attic. To work on some new clothes if we're going to put on a fashion show."

"Okay. Want to watch a movie first?"

"No, thanks. Not in the mood." Taylor walked to my door. "Goodnight, Ethan. Hope you sleep well."

As she left my room, heading upstairs to the attic, I sat down on the bed and slapped my forehead. Any guy would've been chastising me for saying no to a woman like Taylor. But it didn't feel right—and I didn't want Taylor to have regrets. Plus, I still feared what she'd think of me when she found out my secret.

I had done the right thing, and I knew that. But I still felt sad that I couldn't get closer to Taylor.

With a sigh, I got up to shower and brush my teeth before getting into bed. I turned off my light and fell into dreamland. Of course, I dreamed about Taylor. About touching her, about tasting her. But only when she was ready for it—and not half-drunk or emotional.

I woke up around 5 a.m., unable to sleep and horny. I turned that energy into something productive instead. I pulled over my laptop, designing posters for Taylor's fashion show. All that was missing was a date.

Once I was happy with the design—an elegant dress with Taylor's name in sparkles above it—I turned my attention to a web creator. The Kennedys website was so old, so lifeless. It needed something new.

I spent the next hour designing a different website, one that was colorful and modern. I listed fun facts about the Kennedy family—like Sharon's recipes, Mark's fishing, Taylor's fashion, and how close-knit the inn was—and hoped they'd like it. When 6 a.m. rolled around, I walked down the stairs with my laptop to the kitchen.

I found Sharon and Mark making breakfast as always, smiling at me as I entered. Taylor was sitting at the table while sipping a coffee by herself. She looked distracted, probably still embarrassed from last night. I hoped I hadn't hurt her.

God, that was the last thing I ever wanted to do.

I noticed Madison pacing outside through the window, kicking rocks and looking angry. I frowned and gestured outside as I approached Sharon and Mark with my laptop still in hand, the new website loaded on the screen.

"Morning everyone," I began. "What's up with Madison?"

"Oh, she's just upset after our talk last night," Mark explained, frying bacon next to Sharon. "We told her how awful her behavior was at Taylor's fundraiser. She isn't taking it too well."

Sharon sighed. "I thought coming here would be good for that girl, but she's just as troubled as ever. I guess losing a mother will do that to you."

I had sympathy for Madison, though I was still angry she wouldn't stop pursuing me. And that she had wrecked some mannequins at the fundraiser. Grieving a parent didn't excuse that behavior.

"Well, I hope she'll learn her lesson," I held up my laptop. "Anyway, I designed a new website for you. Thought you could use an upgrade. Taylor, do you want to see?"

Taylor looked over, putting her coffee down. She rose to her feet and headed toward us. I showed Sharon, Mark, and Taylor the new website, scrolling through all the features.

"Wow, it's incredible!" Sharon cried. "Thank you so much for doing that, Ethan. It's much better than our old website."

"Indeed," Mark added. "How much do we owe you?"

I shook my head. "Nah, it's free of charge. Hopefully you'll get more traffic and that'll translate into more guests."

"Sounds good to me." Sharon smiled. "Breakfast is almost ready, by the way. Feel free to grab a seat."

I nodded, setting my laptop down. Taylor walked over and sat across from me while sipping her coffee. Things between us were awkward, no doubt after last night. But I was determined to patch things up.

I cleared my throat. "So, heard from Drew again after last night?"

Taylor shook her head. "I haven't. I hope he's going to stop following me. I'm trying to give him the benefit of the doubt since I've known him forever, but...I have to admit, it's a bit weird. If he doesn't stop, I'll have to get the police involved or something."

"Agreed. If he doesn't leave you alone, let me know. I want to make sure you're safe." I glanced over, making sure Sharon and Mark weren't listening to us. They were busy cooking and in their own world. I turned back to Taylor. "I hope things are okay between us. After...after what happened in my room."

Taylor nodded. "I'm fine, Ethan. You were right—I was tipsy. And a bit hungover this morning. Hence the coffee. I'm glad you refused."

I breathed out. "Okay, good. I feared I'd let you down. And I don't want to do that."

"You? Let me down?" Taylor shook her head. "You could never do that, Ethan. Trust me."

I didn't know about that. But it felt good hearing Taylor say it.

"That's a relief. I didn't want you to regret it," I replied. "I still want to keep seeing you. Even take you on another date. There's a hockey game at the community center tonight. Want to go together?"

Taylor smiled. "Sounds perfect. We can get some snacks and make it an official date."

Finally, everything was right in the world again. Taylor wasn't mad at me and our dates were back on. I wanted to get up and cheer. I kept my cool, though.

A few minutes later as we chatted, the guests trickled into the dining hall. Sharon and Mark plated the food and we helped ourselves. Madison eventually came in, grabbed a plate, then headed up to her room while scowling at us. I hoped both she and Drew stayed far, far away.

I pulled over my laptop. "Oh, and I designed some posters for the fashion show. Here they are."

After I opened the document, showing Taylor across the table, she nodded. "Looks amazing. I got a lot done last night, actually. Couldn't sleep much. I should be ready to go in a few days."

"We can't wait." Sharon glanced around the table. "Will everyone come to show their support?"

"And I'm looking for models," Taylor added. "Hint hint."

"I'll be there," Sophie called, feeding eggs to her son. "And I wouldn't mind modeling some clothes."

Taylor's eyes lit up. "Perfect! Anyone else?"

"I can't, darling," Victoria lamented, finishing her breakfast. "I have some important business calls these next few days. I'll be terribly busy."

"Me too," Eric added. "Still trying to find a caretaker for my parents. I wish you all the best, though."

Taylor looked a little disappointed but nodded. I cleared my throat. "You'll have me as a model, of course. Can't wait to wear one of your suits. What about your parents?"

"Oh, I'm not model material," Sharon joked.

"Of course you are, Mom. You too, Dad." Taylor glanced at them. "I'll take your measurements later and find something you can wear. If that's okay."

Mark shrugged. "Anything to support you, dear. We're in."

As Taylor beamed, I turned to Mrs. Cabot. "And you? I think your husband would be delighted to see you in a fashion show. Having fun and looking stylish."

"Hmm." Mrs. Cabot sipped her tea. "Perhaps he would. All right, Taylor, I'll do it."

"Great!" Taylor cried. "At least I'll have some models. I'll be wearing a piece too. Breanna, Abigail? Would you like to walk a runway? For being so helpful, I'll even let you all keep the outfits later."

The table looked excited at that. Breanna just shrugged. "Yeah, whatever. Could be fun."

I turned to Abigail. "What about you?"

She looked down at her plate, taking small bites. "Um, I don't know. I'll think about it."

"Okay, just let me know," Taylor replied. "Mom, Dad, me and Ethan will help you do the dishes."

Sharon and Mark thanked us, then we gathered all the plates and brought them to the sink. The guests finished their drinks and headed back to their rooms. As I soaped up the plates and Taylor washed them, leaving Sharon and Mark to wash the dining table, Sharon glanced back.

"What about your cousin? Going to ask her to join your fashion show? She does love fashion."

Taylor's face fell. She clearly didn't want Madison anywhere near her clothes. And I couldn't blame her after last time.

"It would be a nice thing to do." Mark refilled the ketchup dispenser. "And you two can make amends."

Taylor sighed. "Oh, I don't know..."

Madison walked into the dining hall, her heels clicking on the floor. She glanced around the dining hall before noticing us. Everything turned quiet. I noticed Sharon staring at Madison, gesturing at Taylor. It looked like she was trying to get her niece to say something.

Madison rolled her eyes, turning to Taylor. "Hey, cousin —can I talk to you for a second?"

"I guess." Taylor dried another plate and set it aside.

"Look, I'm...I'm sorry about what I did last night. It wasn't cool. And I hope you can forgive me."

Taylor narrowed her eyes. "Okay. You're forgiven."

Sharon walked over, patting Madison's shoulder. "That was a great apology, Madison. It took a big person to say that. Now, Taylor, why don't you show Madison you forgive her by letting her model in your fashion show?"

"A fashion show?" Madison's eyes widened.

Taylor sighed. "All right, fine. I'll get to work on a piece for you."

Madison beamed. "This is pretty exciting! I've never been in a fashion show before. I'll go take my measurements for you."

Madison took off upstairs, heading to her room. Mark walked over with a smile. "Well, she was ecstatic about that. I guess you two have made up."

Taylor shot me a sideways glance, skeptical about Madison just like I was. Was she sorry or was she just forced to apologize by Taylor's parents? And more importantly, would she ever change?

When a bell rang at the front desk, Sharon rushed out to greet the visitor. Me and Taylor finished washing and drying the dishes as Mark went to see who was there. After we were done, we walked into the foyer, finding Taylor's parents chatting with a dark-haired woman in a pantsuit. A man with a camera on his shoulder stood behind her.

"Oh, of course we know who you are!" Sharon cried. "What an honor. Oh, there's my daughter and our newest employee, Ethan."

Taylor walked over first, shaking the woman's hand. "Nice to meet you. I'm Taylor Kennedy."

"Yes, I've heard about you. Your fashion's making a name for itself," the woman said before glancing at me. Her eyes narrowed. "You look familiar. Have we met before?"

I shook my head. "I don't think so. Who are you?"

"You must not be from Bridgewood, then. Everyone here knows who I am." The woman smiled. "Lisa Remy. I'm the lead reporter for the Bridgewood news station."

Great, a reporter. Just what a guy harboring a secret needed.

"Ms. Remy just told us she wants to film an interview about our inn," Mark explained. "And feature Taylor's fashion, if that's okay with her."

Taylor nodded. "I like that idea. I'm actually planning a fashion show, so it'll be great for exposure."

"Yes, absolutely," Lisa replied. "So, where should we do the interview?"

"In our dining hall. It's got some fireplaces. Real cozy," Sharon answered with a smile. "Then, for the fashion portion, my daughter can give you a tour of her attic. It's where she does all her sewing."

"Excellent," Lisa declared. "My cameraman, Gary, will

record the whole thing. Just act natural and pretend the camera isn't even there. Lead the way, please."

As Sharon and Mark led Lisa and her cameraman into the dining hall, I reached for Taylor's arm. "Uh, I don't think I'm going to sit in on the interview. It's a family inn, after all. I'm just a nobody."

Taylor scoffed. "What? That's not true. You've helped this inn more than anyone before, Ethan. You definitely deserve a spot at the table."

That was sweet of Taylor, but I disagreed. And I didn't want my face on television where anyone could recognize me —and tell Taylor who I was.

I shook my head. "It's fine. Go ahead without me. I'm going to get started on my chores for the day."

"Okay. Are you sure you're all right? You look a bit flustered."

I racked my brain for a lie. "Actually, the truth is...I'm a bit camera-shy. It gives me anxiety. So I think I'll keep my distance. If that's okay."

"Of course. You didn't judge me when I told you I was scared of heights so I won't judge you for this. I'll let you know how the interview goes."

I nodded, walking away to check off the usual tasks on my chore list as Taylor entered the dining hall. I could hear Taylor and her parents chatting about the inn and its history to Lisa who was asking a lot of questions. About twenty minutes later, just as I was sweeping the floors, I heard them walking out of the dining hall.

"Where's that handsome employee of yours?" Lisa asked.

"Oh, he's busy with chores at the moment," Taylor explained. "Anyway, the attic is up here. I can show you what I've been working on."

"Perfect." Lisa and her cameraman followed Taylor,

climbing the stairs. "What's your favorite piece been so far? And where do you get your inspiration from?"

Taylor handled the questions like a pro, answering them as she walked up the stairs. Then I could hear her giving them a tour of her attic. As Sharon and Mark got back to work and I kept sweeping the floors, I was happy for them. No doubt getting on TV would do wonders for their inn. And for Taylor's fashion.

When I heard someone clearing their throat, I turned around, noticing Victoria standing there. And she was holding up a news article on her phone. It was of me—my brother announcing my departure from the Miles company.

And that was when I knew my secret had been found out.

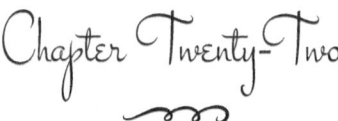

Chapter Twenty-Two

"I finally know where I recognize you from." Victoria held her phone up. "You're Ethan Miles from—"

"Shh!" I whispered, grabbing her arm. "Come with me. We can talk about this in private."

I dragged Victoria down the hallway, opening the door to the storage closet. Checking around to make sure no one was looking—especially Taylor, since I didn't want her to get the wrong idea—I gently pushed Victoria inside. Then I entered, flicking the light on and closing the door behind me.

"What are you doing?" Victoria demanded. "Let me out!"

"Relax," I replied. "I'm not going to hurt you. I just want to keep my identity a secret—that's all. Thought we could talk quietly in here."

Victoria crossed her arms. "I see. Why are you going to so much trouble to hide who you are? Is it because you failed your father's company?"

I had never been called a failure before. And honestly, it hurt. And since Victoria already knew my secret, I figured I could tell her the truth. And hoped she'd keep it all quiet.

"I didn't actually," I explained. "You see, it was all a plan for me to find true love. As cheesy as it sounds. Women kept dating me for my money and not for me. I figured if I lost it all—or pretended to—I might have a chance to find someone great."

"Ah, I see. Like that Taylor girl. I've seen how close you two are."

"Exactly. She doesn't know that I'm Ethan Miles." I stared at my feet. "But my brother took advantage of me. He had me sign a contract that gave him the entire company. So now, I am broke, all thanks to him."

"Oh my." Victoria gasped. "That is truly awful. Does your brother hate you?"

"He just might," I grumbled. "How did you find out about me?"

"Well, I knew I recognized you from somewhere. It kept bothering me. It wasn't until I was on a business call that mentioned your company. Something about it struggling."

I raised an eyebrow. "How so?"

"It seems other companies don't like dealing with your brother. They say he's irresponsible and childish. Bossy and ignorant too. Anyway, that was when I remembered you and looked you up online."

People didn't like doing business with my brother? That made me feel a bit better. Maybe he'd be the one to destroy the Miles Marketing Company for good. Dad wasn't going to like that.

"I didn't know that. Thanks for telling me," I replied. "Look, I want to keep who I am a secret. Can you keep this quiet?"

Victoria paused, thinking it over. "All right, I will. But you'll have to tell Taylor one day, especially if things continue to get serious with her. A relationship can't be built on lies."

"I know," I huffed. "Still working up the courage to tell her. I...I think I'm falling in love with her. And the worst part is, she hates rich people. She has some bad history with them."

"Yes, most people do." Victoria shook her head. "Looks like you got yourself in a bit of pickle. Well, honesty is always the best policy. Just be upfront with her and maybe she'll accept it."

Or maybe she wouldn't. It was a big risk—and I still wasn't sure how to tell her.

"Right. Just gotta find out the best way to drop that bomb. Have you ever been in love? Got any advice for me?"

Victoria looked awkward. "I can't say that I have, no. I put my company first. Sometimes I wish I hadn't. So my advice is this—work can be wonderful and fulfilling but love is truly what life is about. Loving ourselves, our family, our friends. And finding the right person to love. But you already know that. You figured it out long before me."

I smiled. "Well, it's not too late to find love yourself. And thanks for being cool about this."

"It's the least I can do. I've done a lot of business with the Miles Marketing Company, and they've helped me a lot. It's just a shame what's happened to it." She shook her head. "I'm not so sure about love for me, but I definitely know it'll happen for you. I admire you, Ethan."

I frowned. "You do? For what, getting the company stolen from under me and losing it all?"

"No, of course not. I admire how far you're willing to go for love. To give up your name and reputation for it. I think that's beautiful."

"Huh, maybe you're right." I shrugged. "It was worth a shot. One last try before I give up on love forever. And I met Taylor, which was pretty lucky."

"Indeed. Do you know the real reason I came here, Ethan?"

"For a vacation?"

"Well, that's part of it. Bridgewood is a lovely town and I'm glad I came across it online. But no, that's not why. Much like you, I was born and raised in Los Angeles, the city of fortune and fame. I've never known anything different. I took this trip to find something real—something authentic—that I didn't have back home. And I think I found it."

"You did?"

She nodded. "Yes. You've inspired me, Ethan. You've shown me that good people still exist, and love is out there. And I wish you the best with it all."

"Wow. Thanks, Victoria. Glad I could be an inspiration."

"Oh, you sure are." She reached for the door. "And I hope you can figure out what to do about your brother. If you don't want to run the company and instead want to be with Taylor, that's admirable. But you'll have to do something about him before he drags down the company your father built."

Victoria was right—Nathan wasn't fit to lead the family company. But if not me, then who? And how could I stop him?

"Tell Taylor I said hello," Victoria continued. "And don't worry, I'll let you tell her the truth. No one will hear this from me."

I nodded. "Thank you. If there's anything I can do for you in return, let me know."

She smiled. "Oh, you've done enough. You've given me hope. See you later, Ethan."

As Victoria left the storage closet, heading back upstairs to her room, I breathed out. At least my secret was still safe—for now. And I had an update about my brother. His hubris was going to ruin the family name.

As I walked out of the storage closet, it sounded like Taylor was finishing her interview with Lisa Remy. They were walking down the stairs from the attic and chatting about their conversation.

"...and you did great," Lisa was telling her. "I'll get back to the studio and edit this right away. It should air tonight."

"Perfect." Taylor led Lisa to the door. "Thank you so much for this opportunity."

"Of course. You take care—and keep working on that amazing fashion of yours. At your next fundraiser, I think I might buy a new pantsuit."

Lisa and her cameraman left, getting into their white van outside. Taylor shut the door and smiled as Sharon and Mark came out of the kitchen. I walked over, hoping it all went well.

"So? How was the interview?"

"Great." Taylor spun around with a grin. "Lisa took the time to get to know me and my fashion. I can't wait for everyone to see it."

"Yes, us too," Mark added. "And not just in Bridgewood but around the world. Think of all the new customers we're going to get!"

As the family looked hopeful, I was glad I had stood my ground and refused to be on camera. I didn't need someone else recognizing me.

"It was a fun experience, that's for sure. We've never had anything like that before." Taylor then turned to me. "Have you ever been on TV, Ethan?"

Yes, many times for my father's company. But I couldn't say that.

"Uh, no," I lied, swallowing hard. "Not my thing. I'm glad it all went well, though."

"Me too." Taylor sighed. "What a relief. And Ethan, if you're not too busy, do you think you could come with me on a little road trip? I need to buy more fabric."

"Of course." I set my broom aside. "I just finished my chores, actually. We'll take my truck."

"And we'll take care of the guests in the meantime. Maybe start putting up those posters," Sharon suggested. "Take a few with you and put them up."

"Good idea," Taylor said. "Come on—we've got a printer in the basement. Let's set a date on the flyers and print them out."

I followed Taylor, heading to the stairs that led into the basement as Sharon and Mark checked on their guests. The basement was dusty—full of cobwebs, old pictures, supplies, and totes. Taylor led me to a small printer before I noticed a picture hanging on the wall. It was of a girl in pigtails in a backyard, holding a pink dress while smiling with some missing baby teeth. If I squinted, it almost looked like Taylor.

"Who's that? Is it you?"

Taylor blushed. "Yeah, it is. I was a funny-looking kid."

"Are you kidding? You were adorable. Still are. With a cute dress. Nothing's changed."

"Ha, it truly hasn't. I made that dress, actually," Taylor chirped, walking toward the picture on the wall. "I was about six years old. My parents wanted to know what to buy me for my birthday and I begged for a sewing machine. I'd seen a commercial for it and thought it was interesting. Plus, I always loved clothes."

"Wow. Then you were always talented with fashion."

Taylor giggled. "Hey, it took me a bunch of tries to make that dress. You wouldn't want to see the disaster that was the first one. And my mom helped a lot—even got a tailor to come over and show me some tricks. I ended up pricking my fingers quite a bit. But yeah, I always loved fashion. Just didn't think I could make a career out of it. Drew always told me it was impossible."

I reached for Taylor's hand. "Nothing's impossible—trust me. Drew doesn't know what he's talking about."

"Yeah, I'm beginning to see that. Thanks for encouraging me to believe in myself."

I smiled. "Of course. Now, let's get these posters printed out. Just let me add a date."

I ran upstairs, grabbing my laptop and heading back into the basement. I finally put a date on the poster—for the day after tomorrow in the park. Taylor was convinced she could make the clothes in time. Once we printed about a hundred copies of the flyers, we headed upstairs, handing them to Sharon and Mark at the front desk.

"Oh, these are perfect!" Sharon cried. "I'll put one outside and leave another at our desk for the guests to see. You're very talented at graphic design, Ethan."

I shrugged. "Thanks to that marketing degree. Are you ready to head to the city now, Taylor?"

Taylor nodded. "Yeah, just give me a sec. I want to take some measurements of my models first. Just so I know how much fabric to buy. Mom, Dad—you're up. Let me get my supplies."

Sharon and Mark looked both excited and nervous, waiting for Taylor to grab her measuring tape from the attic. She took measurements of their hips, waist, and shoulders, then scribbled them down in her notebook. I noticed she was sketching out some new dresses on the pages. And a familiar face had been drawn underneath.

It was me. Taylor had captured my likeness perfectly.

"Is that me?" I gestured toward the notebook.

Taylor looked toward the page, blushing. "Oh, you saw that, huh?"

"Sorry—didn't mean to pry. Just thought he looked familiar."

She laughed. "Yeah, it *is* you. I just...I don't know, was

bored one night and started doodling you. You have a great face."

"Thanks." I blushed, touching my forehead. "I grew it myself, you know. Well, my mom and dad helped a little."

Taylor snorted. "That was a bad joke."

"Definitely. No one's ever drawn me before, though."

"Well, there's a first time for everything, isn't there?" Sharon glanced between us with a glimmer in her eyes. "How sweet."

"Absolutely. Hope you don't mind," Taylor replied. "Or that it makes you uncomfortable. If it does, I can stop."

"Oh, I don't mind at all. I give you permission to draw me anytime. And if you want to turn me into some cool wizard or vampire, I won't stop you. I'd just like a copy."

Taylor giggled. "Got it. All right, I'm done taking your measurements, Mom and Dad. Thanks for agreeing to be in my fashion show. I know it's not your thing."

"Anything for our little girl," Mark crooned. "Drive safely."

We promised we would, then headed upstairs to knock on the doors of Taylor's models. We started with Mrs. Cabot. She was a little insecure about her body—apologizing for sagging skin and wrinkles—but we didn't care one bit.

"You're beautiful, Mrs. Cabot," Taylor told her. "And when you see yourself in the dress I'm adjusting for you, you're going to think so too."

"You're too sweet, my dear," Mrs. Cabot gushed. "I just know my husband would've loved staying here. And he would wish you two the best with your relationship."

An awkward silence spread between us. Taylor and I hadn't agreed on anything yet—no labels. Were we moving toward boyfriend and girlfriend, then possibly husband and wife? Or would it never happen when my secret came out?

Taylor cleared her throat. "Yes, thank you. Your husband

sounds like a great man. I'll give you more details about the fashion show when I have them."

Mrs. Cabot thanked us, then got back to reading and talking to her urn. We went to Sophie and Jacob's room next, taking their measurements. Jacob kept squirming and moving around but Taylor managed to get his height and width. Then we went to Breanna's door, measuring her for Taylor's show.

"I usually only wear hoodies and cargo pants," Breanna muttered. "This is going to be different."

"Oh, definitely. I'm all about the sparkles and glitters," Taylor chirped, finishing measuring her. "But who knows? Maybe you'll find you like my style a little more. It'll be a unique experience, at least."

"Yeah, I guess. And hey, I wanted to talk to you two."

We stopped in Breanna's doorway, wondering what was going on.

"I just...wanted to thank you," she mumbled. "For not judging me when I told you about my past. People usually freak out when I tell them and think I can't be trusted. In reality, I just got off to a bad start. So...thanks for treating me like I'm human."

"It was our pleasure," I replied. "For what it's worth, we think you're a good kid."

"And everyone deserves to be treated like they're human," Taylor declared. "Don't forget that. Anyway, I'll let you know when the fashion show's happening."

Breanna nodded, showing us out as we headed to the last door. Abigail's room. When we knocked on the door, she let us in a second later, then I noticed some pamphlets on the bed behind her. She was researching different diets.

"Hey, guys." She still wore an oversized hoodie. "What can I do for you?"

Taylor held up her measuring tape. "Mind if I get your measurements for my upcoming fashion show?"

Abigail gulped, staring at the tape in Taylor's hands. "Uh, sure. Come on in."

She walked toward the bed, clearing off the pamphlets and throwing them in her nightstand. I noticed the scale moved in the bathroom, knowing Abigail was probably weighing herself again. That poor girl.

"All right, just stay still and I'll measure you." Taylor bent to measure Abigail's legs. "You have great posture, you know. I think you'll be an excellent model."

Abigail snorted. "I doubt that, but thanks. I'm way too short and chunky to be a model."

"Nonsense," I cried. "You're not chunky at all. And besides, it'll be nice to see real people modeling these clothes instead of those super skinny models. Starving yourself isn't healthy."

"Agreed." Taylor rose to her feet. "I want my fashion to represent all bodies and sizes because they're beautiful—not just size zeroes. Once you're in your dress, you'll see what I mean."

Abigail looked down at her body, running a hand over her stomach. "Okay. If you say so."

I noticed an idea flash across Taylor's face. "Come with me for a sec. I want to show you something."

Abigail was confused but followed, letting Taylor lead her up to the attic. I went along with them, also confused. Taylor opened the door to the attic and brought Abigail over to a stand-up mirror. Abigail recoiled at herself, looking down.

"Uh-uh." Taylor lifted Abigail's chin and making her look in the mirror. "You're beautiful, Abigail. Look at yourself—so wonderfully made. Don't you think so?"

When Abigail hesitated, not saying anything, Taylor grabbed a piece of long, shiny blue fabric off her workstation.

It looked like she was in the process of turning it into a dress. She held it up over Abigail, letting her see what it would look like on her body.

"See?" Taylor glanced between her and the mirror. "Don't you look just gorgeous? The dress brings out the blue in your eyes. I think this is your outfit."

Abigail looked mesmerized, staring at the dress. "Well, it *is* beautiful. I've never worn something so glamorous before. Are you sure it'll fit?"

"Of course. And now's your chance," Taylor enthused. "Trust me, once that dress is on you and you're walking down the runway, you're going to feel like a million bucks."

As Taylor continued, making Abigail feel better about herself, I realized all the good I had done. Helping Mrs. Cabot, then Abigail and Breanna. Even helping Taylor bring her fashion to the town.

My brother could keep the company—if he wasn't too busy running it into the ground. He could keep all the money, fame, and women if he wanted too. I had something beautiful that I was building here. Community, friendship, kindness, love.

Things way better than the fake glitz and glamor back in LA.

Chapter Twenty-Three

After pumping her up for a little while, Taylor lent the fabric to Abigail for now. She was still staring at it as she headed back to her room. I knew that girl was struggling with an eating disorder and food, and clothes were probably hard for her. I hoped this fashion show would be good for her, helping her become more comfortable with her body.

"That was a nice thing you did," I praised Taylor after Abigail had walked downstairs. "Encouraging her like that."

Taylor shrugged. "She's not the only one who's had a bad relationship with their body—trust me. I think all teenage girls go through it thanks to peer pressure and the media. It's pretty clear she's struggling with an eating disorder."

"You know?"

Taylor nodded, fiddling with a dress on a nearby mannequin. "Of course. That's why she was so obsessive about food. And I had one too when I was younger."

"Oh," I whispered. "I'm so sorry."

"It's all right. I'm much better now." Taylor stared after Abigail. "And I hope Abigail will be too."

"Yeah, same. She confided in me that she was struggling. I walked in on her weighing herself."

Taylor shook her head. "Poor girl. If she needs to talk, I'm here. And I'm going to make her feel like a million bucks in my fashion show."

I smiled. Taylor was so kind, so thoughtful. That was another reason why I loved her. She was genuinely nice, and not that fake niceness that people were back in Los Angeles when they wanted something. Taylor didn't realize how special she was.

"Anyway, let's head into town." She turned from the mannequin. "Just have to pick up a few things and then we'll be ready for the fashion show."

I patted the outline of my keys in my pocket. "I'm ready if you are. Lead the way, Ms. Fashion Designer."

Taylor smiled, heading out of the attic and down the stairs. I followed just as Madison was coming out of her room. She looked excited and happy, making me fear another confrontation was coming.

"Taylor! There you are." Madison handed her a piece of paper. "Here, I took my measurements for you. Let me know if you need anything else."

"Great, thanks." Taylor took the paper. "This'll help when it comes to finding a dress for you. I've got a few I think might fit you."

"You're welcome. And... I have something to say." Madison closed her eyes. "Look, I hate apologizing, so I'll just come right out. I'm sorry I knocked over your mannequins. And I'm glad you're giving me another chance."

"Taylor's kind like that." I sighed. "It's one of many things to love about her."

Taylor smiled. "Thanks, Ethan. And thanks to you too, Madison. But you already apologized."

"Yeah, but your parents made me. I wanted this one to

come from the heart. If the roles were reversed, I'd probably never speak to you again. So thanks for not completely turning your back on me."

Taylor sighed. "We haven't always seen eye to eye—especially lately—but we're still family. At the end of the day, that's all you have. We have to look out for each other and forgive each other. Even when it's hard."

I thought about that for a moment, my brother popping into my head. Could I ever forgive him for what he had done? And would he ever be truly sorry?

"Yeah, agreed," Madison added. "And I'm sorry for everything I put you through too, Ethan. I promise—I'll leave you both alone from now on. I kinda had a change of heart last night."

I nodded. "Thanks, Madison. That's big of you. We appreciate it."

"No problem. And just between us," Madison glanced downstairs, "I didn't want to be with Ethan or ruin your show, Taylor. But Drew put me up to it."

"What?" Taylor raised an eyebrow. "What are you talking about?"

"He came to me a few days ago, right after Ethan arrived. He instructed me to seduce him. Even though I told Drew that Ethan really liked you, Taylor. It was more than obvious. Drew was *not* happy about that."

I shook my head. "That guy...he's more trouble than he's worth. No wonder you two were whispering at the carnival."

"Yeah, he was telling me what to do next. He had a plan and everything."

"What did he want you to do exactly?" Taylor demanded. "Harass us?"

"Yeah, basically. To get between you two and ruin your fashion. He was adamant that I destroy your clothes and make you think you didn't have a future. I didn't want to go that far, though. I only knocked over the mannequins."

"Oh my God." Taylor slumped onto the stairs. "I can't believe this. Drew must've been scheming for a while."

I shook my head. "He's scum—and I'm glad he hasn't come back around. Anything else, Madison?"

"Just that he's madly in love with Taylor. It's almost, like, obsession or something. He's got her picture in his wallet and everything," Madison wailed, turning to me. "And he loves Taylor as much as he hates you. So be careful, Ethan. His temper can be scary."

"We will be. You too." I faced Taylor. "You okay?"

Taylor rose to her feet, sighing. "Yeah, I'm okay. Just upset my oldest friend is trying to sabotage my life. What have I ever done to him?"

Madison shrugged. "I don't know, but he's dedicated to this. Staying away from him is probably a good idea. I know I'm going to. I told him last night on the phone that I didn't want to do this little plan anymore."

"What did he say?"

"Oh, he was pissed. Yelled at me for a bit. Then I just hung up. He's starting to scare me, actually. I don't want to see him anymore."

"That dude's crazy," I scoffed. "But what were you getting out of it? What was he promising you?"

"Money, actually. He promised he'd give me a few thousand if I successfully broke you two up. He was going to steal it from his uncle's safe. And since I needed the money, I agreed."

Madison's cheeks flushed. I raised an eyebrow. "You do?"

She nodded, playing with her necklace. "Yeah. Since my mom died, me and my dad are struggling to make ends meet. She was the breadwinner, not him. And we're close to losing our house so the money would've helped. But the cost was too high, and I'm sick of doing Drew's dirty work. It's making me feel used."

"Thank you, Madison," Taylor replied. "You could've taken that money and not told us anything. But you chose to be the bigger person. I think you've finally grown up."

"Yeah, I guess I have." Madison smiled. "It feels good."

"I didn't know you and Uncle Dave were struggling though," Taylor continued. "I can give you some money—"

"No, Taylor. You've done enough," Madison cut in. "I don't want your hard-earned fashion money. I'll find a way to help my dad. But, like, the honorable way and not by helping some creep destroy his so-called friend's life. At first, he tried to convince me that Ethan wasn't good for you. But seeing what I've seen...Drew's wrong. And a jerk."

"We can agree on that." Taylor sighed. "If he doesn't stop, I'll have to go to the police. Would you tell the cops what you told us?"

"Sure—as long as they promise to protect us. I don't want to be on the receiving end of Drew's wrath."

"Yeah, it's not pleasant." I bit my lip. "He already jumped me. Left me bleeding pretty bad."

Madison winced. "I hope he doesn't do that to me. My face is too precious for that."

"Well, let us know," Taylor offered. "Anyway, me and Ethan have to head into town now. Portland has some great fabric shops. We'll see you later."

"Okay, cool. I'll be around. Should I tell Aunt Sharon and Uncle Mark what's going on with Drew?"

Taylor paused. "No, not right now. We don't want to tip him off that we know. But tell Mom and Dad to stay away from him for now. For everyone's safety."

Madison promised she would, heading back into her room to watch some movies. I followed Taylor down the stairs before we said goodbye to her parents and headed outside. I led her to my truck, looking over my shoulder.

There was no one—Drew or otherwise. I hoped it would stay that way.

"Paranoid?" Taylor asked, getting into the passenger seat.

"After what Madison told me, yeah." I got in and turned my key in the ignition. "Your best friend's dangerous."

"It's taken me too long to realize that," Taylor lamented, staring out the window. "But let's not talk about him the whole ride. I want to enjoy our road trip. So, what kind of music do you like?"

On the drive to Portland with Taylor pointing the way, we chatted about our interests and the upcoming fashion show. Drew stayed out of our vocabulary completely. I liked it much better that way.

When we saw the sign that read WELCOME TO PORT-LAND, MAINE, we kept driving, heading into the quaint town. It was a charming, seaside little place with plenty of fishermen walking around. I could smell the scent of fish and lobster as we drove through the cobblestone streets.

"Maine has some incredible seafood," Taylor told me, pointing out the window. "We should stop and get some lunch. There's a food truck over there."

I nodded, pulling off to the side of the road. We headed toward the food truck and greeted the vendor before placing an order. Taylor and I got the seafood boil, eating and chatting on the nearby picnic table. The seafood was flavorful and buttery —much better than anything I'd had back in Los Angeles.

Then we got back in my truck with Taylor pointing the way to her favorite fabric shop. It was called *Rapunzel's*, named after the Disney character, and it had a long strip of fabric hanging from the front door. It was blonde and supposed to look like Rapunzel's hair. I thought it was clever and had a strong marketing hook. Taylor's family needed something as charming as that to promote their business.

I followed Taylor inside, letting her chat with the shopkeeper for a bit. They knew her by name. She bought some fabric, using the measurements she had taken as reference, then we left the shop with tons of materials in our arms. I was surprised at how heavy it was.

"Sorry for making you carry all this," Taylor apologized as we headed to my truck. "Usually, I don't buy this much but I want to be prepared for the show."

"Hey, there's no one I'd rather break my arms carrying stuff for." I winked and placed all the materials in my backseat. "So, what's next? Heading back to the inn?"

"Actually, can we stop at one more place? If it's not too much trouble."

I closed the back door, shaking my head. "For you, nothing is too much trouble. Where do you need to go?"

"The Sunnyside Retirement Home. It's only a few blocks from here."

"Of course. But first!" I reached into the backseat again. "Let's hang up your posters. Gotta let everyone know about your completely awesome fashion show."

Taylor smiled, helping me nail some posters to nearby signs and trees. Then we went back into the fabric store and the shopkeeper agreed to let Taylor put her poster in the window. A lot of the nearby shops were also onboard, making me realize how nice everyone was in small towns. It had a comradery that you just didn't find in bigger cities.

"There, that should be enough for now." Taylor put the rest of the flyers onto the backseat. "We'll finish putting these up back in Bridgewood. And the posters are just gorgeous. Thanks again for making them, Ethan."

"My pleasure. Gave me something to do too. So, the retirement home, huh? You know someone there?"

Taylor nodded, getting into the passenger seat. "Yeah, I do. Evelyn Beadle—she used to work at my parents' inn back in the day. She was old then and needed the money. Besides my parents, she practically raised me."

"Aw, that's sweet. I'm glad she's still around."

"Yeah, me too. It'll be rough on our family when she passes away." Taylor shook her head. "But let's not think about that. I'm excited you'll get to meet her—someone so important to my childhood. Did you have someone like that growing up?"

I got into my truck, stepping on the gas and pulling away as I cooked up an answer. Nate and I were raised by a slew of nannies and butlers, all of whom were just trying to make a living. I don't think my parents paid them enough for putting up with two rambunctious boys.

But I couldn't tell Taylor that, so I shrugged. "Nah. It was mostly my brother and I as kids. My parents worked a lot."

"That's too bad," Taylor murmured. "I mean, my parents worked a lot too with the inn. But they always made time for me. We were close growing up."

"I can see that." I glanced at Taylor. "You have a beautiful family. And hopefully, now that Madison's admitted what she was up to, she can be a part of it too."

"Yeah, let's hope. I guess she *has* matured."

We continued chit-chatting before we arrived at the retirement home. I parked around the back, then headed toward the glass doors with Taylor. The elderly residents were walking around the garden and being pushed in wheelchairs by nurses and family members. They smiled at us, glad to see new faces.

"The nurses know me here." Taylor opened the door for me. "I visit Evelyn every time I buy new fabric. After you, sir."

"Why, thank you, miss," I joked, entering the retirement home. "You lead the way."

Taylor nodded, heading up to the front desk to speak with the nurse. She knew Taylor and gave us both permission to see Evelyn. After we had put our visitors passes around our necks, I followed Taylor down the white, sterile hallway. At least she knew where she was going.

After passing many rooms and taking an elevator to the third floor, Taylor led me down the hall. We stopped at door 319 and she knocked twice. A minute later, a nurse opened the door.

"Ah, Taylor. Nice to see you again," she chirped. "Here to see Evelyn?"

Taylor nodded. "I am. How is she doing?"

"Not good, I'm afraid," the nurse regretfully explained. "She just finished her chemo. She's a bit confused but maybe seeing you will be good for her. Go ahead in—just be gentle."

We nodded, stepping around the nurse to enter the room as she left. I noticed a very old woman—at least in her nineties—sitting in a chair, wearing a blue nightgown. She was connected to a chemotherapy machine and looked exhausted. She had white hair, wrinkles underneath her sparkling blue eyes, and was very thin. The room was plain with only a bed, wall television, and a small dresser. Taylor approached her slowly.

"Evelyn?" she asked. "It's me, Taylor."

"Oh, dear, is that you?" The old woman reached for a pair of glasses on the nearby table. "Let me take a good look at you. Ah, as beautiful as ever."

"Thanks, Evelyn. I came to see you. And I brought someone with me. This is Ethan, the inn's newest employee. And...he's special to me."

I smiled. "Special, huh? I feel the same way. Nice to meet you, Evelyn."

"What a handsome man you are." Evelyn squinted. "Nice to meet you. I'm afraid you caught me after chemotherapy where I'm a bit weak. Usually, I'm a lot more energetic than this."

"Chemo?" I asked. "Do you have cancer?"

"Yes, unfortunately. Breast cancer." Evelyn removed her white wig. She was bald, her head shiny. "I use this to hide it."

"I actually brought you something for that. A gift." Taylor reached into her bag. "A scarf."

She pulled out a beautiful red and gold scarf. The old woman's eyes lit up as Taylor placed it around her head, hiding the baldness.

"My goodness." Evelyn grinned. "It's beautiful! Are you still working on your fashion, dear?"

Taylor nodded. "I am. Thanks to Ethan, I've gotten a lot more confident about it. I just had a fundraiser where we raised a lot of money for the inn. People are buying and wearing my clothes now. And I'm putting on a fashion show soon. We're going to do it all ourselves."

"Oh, how wonderful! I so wish I could be there. You've always loved fashion, ever since you were a little girl. I'm so glad you're living your dream." She paused to cough, then looked up at Taylor. "Well, go on—tell me everything about it. I'll try to keep my eyes open as long as I can."

Taylor nodded, sitting on the nearby bed as she told Evelyn about the fundraiser. She left out the parts about Drew and Madison. As she went on, I felt someone staring at my back.

I turned around, noticing an old man in the hallway. And he was staring at me intensely—like he recognized me.

And the worst part was, I recognized him too.

Chapter Twenty-Four

The elderly man was the father of a client I had worked with once, owning a restaurant chain in California. They had their origins in Maine. It was a family-owned business, one the elderly man had started, but then had come down with Alzheimer's and needed more care. And it turned out my client had placed his father here.

I winced. Was this the future my father had to look forward to?

The man—dressed in a blue robe and slippers, using a cane with his hair unkempt—staggered over to me. "You. I recognize your face."

"I'm sure you don't," I stammered. "We've never met before."

"No, I'm sure I know you," the man insisted. "Some... some businessman..."

Taylor rose to her feet, walking over. "Ethan, what's going on? Do you know this man?"

"No, he's a total stranger," I lied, staring at the elderly man. "Do you need help getting back to your room, sir? I can take you there."

When I reached for his arm, he wiggled out of my grasp. "Don't touch me! I know that face. At least, I think I do..."

As the man struggled to place me, I gulped. Just mentioning my family's company would blow my cover. Taylor already knew about them thanks to the community center.

"Mr. Morris, there you are," a nurse cried, running over. "You're due for a sponge both, you know."

"I know." The old man wrinkled his nose. "That's why I left. I can't stand those damn sponge baths."

The nurse shook her head. "I know, but you need one. Come on—I'll help you back to your room. And I'm terribly sorry if Mr. Morris bothered you. He's got Alzheimer's and is very fragile."

I faked a smile. "It's all right—no worries."

"I swear it, I know you!" the man continued to yell. "I've seen you before. Back in Los Angeles."

The nurse gently reached for his hand, guiding him down the hallway. She led him into a quiet room where she prepared him for a sponge bath. As I watched them go, Taylor turned to me.

"Aren't you from Los Angeles? Is it possible he knew you back there?"

I shrugged. "No idea. So, what did I miss?"

Taylor led me back into the room, dropping the subject for now. I was grateful I had kept my past life a secret a little longer. We chatted with Evelyn for another twenty minutes, then Taylor checked her watch.

"We should get going." She rose to her feet. "But it was so nice to see you again."

Evelyn smiled. "You as well, Taylor. It was just like all those times when you were a child. Oh, how I miss working at the inn. I wish I could come back."

When she sniffled, Taylor reached for her hand, caressing

it. "I know—I do too. And Mom and Dad. But this is the best place for you in your condition."

Evelyn nodded, looking down at the scarf. "Yes, I know. Thank you for this lovely scarf. I'm going to wear it all the time and think of you."

Taylor beamed. "Perfect. I'll be back to visit you again soon, Evelyn. Don't worry."

"I look forward to it." Evelyn turned to me. "Keep my girl safe, will you? Taylor means a lot to me."

"Of course," I insisted. "She means a lot to me too. Take care, Evelyn. A pleasure to meet you."

After we said our goodbyes, we headed out of the room, closing the door behind us. Taylor slowed down as we walked down the long corridors. More elderly people with canes and wheelchairs greeted us. As we walked past the front desk, I noticed a familiar face on the television.

Me. The local news was talking about how I had lost the company and my brother took over, though it wasn't doing as well as when I had run it. That was revenge in itself. But I couldn't let Taylor see the screen.

I needed a distraction.

I paused, touching the outline of my pocket. "Oh, crap—my keys. They're not in my pocket."

Taylor stopped. Her back was turned away from the front desk. "Oh no. Can you remember where you last had them?"

"Yeah, back in Evelyn's room. Maybe I dropped them or set them down or something. Can we go back and check?"

"Of course—come on."

Taylor headed down the hallway, back to Evelyn's room. I followed and sighed in relief. Hopefully when we got back to the front desk, the news would be talking about something else. Something without my face plastered across the screen.

Taylor knocked on the door, waiting for an answer, but none came. She opened the door with a creak and peered inside. Evelyn was sleeping, snoring soundly in her chair. She had placed the scarf around her head. It was a sweet gesture, one that kept Taylor with her all the time.

"We'll have to be quiet," Taylor whispered, turning back to me. "Let's search for your keys without waking her up."

I nodded, tiptoeing inside the room behind Taylor. I pretended to help her search before I gently set my keys down on Evelyn's bed. Then I picked them up, making sound on purpose.

"Over here," I whispered. "Found them. Must've put them down for a sec."

"Good," Taylor whispered back. "Let's get out of here before we wake Sleeping Beauty."

I headed toward the door, opening it quietly. Taylor followed and shut it behind us. Then she paused, pressing her ear against the door. The old woman was still snoring.

"We did it," Taylor gasped. "Without waking her up. Go us."

"We *do* make a good team." I winked. "Come on— Bridgewood's waiting for us."

Taylor followed, stealing glances over her shoulder every few seconds. I could tell she missed Evelyn. If only there was some way she could come and live at the inn again.

As we passed the front desk, I held my breath, hoping my face wasn't on the TV. The news reporter was now talking about a local animal shelter that needed help. I sighed in relief. My secret was safe—for another day. Even if I felt terrible that I was still keeping it from Taylor.

But then I remembered her hatred of rich people and thought it was better to keep my mouth shut.

"Evelyn's the closest I ever had to a grandmother," Taylor sighed as we left the building, interrupting my worrying thoughts. "All of mine died when I was young. She was a great surrogate grandma."

"I bet. You two looked close."

Taylor sighed. "Very. I try to come out to see her whenever I can. She doesn't get any other visitors, you know. No family or friends, never had kids. I owe so much to her."

"She appreciates it—I could tell. And she's lucky to have you."

"I'm lucky to have her." Taylor gestured at my truck in the parking lot. "We'll have to come back soon. But for now, I need to get back to the inn to put a few finishing touches on my clothes."

"Sounds good. The fashion show will be a hit—just you wait."

Taylor smiled, thanking me as we headed to my truck in the parking lot. After we got in, driving down the street, I noticed a billboard. It read: YOUR SIGN HERE. ADVERTISE TODAY!

That was the exposure the inn needed. I pulled over, looking closer at the sign. It listed the details of where you could buy the billboard. When I realized the address was only a few blocks away, I stepped on the gas.

"What are you doing?" Taylor asked. "The way out of the city is behind us."

"I know—but I've got an idea. We can buy a billboard for the inn." I glanced at her. "Should draw in even more guests. Can you imagine if you got as many people as say, the Hilton Hotels?"

Taylor snorted. "Our place isn't big enough for that— we'd have to pitch tents in the backyard. But if you think a billboard is a good idea, then I do too."

"I do. The success of a business is usually all in the marketing. And I want the inn to succeed, no matter what."

Taylor smiled. "I appreciate that, Ethan. How you've always been looking out for us. The inn is fortunate to have you. I am too."

I fell silent, though I blushed. Taylor had a way of turning me into a lovesick teenager. I didn't mind it.

I found the shop that sold the billboards, pulling over. As we entered with the chime of a bell, a salesman in a suit stopped us. He proceeded to tell us all about their billboards and signs.

"We just want something simple," I told him. "To advertise the Cozybrook Inn over in Bridgewood."

"I've heard of that place," the man remarked. "My brother stayed there once. Claimed the food and the ambience were five stars."

Taylor grinned. "I'm so happy to hear that. So, how much to advertise our inn on your sign?"

"The basic fee is 1,000 dollars. But trust me, it's worth it. We get tons of traffic down that road."

Taylor hesitated. "I don't know—that's a lot of money. And I've been trying to save more. For the inn *and* my fashion line."

"Tell you what? You seem like nice folk." The man glanced between us. "I'll give you a discount since you're a first-time buyer. 500 bucks for the sign, take it or leave it."

"I guess I could dip into the money I got from the fashion sale." Taylor reached into her pocket. "If you think it'll be a success."

Just in case it wasn't, I didn't want Taylor spending her own money. I reached into my pocket and pulled out the rest of the cash her parents had given me. I had just enough—570 dollars.

"It's all right," I told Taylor, handing the money to the businessman. "I'll cover it. My treat to you."

Taylor's eyes widened. "No, I can't let you do that. You need that money to pay off your truck."

"I'll find another way, trust me. I'll make your inn

successful, no matter what. If this is what it takes, then so be it."

"You've got a keeper, ma'am," the businessman said, counting my cash. "Yep, it's all here. We'll get started on your sign right away. Anything special you want on it? I got a graphic designer in the back."

"Keep it simple with the font easy to read," I explained. "Maybe with a lodge, some birds, and sunshine. That'll reel people in."

"Good idea. You should've been a graphic designer," the man replied, putting my money in the cash register. "I'll get my designer on it ASAP. Should have that sign up in a few days. Then, with luck, new guests will roll in and you can thank us for the help."

"Sounds good." I backed away from the counter. "Thank you."

Taylor stayed silent as we left the shop, getting into my truck. Once I had put the keys into the ignition, pulling into traffic, she turned to me.

"I just...I can't believe you did that," she cried. "Gave the money for your truck to help the inn. What if you can't pay off your truck? What if it gets taken away?"

"Then it's a good thing you have a car. Might need to hitch a ride with you," I joked. "You deserve it, Taylor. Your parents too. That's why I did it."

Taylor leaned over, kissing my cheek. I felt warmth spreading through my body like a jolt of sunshine. That was what Taylor was to me—the sun. And my life before her had been nothing but darkness.

"What was that for?" I asked, forcing my eyes back to the road.

"For being you," she said. "One of the best men I've ever met. I didn't think gentlemen still existed. Full of loyalty and honor. You're a rare breed."

But would she still think that after my secret came out?

"Thanks." I smiled. "I think you're pretty extraordinary too."

"Look at us—two extraordinary people. The world better watch out."

When she started doing superhero poses, I chuckled at her silliness. I couldn't remember my problems as I drove us back to Bridgewood. The welcoming sign brought a smile to my face. It felt comfortable, safe. Like nothing could hurt me.

"Don't forget we have that hockey game tonight." I pulled into the parking lot of the inn. "If you're still up for it."

"Of course." Taylor reached for her door. "With luck, we'll get to see a good fight. I love it when hockey players get physical."

"You *like* all the blood and fighting?"

"Are you kidding? Best part of hockey. Besides scoring a goal."

I grinned. "You are one of a kind, Taylor. And I'm done with my chores for today. Need my help with anything?"

"Yes, actually—up in the attic. Still have a few more outfits to finish. Come keep me company?"

"I wouldn't like anything more," I murmured.

We spent the next few hours in Taylor's attic, going over her fashion for the upcoming show. I gave her my opinions of colors and fabrics and held sewing needles while she worked. We started to feel like a team—I handled the business side while she worked on the fashion. It was already a million times more enjoyable than my old job.

When Sharon and Mark called us downstairs for dinner, we paused our work, joining them in the dining hall. The guests came down with us and we shared a hearty stew for dinner. Abigail was still beaming about her dress, thanking

Taylor for the opportunity. I was just happy to see that girl enjoying herself.

After helping her parents wash and dry the dishes, me and Taylor hopped in my truck and headed for the community center. The way the employees changed the convention halls so quickly for different exhibits made my head spin. We followed the sign on the door, heading to the hockey rink inside the community center.

"It's only a friendly game—not the NHL or anything," Taylor explained as we entered the rink, the chill from the ice spreading through my body. "But it's still fun to watch."

I sat down on the bench, watching as the hockey players lined up on the ice. Other people came in and sat around us. I shivered, clinging to my tiny shirt. I knew I should've brought a sweater or something.

"Yeah, hockey's awesome. I just wish I'd brought a blanket. I forgot how cold these arenas are."

"Don't worry." Taylor scooted closer, placing her head on my shoulder. "I'll keep you warm."

I definitely felt warm in certain places when she was next to me. God, did that girl even know the effect she had?

We watched the game for a while, cheering whenever someone scored. I didn't know the teams or the players but still had a great time. Halfway through during the intermission, Taylor got up to get us some popcorn and sodas down the hall. There was a little booth for snacks and drinks.

She returned a few minutes later, handing me a large popcorn and soda. "Here—my treat. It's the least I can do since you bought the billboard."

"Thanks." I stuffed popcorn into my mouth. "Popcorn is the way to my heart, actually."

Taylor sat down with a playful glint in her eyes. "Good to know. Here, catch!"

She threw a piece of popcorn in my mouth, making me

move to catch it. We had fun during the intermission by trying to throw popcorn in each other's mouths and keeping score. Taylor won—she had a much better throwing arm than I did.

When the next period started, Taylor set her popcorn aside, placing her head on my shoulder again. My heart was pounding with excitement. I loved having her close—the only problem was I never wanted to let go. As I placed my head on hers, watching the hockey game, I felt like I was in a perfect moment.

Until I felt someone watching me. I glanced around, noticing a man in his fifties standing near the door to the arena. He wore a leather jacket with dark jeans and boots while carrying a camera around his neck. Once he had snapped a picture of us cuddling on the booth, he turned, leaving the arena.

Who was that guy? What did he want? And why was he watching us and taking pictures?

I needed to find out.

Chapter Twenty-Five

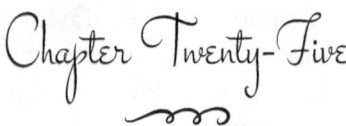

I rose to my feet, slipping out of Taylor's grasp. She moved her head off my shoulder and looked up at me in confusion. I didn't say anything as I pushed through the crowd of people sitting on benches to make it to the exit door.

I ran out of the hockey arena, then sprinted down the corridor. Once I reached the front door, I walked out of the convention center, looking left and right for the man. I caught him getting into a black sedan and pulling away.

"Wait, stop!" I cried, chasing after his car.

But it was no use—I wasn't fast enough. His car took off down the road, turning right and vanishing. I sighed. It seemed like I would never find out who that man was—or why he was taking pictures of me and Taylor.

But I didn't like it one bit.

As I turned, heading back to the convention center, I stepped on something. It crunched underneath my feet. I bent down, realizing it was a business card. And it finally explained who that man was after I smoothed it out.

It read CHARLES LANE, PRIVATE INVESTIGA-TOR. And it listed his phone number and email. Jackpot. I finally knew who was watching us. He must've dropped the card as he got into his sedan.

I was going to have to investigate this private investigator. I needed answers—like who hired him. I wondered if it had anything to do with my brother.

Stuffing the card deep inside my pocket, I walked toward the doors of the convention center, entering the building. I nearly crashed into Taylor as she came walking around the corner. She looked concerned, her eyes wide.

"Ethan, there you are," she exclaimed. "You ran off pretty fast. Is something wrong?"

"Uh, no," I lied, faking a smile. "Just thought I saw Drew poking around. False alarm—it was just a guy who looked like him."

I didn't know why I had lied to Taylor about the private investigator. For the most part, I didn't want to worry her. She had been through enough with Drew and Madison. But if the PI was hired by my brother, I didn't want my secret getting out. For now.

"Oh, that's a relief," Taylor replied. "You want to head back to the hockey game? A fight broke out just as I was leaving."

I locked my arm with hers. "Well, we can't miss that. Come on—let's watch hockey players punch each other for a while."

Taylor laughed, walking hand-in-hand with me back to the hockey arena. We found our old seats after pushing through the crowd. Two hockey players were still fist-fighting on the ice. People were cheering it on, including Taylor. I chuckled at her enthusiasm before the game started up again and the two players got a penalty.

The game ended shortly after that, though me and Taylor were too busy talking and joking around to notice. We left the community center with the rest of the crowd, heading to my truck in the parking lot. There was still no sign of that private investigator.

"Want me to take you home?" I opened Taylor's door.

"What a gentleman." She winked. "And yes, please. Still finishing up some stuff for the fashion show. I can't believe it's happening."

"Hey, you deserve it." I smiled as I got into my truck. "And I'll be right there along the way, helping you through it."

Taylor grinned, then we chit-chatted on the drive back to the inn. Once I took her inside, walking her up to the attic, she leaned in and kissed me on the lips. It was nice—soft and unexpected.

She pulled away, blushing. "Sorry, I kinda sprang that on you."

"Oh, I'm all for being sprang on," I joked. "Anyway, I'll let you get some rest. See you tomorrow."

She nodded. "See you then. And Ethan, if you ever want to spend the night...you know where I am. Just saying."

She shut the door to the attic with a smile, leaving me breathless in the hallway. I had a beautiful woman willing to be with me and I was still holding back. If it weren't for my secret, I would've told her I loved her already. But I had to be careful.

And before I could sleep, I had to know who that private investigator was.

I snuck downstairs, walking outside for some privacy. The sky was pitch black and all the guests were snoring upstairs. I heard nothing but crickets in the nearby forest as I pulled out my smartphone. After finding the number on the card, I called the private investigator.

He answered after a few rings. "Yeah? Who is this? You're calling awfully late. Good thing I'm a night owl."

"Sorry," I began. "But I found your card. This is Charles Lane, the private investigator, right?"

"That's right. And who are you?"

I paused, thinking. I didn't want to give my actual name —just in case he knew me and refused to help. So I made something up.

"Nick. Nick Hartford," I lied, thinking on the spot. "Can we meet tonight? I'd like to hire your services. I heard you're in the Bridgewood area right now. So am I."

"Well, I won't turn down a potential client. I'm actually only in this small town because I'm doing surveillance for another client of mine. Came all the way from Dallas."

Surveillance for another client? I had to figure out who it was.

"Well, looks like you'll have another job lined up," I remarked. "Where can we meet?"

"I'm staying at a cheap motel just outside Bridgewood. The Sleepy Cat Motel. You can't miss it—it's got a big neon sign of a cat in front of the building. Let's meet in the parking lot. And in case you're trying to play me, I want you to know I'm licensed to carry. And fully loaded."

I gulped. "Uh, got it. See you soon."

After we hung up, I got into my truck, pulling out of the inn's parking lot. I hoped meeting with this private investigator wasn't a bad idea. I drove about half an hour, using my truck's GPS to point the way. When I noticed a giant neon sign of a cat, I pulled into the parking lot of the motel and waited.

As I sat there, I noticed the PI's familiar sedan parked a few cars away. This was definitely the spot. The same man I saw at the hockey arena walked out of a room and glanced around the parking lot. I flashed my lights, letting him know I was there for him. He nodded and walked toward my truck with one hand on his belt. A small pistol poked out of the side.

I unlocked my doors, letting the private investigator jump in. When he turned to me, his eyes widened, looking me over. "Well, you ain't no Nick Hartford."

"No, I'm not. I take it you know who I am?"

He nodded. "Yeah—Ethan, the guy I've been asked to follow around. Well played."

"I had to meet you and find out why you're following me. Who hired you?"

He smirked, lighting a cigar in his mouth. "I'm afraid I can't tell you that. Client confidentiality and all that jazz."

I had a feeling my brother put him up to this. But in case I was wrong, I didn't say anything. I didn't want to give the private investigator more ammunition against me.

"Uh-huh. What were you hired to do?" I demanded. "Stalk me? Isn't that a crime?"

"Hardly" Charles blew smoke. "You were out in a public place. So was I. Trust me, I know the law. Been in the PI game for thirty years now."

Thirty years? So he was a professional—and probably not cheap. Someone wanted dirt on me. Or, at the very least, to make me squirm.

"Look, I want you to leave me alone," I insisted. "I haven't done anything wrong. I'm just trying to live my life."

He shook his head. "No can do. I signed a contract, and I intend to fulfil it. Besides, my client thinks you're bad news. They want to know about your past. And I'm going to find out."

I gulped. What if he found out my last name was Miles? What if he told Taylor and ruined everything?

"Isn't there any way I can get you to back off? Maybe pay you double what your client's paying you?"

Charles snickered. "You don't want to know how much

money my client spent to follow you around. Trust me, you can't afford that, let alone double."

I sighed, tightening my grip on the steering wheel. There seemed to be no way to get this man to back off.

"If I were you, I'd just take it easy. There's nothing to worry about if your past is clean." Charles took another drag of his cigar. "And if you're not, well...I guess I'll find out soon. It's only my first day on the job, after all. I need time to put together a report."

"And then what? You report back to your client? What are they going to do with this information?"

He shrugged. "Beats me. I was just paid to follow you and report back. What my client does after that is their business—not mine. Why? You hiding something big?"

I glared at him. "No. I was just curious. Secrets or not, no one wants to be followed. You wouldn't like it either."

"Probably not. But as I said, I've done nothing illegal. And I'm loyal to my client so I'm not telling you a damn thing." He reached for his door handle. "But it was nice meeting you, Ethan. See you around."

He got out of my truck, heading back to his motel room. I scowled when he vanished inside. My meeting with the private investigator had gotten me nowhere—I still didn't know who had hired him or what he would do with my information. If he found out that I was in fact Ethan Miles.

Of course he would. What kind of private investigator would he be if he couldn't? My face and name were all over the news. It was a miracle Taylor hadn't seen it yet.

There was a part of me that just wanted to run—to head home and escape all this drama. But I couldn't leave Taylor. Not only did I love her, but she needed me for the fashion show. I couldn't turn my back on her and the inn.

With a sigh, I started my truck and pulled out of the parking lot of the sleazy motel. I followed the GPS back to the inn and approached the rustic cabin with my headlights on. As I drove closer, I noticed Taylor on the step, pacing. She had gotten dressed and looked upset. What was going on?

I pulled over, rushing toward Taylor on her porch. "Taylor? Are you all right?"

Her head snapped toward me. It was then that I noticed the tears in her eyes. "Ethan, there you are. I went to your room but you weren't there. Where did you go?"

"Just for a little drive. It's good for my mental health," I lied, then frowned. "You're crying. What's wrong?"

She sniffled, then took a deep breath. "I just got a call from Portland. It's Evelyn, Ethan. The nurses say she doesn't have much time left. The cancer's too vicious."

"Oh my gosh," I cried. "Taylor, I'm so sorry. Did you want to go see her?"

Taylor nodded, wiping her eyes. "Yes, if you could take me. I don't think I'm in the right mental state to drive."

"Of course, of course. Do your parents want to come too?"

"Yeah, Mom and Dad are just getting dressed. We told the guests we'll be gone for a little while but they can help themselves to the food and toiletries in the meantime."

"Good, good. Come here." I offered my arms. "I'm so sorry."

Taylor leaned in for a hug, then I stroked her hair and tried to comfort her. She cried on my shoulder for a little while before the door to the inn opened behind us. Her parents came out in their regular clothes, looking somber.

"Ah, Ethan. There you are," Mark cried. "Taylor told you what's going on?"

"Yes, she did." I kept my arm around Taylor. "I met Evelyn when we took a trip to Portland. Taylor told me all the good memories—how she worked at the inn for so long. She seems like a nice lady. I'm sorry you're all going through this."

"Thank you." Sharon patted my shoulder. "I'm so glad you're here with us, Ethan. Especially for Taylor's sake. You're a great comfort."

Taylor nodded. "Agreed. Thanks for taking us, Ethan."

I smiled and told them no problem, though I still felt guilty about my secret. And I hoped the private investigator wouldn't get between us. Or anyone else for that matter.

"Well, we should get going." Taylor dabbed her eyes. "We don't know how much time she has left."

I nodded, leading Taylor and her parents to my truck. We hopped in and pulled away from the inn while following the GPS back to Portland. After a few miles, I saw a familiar car in my rearview mirror.

It was Charles. Yet again, he was stalking us.

When I took a left with the sedan following us, Taylor frowned and looked in my rearview mirror. "Okay, am I crazy or is that car following us?"

"I'm sure it's nothing," I lied, not wanting to upset her. Taylor was already deeply emotional. "Why don't we talk about Evelyn a little bit? What is your favorite memory of her?"

Taylor shared some details about her childhood, then her parents added what they liked about Evelyn. She always had an old, wise lady vibe to her and was a great help at the inn for decades. They were all deeply sad when she got old and sick and had to move into the retirement home. I could've listened to Taylor talk all day, especially about things she loved.

When we reached Portland, it was still pitch black outside as I parked around the back of the building. The sedan had faded from my rearview mirror, but I knew Charles had to be somewhere. He didn't seem like the kind of private investigator to lose a target.

As we walked toward the front doors of the retirement

home, we saw an ambulance parked outside. Taylor's eyes widened. "No, no, no..."

She took off running, entering the building and rushing down the hallway. Me and her parents followed. The nurse at the front desk tried to stop her but Taylor didn't listen. I ran to keep up with her with Taylor's parents behind me as I headed to the third floor where we had met Evelyn.

After I stepped off the elevator with Taylor's parents, I noticed other senior citizens were awake, peeking out their doors and murmuring. Something big had happened. I rushed down the hallway, finding Evelyn's room where the paramedics were. Taylor was crying in the doorway as the two paramedics lifted Evelyn's lifeless body onto a stretcher and placed a white sheet over her face.

"I'm sorry," the paramedic told Taylor. "She's gone."

I was glad I was standing there, because Taylor collapsed and started to sob. I could only embrace her as she wept before her parents caught up and followed suit.

Chapter Twenty-Six

W e stayed at the retirement home for a little while, sitting near the front desk. The paramedics had wheeled Evelyn's body out of the home and into the ambulance. They promised they'd let us know when the autopsy was complete so we could hold a funeral. Other people in the home liked Evelyn and were sad to see her go.

I brought Taylor a cup of coffee from the vending machine, sitting next to her in the foyer. "Hey, how you holding up?"

"Okay, I guess." She sipped her coffee. Her cheeks were still stained with tears. "I feel like I lost a grandmother. Me and Evelyn were close."

"Yeah, I know." I placed my hand over hers. "Again, I'm sorry."

She took a deep breath. "Thanks, Ethan. I'm just glad we went to see her before she died. And that you got to meet her. I'll remember that final day forever."

When her parents were done chatting with the nurses and other elderly residents, we left the retirement home, heading to my truck in the parking lot. The private investigator was snapping pictures of us again from his car before driving off. With Taylor and her parents so upset, I was the only one who noticed. Did he have to take pictures at such a terrible time?

I shook my head, driving back to Bridgewood. Taylor's parents thanked me again for coming and headed to bed. I paused with Taylor in the foyer, gesturing at the stairs.

"Are you going to sleep?"

She shrugged. "I'm not tired. Too much on my mind. Maybe I'll go on a drive like you did."

"Okay. Just be careful." I recalled the private investigator. "Plenty of messed up people out there. What about your fashion? Are you almost ready for the show?"

She sighed. "I think so. I should probably work on it tonight, but...I just don't have the strength. Maybe we should cancel the show. I'm not sure I'm ready just yet."

With Taylor on the verge of tears, I reached for her hand. "I think Evelyn wouldn't want her death to get in the way of your dreams. She loved your fashion. And she was very encouraging."

"Yeah, she sure was," Taylor replied. "I just don't know..."

"How about this? You can take a moment at the fashion show to honor Evelyn. Hold it in her memory. Maybe pass around some pictures of her, talk about her to your audience. That way, everyone will remember her."

Taylor looked up, smiling. "Yeah, I like that idea. Okay, Ethan—you've convinced me. The fashion show is back on. And I should finish up some stuff."

I beamed. "Perfect. Can't wait to see it. And if you ever need me, you know where to find me, Taylor. I'm always here for you."

"I know, Ethan. It's one of the things I love about you," she confessed, then paused. Her cheeks were bright red. "Uh, anyway, I should get back to my attic slash fashion studio. See you in the morning."

She turned, heading up the stairs. I couldn't believe what had slipped out of her mouth. She loved me—the feeling wasn't just one-sided. I wanted to dance and panic at the same time. My secret always came back, weighing on me.

I headed up to my room, on cloud nine and worrying when I turned on the television. The interview Taylor and her parents had done with the local news had aired. They looked great—they gave perfect answers and a tour of their inn. Even Taylor's fashion made an appearance. I hoped it would bring in more business for their inn. And the best part? They left me out of it, making me glad no one would recognize me. Especially that nosy private investigator.

I must've fallen asleep after that, exhausted from running around. I woke up to someone knocking on my door. I rolled over in bed, still in yesterday's clothes. It was almost 6 a.m. I got up—throwing on a fresh set of clothes—as I rushed to answer the door.

It was Taylor in my doorway, looking sad. "Hey, Ethan. I got a call from the retirement home."

"Oh? Is everything okay?"

"Yeah, everything's fine. As much as they can be right now. It turns out Evelyn had pre-paid for her funeral and planned it out a few years ago. She requested to be buried a day after her death. With the autopsy completed last night, we're able to go ahead."

"I see. What was the cause of death?"

"The cancer killed her, ultimately. Stopped her heart while she slept. With my scarf around her head." Taylor sighed. "I fucking hate cancer. Anyway, she already paid for the plot at the local cemetery. In her will, she wrote that she didn't want to burden me or my parents since we were her only contacts."

"That was nice of her," I whispered. "She was looking out for you, even after death. It proves how much she loved you and your family."

Taylor sniffled. "Yeah. I miss her so much. My trips to Portland just won't be the same."

"I know. But you could visit others in the retirement home," I suggested. "Bring them some homemade scarves and clothes. I bet they would love that, especially in Evelyn's memory. I'm sure some elderly folks don't have anyone."

Taylor nodded. "You're right—that is a good idea. Maybe in time. Right now, I'm too upset to go back there. But we do have to get back to Portland for the funeral. Are you able to come with us again? I...need you there."

"Taylor, you don't have to ask twice." I reached for her hand. "I'll come with you. Just let me eat breakfast and do some chores."

Taylor thanked me, heading downstairs to help her parents with breakfast. They were quiet and sniffling as they fried eggs and bacon. The guests gave us their condolences when they found out what happened. After eating breakfast and washing the dishes, I did a few quick chores before leading Taylor and her parents out to my truck.

The social worker assigned to Evelyn texted Taylor all the information on the funeral. We arrived at the cemetery a few blocks from the retirement home, finding the tombstone that Evelyn had paid for in advance. We met the social worker in person and the priest performing the last rites over the casket.

Evelyn laid there, her eyes shut and looking peaceful. Taylor placed some flowers inside the casket and stepped back. She let her parents say their goodbyes as she held my hand. I squeezed three times, letting Taylor know everything would be okay.

"We therefore commit this body to the ground, earth to

earth, ashes to ashes, dust to dust," the priest read aloud. "In sure and certain hope of the Resurrection to eternal life."

We then watched the cemetery workers lower the casket into the ground, the sun beating down on us. It was a beautiful day of sunshine and birds chirping. After it was over, we walked through the cemetery, heading to my parked truck.

"Well, I guess that's it," Taylor lamented. "It's over. Evelyn is gone."

"I don't think anyone is ever *really* gone." I gripped her hand. "Not as long as we remember them. And it seems Evelyn left a mark on everyone she met."

"Yeah, she sure did," Taylor sniffled. "I'm going to make sure everyone at the fashion show knows her name."

"That's tomorrow, isn't it?" Mark asked. "In the park?"

"Yep—and hopefully, it'll attract a huge crowd," I answered. "Today is also the day the billboard we bought for the inn in Portland should go up. Even more guests should be checking in soon."

"A billboard? How fancy," Sharon gushed. "Ethan, we can't thank you enough for all you've done for us. It's like... one day, you just showed up and made our lives better."

"I think he's an angel," Taylor sighed, winking at me.

I snorted. "Oh, definitely not. But I'm starting to believe in fate. I think I was meant to meet you guys."

"Funny—I was just thinking the same thing," Taylor replied with a twinkle in her eyes. "Without you here...I think I would've fallen apart. Thanks for holding me together, Ethan."

"I'll gladly be your glue any day of the week," I flirted. "Come on—let's get lunch on the way back to Bridgewood. My treat. I spotted a tasty-looking French fry truck a few miles from here."

After getting into my truck, we went out for lunch, chit-chatting and keeping the mood light. I tried to stay upbeat and cheery for Taylor since the funeral had been so hard. We got back to the inn shortly after that, finishing up more chores and taking care of the guests while Taylor worked in the attic. More guests slowly started to trickle in.

A middle-aged woman with two kids and a husband entered, walking up to the front desk. "Is this the Cozybrook Inn?"

"The one and only," Sharon replied with a smile as I mopped the floors. "Checking in?"

"Yes, please," the husband replied. "We heard so many good things about your inn on the news. We had to see what the fuss was about."

Sharon and Mark were thrilled to have new guests, showing them to the empty rooms upstairs. I even checked in a few more people when they were swamped. We were quickly running out of rooms, having to resort to letting people sleep in the basement.

"My goodness, we're going to need a bigger inn soon!" Sharon cried, walking back to the front desk. "I wonder if we could expand upstairs—add a new wing."

"With more money coming in, that's something to think about." I finished my mopping. "I'm happy things are working out for you guys."

Sharon beamed. "We have you to thank. We really struggled before you came along. In fact, Mark and I were talking last night, and we'd like to make you a partner in the inn. Since you've worked so hard for us."

Mark came down the stairs, overhearing our conversation and nodding. "Yes, we owe all our marketing success to you. Taylor was onboard with making you a partner. What do you say?"

I smiled. "Well, I'm honored. But can I think about it? It's a big step."

"Of course, of course. No rush," Sharon assured me.

"Whatever you choose, we're just glad you came to Bridge-wood. Now, we'd better get started on dinner. Mark, if you could help me with the pork chops?"

"Ooh, my favorite." Mark licked his lips as he followed his wife into the kitchen.

I put my mop away, thinking about their offer. If I accepted, I could have another business. I was good at running those. But it would mean saying goodbye to Los Angeles forever—making my home here permanently. If that private investigator didn't expose and ruin me.

Decisions, decisions.

I was just about to enter the dining hall and ask Taylor's parents if they needed help when my phone rang. As I pulled it out of my pocket with only one bar as usual, I realized it was my mother's number. She and Dad had avoided my calls up until now. What had changed?

I answered, placing the phone up to my ear. "Mom, is that you? I've been meaning to talk to you about—"

"Ethan, your father's in the hospital," Mom interrupted. I could hear the beeping of a hospital machine behind her. "He's suffered a stroke, I'm afraid."

"A stroke? Oh my God!" I plopped onto the nearby bench in the foyer. "How? When?"

"Last night. You haven't heard? Ever since your brother took over the company, it's been nothing but a disaster. That boy can't lead a project to save his life. Anyway, the Miles Marketing Company went down a few points on the DOW."

"Shit," I cursed. "And that caused Dad's stroke?"

"I think so, yes. All the stress from you leaving and your brother taking over the company. And his Parkinson's isn't doing too well either. How could you do this, Ethan? How could you abandon your family's company?"

"Look, that wasn't my intention. Nate tricked me—made

me sign a bad contract. What did he say to you when he called?"

"That you always hated working at your father's company. That you wanted it to fail. He claimed you called your father and I some awful names behind our backs too."

No wonder Mom and Dad hadn't wanted to speak with me. My brother had painted me out to be the villain when in reality, it was the other way around.

I scoffed. "What? That couldn't be further from the truth. Nate's playing you, Mom—playing everyone. Including me. Can't you see that?"

Mom hesitated. "I... I don't know what to believe. I just think you should get back to Los Angeles. In case your father doesn't have much time left."

"Okay. I can get home." I paused. "I, uh...might need a loan for a plane ticket. Nate cut off all access I had to the family account."

"He did? I had no idea," Mom cried. "All right, I'll help. What airport is closest to you?"

"Well, Bridgewood is too small to have an airport. But Portland would."

"All right, I'll call them and have a ticket to LA waiting for you. When you get here, you can explain everything your brother's done."

"With pleasure. See you soon."

After I hung up, I headed upstairs, packing some of my things for the flight. I made sure I had my passport before heading up to the attic. I knocked on Taylor's door, waiting for her to answer a second later. She was holding a piece of blue fabric and measuring tape.

"There you are," she said. "I've got your suit ready for the fashion show. Want to see?"

"Uh, actually, there's something I need to tell you." I

scratched my neck awkwardly. "There's been a family emergency back home. My dad had a stroke."

Taylor's eyes widened. "Oh my gosh—how awful. First Evelyn, now your dad. So much sadness lately. Are you heading home?"

"Yeah, just for a little bit. In case he doesn't have much time left. My mom already bought me a ticket at the airport. She knows money is tight."

"I understand. Need me to come with you? You were there for me when Evelyn died, so it's only fair."

"I appreciate that, Taylor, but I think this is something I have to do on my own. Besides, my family can be a lot to handle. But I hope I'll be back for your fashion show. I don't want to miss that."

"All right, I get it. Be safe, Ethan, and call me if you need me." Taylor kissed my cheek. "I hope your dad makes a full recovery."

I did too. The last time I spoke with my father, he wasn't happy with me, all thanks to my brother. And I would be damned if I was getting to let that be our final conversation.

I had to get home—had to tell my parents everything. As much as I dreaded running into my conniving brother again.

Chapter Twenty-Seven

I packed my suitcase into my truck, then started my long drive to the airport in Portland. After giving my keys to the valet, I checked in, grateful that Mom had bought me a ticket. I boarded the plane shortly after that and took my seat.

It was an eight-hour plane ride from Maine to California. During that time, I ate, napped, and worried about my father. And what it would be like to see my brother again. As the plane hovered above California, the sky turning orange from the dawn, I found myself growing nervous.

I didn't want to be in California again. I missed Bridgewood—and Taylor. As the plane landed and we were allowed to disembark, I wondered if the private investigator would follow me all the way here.

No, that was insane—he wouldn't do that. And I didn't spot him anywhere on the plane. For now, I was safe from that guy.

I grabbed my suitcases, then walked off the plane with the other passengers. After making my way through the crowded airport, I walked outside, intending to hail a taxi when I spotted a black limousine. The chauffeur was carrying a sign that read FOR ETHAN MILES.

I walked over, clearing my throat. "Hey, that's me. Is this my limo?"

The chauffeur nodded, opening the back door for me. "Yes, it is, sir."

I hadn't been called sir in a long time—not since I left my office. As I got into the back seat, I noticed my mother sitting there, a glass of champagne in her hand. She was still wearing her fur coat and boots and looked in good spirits. Despite the fact that her husband and the father of her children was in the hospital.

"Mom," I blurted. "You came to pick me up."

"Well, how else were you going to get to the hospital?" she asked, sipping her drink. "Since you're living like a commoner now."

"Yeah, I guess I am." I stared out my window as the limo driver stepped on the gas. "And you know what? I actually like it. I'm enjoying Bridgewood."

Mom raised an eyebrow. "Hmm. Well, not me. I much prefer life in Los Angeles."

I had once too. But things had changed—thanks to Taylor. She had woken me up to a whole new life, one I liked much better than my old one.

"Right. Anyway, how's Dad doing? Will he make it?"

Mom shrugged. "I don't know, darling. I hope so. Rest assured, he's getting the best medical care in the city."

"Good. You don't sound too upset about it, though."

She turned to me. "Of course I am! I do love your father. But life must go on, even if someone we love gets sick."

I shook my head. Taylor had mourned harder for an employee than my own mother did for my father. It was at that moment that I realized my family was truly messed up.

"Uh-huh." I narrowed my eyes at Mom. "How's Nate doing?"

"Pretty well for someone who's running our company into the ground," Mom mumbled as she sipped her champagne again. "No wonder your father had a stroke. You should've never left the company, Ethan."

"I didn't mean to leave permanently. Nate tricked me."

Mom turned to me. "You should've been smart enough to see through his lies. If you ask me, this trouble is your own doing. And now, the company your father worked so hard to build is going down in flames."

Despite my mother's best attempts to make me feel guilty, I didn't. I blamed Nathan for what he had done. It wasn't my fault he had made up a contract to take over the company and then couldn't run it.

I knew getting through to my mother was pointless so I didn't say anything else on the ride to the hospital. Once we arrived, the limo driver let us out at the front doors. Mom set her champagne glass down and headed for the building. I followed as we walked through the parking lot. I inhaled the fresh California air, but even that smelled wrong to me now.

I missed Bridgewood more with every passing second.

We entered the hospital's foyer, looking around. This was clearly a rich hospital—only for the upper echelon of society. I noticed important businessmen and celebrities staying here for different surgeries and illnesses. Mom started walking off down the hallway, heading left toward a separate wing.

"This way, darling. Your father's recovering down here."

As I walked behind her, my phone buzzed. It was Taylor when I pulled it out of my pocket.

TAYLOR

Everything all right? Did you make it back to LA okay?

ME

I did. Just about to see my dad now. I'll text you later.

She sent me a smiley emoji back as I placed my phone in my pocket. She was so sweet to check on me. Thinking about her, I followed Mom into a private room. I winced when I saw Dad lying in the bed while connected to a machine and IV.

He looked up, wearing a hospital gown with a long, weary face. The left side of his mouth was a bit droopy. His eyes widened when he noticed me. "Ethan..."

"Hi, Dad," I whispered, leaning against his hospital bed. "Mom told me you had a stroke. You doing okay?"

"So far," he mumbled. "What happened? Why did you leave the company?"

I sighed. "It's true what I told you before—I faked losing all my money and fame to find a woman who truly loved me. But my brother took it too far. He tricked me with a contract that gave him total control of the company. Essentially, he ruined me. Cut off my access to the family account too."

"Oh, Ethan. Always telling lies, aren't you?"

I spun around, noticing my brother standing in the door-way. He was wearing one of my blue suits with a wide grin on his face. And Anna was hanging off his arm in a very tight, red dress.

I scoffed. "It's not a lie. You wanted me out of the picture so you could take over Dad's company. And since you couldn't do it legitimately, you resorted to sabotage and treachery."

"Ethan, is this the appropriate time to talk about this?" Nathan glanced at our father. "Dad's in the hospital. You don't want to stress him out even more, do you?"

"Seems you did that all on your own," I muttered,

crossing my arms. "Something about the company losing DOW points? Not so good at being a big, famous business-man, are you, older brother?"

His jaw clenched at that. Anna rolled her eyes, petting his arm. "Don't listen to him, baby. Ethan's just jealous of you."

"Hardly," I grumbled. "Anna, there you are. Hanging off my brother like a parasite. You'll date anyone as long as they've got money, huh?"

As her face turned into a snarl, Mom stepped forward. "Stop—your brother's right. We're here to check on your father, not argue. So stop it, both of you."

Me and Nathan turned quiet, though we continued to glare at each other. A minute later, a doctor in a white coat entered the room, wanting to speak with us. The prognosis wasn't very good.

"I'm afraid the stroke was extensive," he explained. "Your father will need more care. I recommend sending him to a care facility in northern Los Angeles. That way, he'll have constant access to doctors and nurses."

Mom's face lit up. "And he'll have to live there? Permanently?"

The doctor nodded. "Yes, I believe so. But you can visit anytime. We recommend that, actually. Seeing family is good for the patient's mental health. It's a miracle he can still speak."

Mom appeared to be thrilled at the idea of finally having the mansion to herself. Maybe her and my brother were more alike than I suspected. Two money-hungry, soulless peas in a pod.

"All right then," Mom replied, trying not to sound too happy. "Let's get him transferred."

"Great, we'll get the paperwork started," the doctor confirmed as he faced my father. "Get some rest, Mr. Miles. And let us know if you need anything."

My dad nodded, then the doctor left the room and shut the door behind him. My brother was still smirking my way and it was starting to piss me off. If he was worried about the company going under, he didn't look like it. Though he was always a good actor.

"I need to speak to Ethan," Dad commanded. "Alone."

"Why?" Nathan asked. "Ethan has nothing to say—"

"Now," Dad grumbled. "Out. All of you."

With a scoff, Nathan turned, leaving the room. Anna followed like a lost puppy. Mom glanced between us, wondering what was going on before she followed. I stepped closer to my father's bedside.

"Yes, Dad?" I asked. "Look, before you start, I want you to know I'm sorry about all this—"

"No," Dad interrupted. I feared a lecture was coming. "I'm sorry. I wanted to say that in case this is the end for me."

"You're sorry?" I asked, frowning. "But...why?"

"Because I realize you were right. I'm sorry I stopped answering your calls and took your brother's side." Dad sighed. "I was at his office a few days ago and found the contract he made you sign. I believe you, Ethan."

That was a relief. "So you know the truth. I left to find love, but I never wanted to abandon your company."

Dad stared out the window at the city. "No, I don't blame you. Perhaps I was wrong to force my business on you boys. I should've let you become whatever you wanted instead of turning you into mini versions of myself. And now, I fear I've created a power-hungry monster in your brother."

"Yeah, he's definitely lost it. Is there anything I can do to help? I'm not sure I can get the company back."

"Probably not—your brother's determined to keep it, even if it is failing. I just want to ask you one thing."

"Of course, Dad."

"Are you happy in Bridgewood?"

I immediately thought of Taylor, unable to stop a smile. "I sure am. I met someone wonderful. I'm in love, Dad. Truly, madly in love."

Dad tried to smile, though he couldn't quite make it with his full mouth. "I'm glad you found someone who loves you for you. Your mother...well, I know she doesn't truly love me. That she only wants my fortune. And she'll have it all soon enough."

I winced. "Dad..."

"It's all right, son. I figured that out a long time ago." Dad sighed. "If I can leave you with one thing, it's this—don't follow in my footsteps. Make your own happiness and don't tie it to money. It's meaningless in the end."

Dad had a point. I nodded, hoping I wouldn't let him down.

"And don't worry about the company. There's nothing you can do now," Dad continued. "When it falls apart completely, it'll be your brother's fault. You did nothing wrong."

My only mistake was trusting my brother. I wouldn't do that again.

"Okay, Dad. Thank you. Do you need anything else?"

"No. Just go back to Bridgewood—live your life the way you want to. Don't be blinded by money and power like I was. Because now, I have nothing."

"That's not true." I reached for his hand. "You have me. Even if I'm a million miles away, you'll always have me."

Dad tried to smile again. It was a nice moment—I hadn't had that many with my dad. He was always busy working. Maybe him having a stroke would be a good thing for our relationship. And I was glad he had seen my brother's true intentions.

I cleared my throat. "But Dad...I need to ask you something. The woman I'm in love with in Bridgewood—Taylor —doesn't know about my past. That I'm Ethan Miles. And she hates rich people with a passion."

"Ah." Dad sat up in bed. "Some people do. I take it you're afraid to tell her?"

"I am," I whispered. "God, so afraid. What if I lose her forever?"

"It's a risk you'll have to take," Dad answered. "You need to tell her the truth, even if it hurts. If she truly loves you, she'll get over it. In time."

Dad had good advice. And it was past time I told Taylor the truth. As I formulated a response, the door burst open. Nathan stuck his head inside, glancing between us. "What's going on in here? Is Ethan feeding you more lies?"

"Actually, I was just on my way home. To Bridgewood," I clipped, turning back to Dad. "I'll call you every day and check on you. Take care, Dad. Love you."

Dad nodded, watching me head to the door. I pushed past Nathan and started walking off down the hallway. Mom and Anna were sitting nearby, watching Dad's room. Then Nathan started following me.

"What—that's it?" Nathan asked. "No more arguing? You're just going to leave?"

I spun around, coming face to face with him in the middle of the hospital's hallway. "What did you expect? A fistfight? I don't want to argue with you, Nate. And I don't want the company back. I'm much happier in Bridgewood anyway. So your big plan of stealing the company from me and ruining my life? It didn't work. I found something much, much better when I got away from this city."

"You don't mean that," Nathan spat. "You miss the company, the fame, the money. Admit it!"

I shook my head. "I don't. And it makes me sad how low you'd go for money and power. How you tricked your own brother for it. Enjoy the company and your new life, Nathan. But all the money in the world can't buy you real friends, genuine love, or fulfilment."

He scoffed as I turned, heading for the doors. I didn't look back as I hailed a taxi. I used what little money I had left to visit Cheyenne at her apartment. She was happy to see me as we caught up, sitting on her couch and chatting with her fiancée. She was still searching for a job but seemed to be doing much better. And she was thrilled I was so happy in Bridgewood.

She drove me to the airport, a kind gesture. Mom had paid for a ticket back—luckily—so I boarded the next plane and left for Portland. When I arrived back in Maine, I nearly kissed the ground. Home sweet home. The life I built and loved was here.

I got the keys to my truck back from the valet, then drove to the inn. It was almost dinnertime when I pulled into the parking lot. As I entered the foyer, I noticed a dozen more guests had arrived. The Kennedys had to turn some away since they didn't have enough room. They were busy setting up a waiting list for future guests.

"Ethan, you're back!" Sharon cried. "Taylor told us you had a family emergency. Everything okay?"

"Yeah, I think so. Is Taylor in her attic?"

"Yes—she's getting ready for the fashion show tonight. You made it back with a few hours to spare."

"Thank goodness. I'm going to check on her."

Sharon nodded, returning to checking in more people as I headed up the stairs. When I knocked on Taylor's door, she was so happy to see me, peppering kisses all over my face. I never wanted it to end. The attic was a mess behind her, but at least all the clothes looked ready to model.

I debated telling her the truth, but the fashion show was so close now. I didn't want to ruin her big day. So I kept quiet for now. But as soon as the show was over, I had to tell her who I was.

And hope with every fiber of my being that she would still love me.

Chapter Twenty-Eight

We ate dinner in the dining hall shortly after, catching up with Taylor, her parents, and the guests. I introduced myself to the new people who had arrived and finished the chores I had missed when I was away. Taylor kept trying to ask me questions about my time in California, though I kept my answers short and sweet.

She'd know the full truth soon enough.

After dinner and chores were done, I helped Taylor pack all her clothes into my truck. Between me, Taylor, and her parents, we all offered her models rides to the Bridgewood Park downtown. Taylor had already asked a local carpenter to build a mini stage with a microphone, set up chairs, and string lights in the nearby trees.

"We got it all done while you were gone," Taylor explained when we arrived at the park. "The townspeople were kind enough to help."

"That's good. Sorry I was away."

Taylor shook her head. "Don't be—I understand. Family comes first. Now, are you ready to walk in your first fashion show?"

I grinned. "Of course. Lead the way."

Taylor took me to the backstage area that sounded fancier than it was. A simple black sheet separated it from the stage. I quickly changed into the blue suit that Taylor had designed for me, checking myself out in the mirror. I looked like a million bucks. Then the other guests joined us.

They all looked good too—from Mrs. Cabot to Breanna, Madison, Abigail, and Sophie and her son. The other guests took their seats as more people began to arrive. Some had even come from out of town for the fashion show, learning about it online or from the flyers we had posted in Portland.

"All right, everyone—showtime," Taylor said, glancing around. "You all look wonderful. And I'm so proud we made it. Are you ready to strut your stuff?"

We nodded, waiting for Taylor to give the orders. She headed toward the stage where she began speaking to the audience at the microphone. I poked my head around the curtain, noticing a full crowd. There wasn't an empty space in the park. I smiled, knowing Taylor deserved it. She had worked hard.

Taylor cleared her throat, speaking into the microphone. "Hello everyone, and welcome to my first fashion show. My name is Taylor Kennedy and I've been into fashion since I was a little girl. I'd like to thank my good friend, Ethan, for giving me the encouragement to do this."

I poked my head around the curtain again, waving at the crowd. Taylor was beaming at me before returning to her speech.

"And before we get started, I'd like to dedicate this fashion show to the late great Evelyn Beadle," Taylor continued. "She just passed away from cancer. She was like a grandmother to me—and a huge supporter of my fashion. I know she'd be so proud of me today. I'd like to share a few happy memories I have of her..."

As Taylor talked to the eager crowd, I noticed Drew

approaching in his truck. He parked on the side of the street and began to walk over. I paused, wondering why he was here. Hadn't Taylor told him to take a hike?

"Without further ado, let's get started." Taylor gestured at the backstage area. "Please welcome our first model, Abigail!"

Abigail walked onto the stage, hiding her face and looking a bit shy. But Taylor gave her a smile and a thumbs up. Abigail walked to the end of the stage, doing a little twirl. People began cheering for her—including me.

"Go Abigail!" I called. "You look amazing!"

Abigail was smiling so wide that I knew her face had to hurt. After she finished walking, showing off the dress as Taylor spoke to the audience about its design, she gestured for me to walk next. I did my best to strut on the runway and smile at the crowd. I noticed Drew rolling his eyes and crossing his arms, looking like he was waiting for something. But what?

Mrs. Cabot walked next, then Sophie and her son. The crowd aww'd when her little boy waved at everyone. Then it was Madison's turn. She swayed her hips, winking and blowing a kiss at the audience. She was a natural. After Breanna walked, Taylor changed into a flowing red gown. She narrated its history as she walked down the runway. Then she paused at the microphone, smiling.

"Well, thank you all for coming again," she chirped. "I know this was last-minute, so I appreciate it. I look forward to designing new clothes and putting on another fashion show at some point—"

Drew rushed onto the stage, grabbing the microphone from Taylor. "Stop! I need to say something."

"Drew? What the hell?" Taylor demanded, reaching for the microphone. "Give that back!"

But Drew side-stepped her, holding onto the microphone. "No—I have to say this. Someone among us is a fraud."

People in the audience began gasping and murmuring, including Taylor's parents. My heart was hammering in my chest. I knew what was about to happen—Drew was going to expose me.

He was the one who had hired the private investigator, not my brother. It all made sense now.

I stepped onto the stage, heading toward Drew as he pointed a finger at me. "There he is. Ethan Miles, the son of multi-millionaires who started the Miles Marketing Company in Los Angeles!"

"The...Miles Marketing Company?" Taylor asked, turning to me. "They were the ones who got the community center to rent a room for me, weren't they? What's going on?"

As people in the audience looked confused, Drew reached into his pocket.

"Oh, don't worry—I came with proof. I hired a private investigator to follow Ethan around. I always had a bad feeling about him. And I didn't like him stealing what was mine."

Drew pulled out a newspaper, one from back in California. It had my face and name on the front page and talked about how much money I had lost at the company. All a fabricated story, but the crowd didn't know that.

"My P.I. had a connection in California. They recognized your face when they saw it," Drew explained, smirking. "Everyone knows who you are now."

Taylor turned to me. "No...tell me this isn't true. You can't be Ethan Miles, can you?"

I hesitated for an answer. "Taylor...I'm sorry—"

"So it *is* true," she said, shaking her head. "Damnit,

Ethan. You knew I hated rich people. Why didn't you tell me?"

"Because I was afraid you wouldn't like me anymore. Look, I never meant to hurt you. The plan was to pretend to lose all my money and fame so I could find a woman who loved me for who I was. Because I wasn't having much luck in LA."

Drew scoffed. "A likely story."

"It's true. I swear!" I cried. "But my brother, Nathan, tricked me. He had me sign a contract that I hadn't fully read. It gave him the company I once ran after my father left. I lost all my friends, my connections. Everything. So I became a regular guy."

Taylor crossed her arms. "You still should've told me. God, I feel like everything I know about you is a lie."

"No, it isn't," I insisted. "Taylor, you know me. Everything I told you was true. The chemistry we had was real—I know it. Okay, I'll admit I should've told you about my background before, but I didn't know how. We were getting closer and then you told me about your past with Oliver. I was worried you'd think I was just like him."

"So you lied to me. The whole time." Taylor scoffed. "I can't believe I thought I was in love with you. I told you everything about me—things I've never told anyone before. I let you see my fashion, even let you meet Evelyn, one of the most important people in my life. We shared intimate, private moments. And you were playing games the whole time!"

I felt like my world was imploding around me. The murmuring crowd faded, leaving just me and Taylor on the stage. And I was losing her. All because of Drew and his private investigator.

"No, no—I wasn't!" I cried. "I love you too. You're the only good thing in my life. I was planning to tell you everything after the show. I never wanted my secret to come out like this—"

"Well, it has. Truth always comes to light," Taylor wailed, shaking her head in disgust. "I knew I should've just left your truck on the side of the road. You're just like Oliver Vaughn. God, I'm such an idiot for falling for it again."

"How can you say that? I'm nothing like that Oliver idiot. I never hurt you, never took advantage. I wanted the best for your inn. And for you!"

Taylor was on the verge of tears. But Drew was still smirking. "Face it, Ethan—you've screwed up. Taylor sees you for who you truly are. Just another lying, scheming rich boy who grew up with a silver spoon in his mouth."

I didn't know what to say. What could I say now that Drew had turned Taylor against me?

"I'm sorry, but that's just not true," Mrs. Cabot interjected, hobbling onto the stage. "Ethan is a good, kind man. He helped me scatter my husband's ashes and gave me such sweet words of comfort. He didn't have to do that."

"And he sat with me and let me talk about my eating disorder," Abigail chimed in, facing the crowd. "He helped. Both he and Taylor did."

"And he didn't judge me when I told him I had a criminal background," Breanna spoke up, looking embarrassed. "He's a real one."

Sharon cleared her throat in the audience, standing up. "And he's a hard worker. He's done so much good for our inn."

"Agreed!" Mark hollered in his seat next to Sharon. "Who cares about his background? Or that he lied? Not telling people about his past was his choice. We know who he is— we've seen it. Taylor, I don't like to meddle in your private life, but Ethan is a good man. I think we should hear him out. Let him explain everything."

"Yeah, I'm with Aunt Sharon and Uncle Mark," Madison added, glancing at us from the side of the stage. "Ethan's a good dude. He was always nice to me, even when I wouldn't leave him alone. And so loyal to you, Taylor. If you ask me, Drew's the freak you should never talk to again."

Drew scoffed at her. "Shut up, Madison. No one needs a slut's opinion."

"Excuse me?" Madison huffed, crossing her arms. "You were the one who asked for my help, remember? You wanted me to stop Ethan and Taylor from getting together. I was just doing what you asked—"

"It doesn't matter," Drew interrupted, turning to Taylor. "As soon as I found out the truth about Ethan, I knew I had to tell you. It couldn't wait. I'm sorry, Taylor. Sorry the man you fell for isn't who you thought he was."

Taylor shook her head, staring at the ground. "Just my luck, I guess. I...have to get out of here. I'm sorry."

She didn't even glance at the crowd as she rushed off the stage, heading to her truck. Taylor stepped on the gas and sped off. After she had disappeared down the street, people were still murmuring.

"Well, I'm glad all that came out," Drew taunted. "Now Taylor can realize I'm the one she's meant to be with, not you. Too bad, so sad, Ethan."

I balled my fists, the desire to punch Drew rising inside me. But what good would that do? I had already lost Taylor. There was nothing left for me in Bridgewood anymore.

I glanced at the crowd, noticing them staring at me. Some were taking pictures—probably to sell to the media. I had become a zoo exhibit again. Without looking back, I headed for my truck, getting in and speeding off toward the airport. I didn't even bother going back to the inn to get my clothes. It would've been too painful.

When I arrived at the airport, I called my mother. "Hey, Mom. How's Dad doing?"

"Okay, I guess. He's being placed in a care facility today. Why?"

"Just wondering. I, uh...have a big request. I want to come back to LA. I'm sick of this small town."

"Oh, thank God." Mom sighed with relief. "Because your brother is in a sorry state. Do you need me to buy you another plane ticket home?"

"Yes, please. See you when I get there."

"Great—meet me at my house. Still getting used to that since your father is gone. And Ethan? Despite everything, it'll be good to have you home again."

Home. It was back in California again, whether I liked it or not.

Mom purchased my plane ticket, then I confirmed it at the gate and boarded the plane. It flew me back to Los Angeles where gossip about our company had spread. I noticed a newspaper at the airport that read NATHAN MILES LOSES 200 MILLION DOLLAR DEAL. IS IT OVER FOR THE MILES FAMILY?

That didn't sound good. I knew I had to find out what had happened.

I took a taxi from the airport, arriving around dinnertime in Los Angeles. After the driver dropped me off at Mom and Dad's house, I paid him with what little money I had left, then knocked on the door. Mom greeted me with a hug in her usual fur coat.

"Hello, darling. So nice to see you again. Now that you're back, you can see what's happened," Mom began. "Your brother lost a big deal to a rival company. The one your ex owns."

"Diana? Oh my God!" I said, entering the house. "How did that happen?"

Mom shut the door. "Isn't it obvious? Because Nathan can't run a business. He doesn't know how. It has to be you, Ethan. You're more qualified. That's why your father gave you the business instead of him."

"So, what do you want me to do?"

"Go check on your brother. Here, take my car." Mom reached into her pocket to pull out the keys to her Lamborghini. "He's been working late nights at the office. Talk with him—see if he'll listen to reason. You may be the only one who can save the company he's ruined."

"All right, but no promises. Nate's stubborn. I'll let you know how it goes."

As I turned toward the door, Mom reached for me. "Just one thing. What about your new life in Bridgewood? Your relationship with some woman? Your father told me you were happy there. That you were never coming back."

I sighed. "Yeah, I know. And I was. But...it didn't work out. I guess it just wasn't meant to be."

"Oh. Well, even though I didn't approve of you leaving— and can't understand why anyone would want to leave this life behind—I'm still sorry, Ethan. For your sake."

"Yeah, I am too. I'll talk to you later."

And then I left the house, heading for my old office building. It was all I had left.

Chapter Twenty-Nine

When I had made it to the Miles Marketing Company headquarters, employees were on their way out, carrying boxes filled with their things. The front desk was empty when I entered. The entire place was like a ghost town. As more employees walked by, recognizing me and murmuring, I headed to the elevator and rode it to the top floor.

After the elevator dinged, I stepped off, looking around. All the cubicles were vacant. It was nothing like the crowded, vibrant office I had been in charge of. When I heard whispers coming from my office, I followed the voices. My brother had replaced my name with his on my office door.

I opened the door an inch, hearing it creak as I stuck my head inside the office. Anna stood there, yelling at my brother. The office was in disarray—papers everywhere, pencils on the floor. It was like a tornado had swept through the building.

"...and it wasn't supposed to go like this!" Anna yelled at him. "How could you let this happen?"

"I don't know!" Nathan cried, putting his head in his hands. "God, everything is a disaster."

I cleared my throat. "Um, sorry to interrupt. But what's going on?"

Anna turned to me, rolling her eyes. "Oh, your brother just bit off more than he could chew. I can't believe I ever saw something in him. Good luck cleaning up this mess, Nathan. I'm done."

Anna stormed out of the office, getting into the elevator. Nathan looked up and snarled. "Fine, go! I never needed you anyway. Stupid skank."

I shook my head at the drama. "Seriously, what's going on? I heard something about you losing a multi-million deal?"

Nathan sighed, sitting at my desk. "That's pretty much the gist of it, yeah. I fumbled the presentation and lost a massive deal. To your greedy ex, actually. I can't stand that woman."

"And all the employees?"

"Gone." Nathan played with a pencil on the desk. "They knew our company was a sinking ship and they wanted off. I guess there's no such thing as loyalty anymore, huh?"

I crossed my arms. "You're one to talk about loyalty, Nate. Was it worth it? Tricking me to take over the company?"

Nathan rose to his feet, looking out at the city. "In the beginning, yes. My whole life, our parents fawned over you. Even though I was the oldest—the one who should've been inheriting the company—they liked you better. And I can't tell you how many decades that's pissed me off."

"Well, that's hardly my fault. And after all this, you can't blame our parents. Dad knew you couldn't run a business. That's not a bad thing either, Nate. It's just not in your blood. And that's okay."

"But it should be," Nathan spat, turning around. "This was supposed to be my chance. And I blew it!"

"So you did." I leaned against his desk. "What now?"

"I have two choices. Either keep leading the company and watch it go down in flames," my brother whimpered, pausing, "or...step away. Let someone else handle it."

"Mom was hoping you'd pick the latter. She sent me here to help you, Nate. And I want to. Even after all you've done to me. As fun as it would be to let you sit in the mess you've made, I have to save Dad's company."

"How? I've already messed it up."

"True—a lot of damage has been done. Unless we admit the truth. Give the company back to me, Nathan. The way it was supposed to be before your ego took over."

And then I held my breath, waiting for his answer while hoping he would make the right choice.

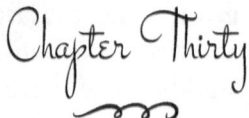

Chapter Thirty

Nathan thought about it for a second. Just when I thought he would refuse—stubborn until the end —he sat down at his desk, typing something out. Then the printer made noise in the corner of the room.

"Sign that paper—it'll give you full reign of the company and the fortune back," Nathan insisted. "Feel free to read it this time."

"I intend to," I replied, walking toward the printer.

My brother was being honest for once—there were no hidden details in the contract. Once I signed it, I slid it toward my brother on his desk. He added his signature reluctantly.

"There, it's done," Nathan cried. "I guess I should get out of here."

"No—we're going to hold a press conference. And you're going to apologize for what you've done. Plus, I need to make an announcement."

To my surprise, Nathan agreed. He had either learned his lesson or just wanted to wash his hands clean of it all. I contacted the local news, telling them I was back in town and wanted to hold a press conference. I set up a podium on the street outside as journalists arrived to livestream us. The flashing of the cameras and intrusive questions weren't things I missed about Los Angeles.

I approached the podium, clearing my throat. Nathan stood next to me. "Thank you for coming. As of today, I'm the CEO of the Miles Marketing Company again. My brother has signed the contract to return it all to me. But I think we owe the public an explanation. Here it comes…"

I ran through the entire story—how jealous my brother was of me and how it was his idea that I pretend to lose all my money to find love. I briefly talked about my time in Bridgewood and apologized for the ruse.

"I had good intentions. My brother didn't, though he's making up for it," I confessed, glancing at him. Nathan only nodded and kept his mouth shut. I turned back to the journalists. "I'm going to attempt to clean up my brother's mess and get our company on the right track again. But I have something to say first."

I looked into the camera, hoping both Taylor and Oliver Vaughn were watching.

"Oliver Vaughn, a prominent businessman who's planning to start a hotel chain, is a lying crook," I declared, making the journalists murmur. "He stayed at the Cozybrook Inn in Bridgewood, Maine and stole their ideas for his hotels. If you need proof, contact the owners, the Kennedy family. They have pictures of Oliver in their town. I just wanted to make sure you know what a thief he is—and recommend the inn. It was a lovely place, something I'll cherish forever."

"What the hell are you doing?" Nathan whispered, leaning toward me. "Oliver's one of our top clients!"

"Not anymore," I snapped, turning back to the camera. "Look, all this lying hurt someone close to me. This amazing woman I met, Taylor. She's mad at me right now—and I get it—but I have to say this. I love you, Taylor. Even if you never speak to me again, I'll continue loving you until my last breath. Thank you for seeing the real me."

The journalists looked confused and so did my brother. But I had to say it.

"Furthermore, I intend to pass along my company to Cheyenne Nichols, a great friend of mine," I continued. "If she'll accept, of course. I just have a few things to do first. Anyway, thanks for listening. And remember this—money isn't everything. I'd give it all up to hold the woman I love again."

As I stepped off to the side, heading to Mom's car, Nathan grabbed my arm. "Are you serious? You're giving the company to Cheyenne, your goddamn secretary?"

"Yes, I am," I spat, wiggling out of his grasp. The journalists continued to snap pictures. "It's the least I can do after all she did for me. Don't think I've forgotten that you fired her."

"Of course I did," Nathan sneered. "She was a spy. But do you seriously think she can lead this company? She doesn't have any experience!"

I shrugged. "She can't be any worse than you. I'm done with the corporate life for good. And if you were smart, Nate, you would be too. It's nothing but poison."

I left Nathan standing there as I walked toward the Lamborghini, heading back to the office. It was empty except for me—and I hoped Cheyenne could get it up and running again. For my father's sake.

With access to the family account, I transferred some money. I sent a large paycheck to Mrs. Cabot, then Sophie, for the care of her son. I didn't forget about Breanna, Madison, Abigail, Eric, or the Kennedys. I hoped they'd accept the large transaction I was sending their way.

After doing all that, I just had one last thing. I picked up the phone and called the president of NYU. That was the only perk to being rich and powerful—the connections. And I hoped I could make some magic.

"Hello, this is Ethan Miles," I began once a secretary answered. "Yes, the owner of the Miles Marketing Company. And yes, I'm aware we're in the middle of a scandal right now but I have to speak to the president. It's very, very urgent. Thank you."

The secretary transferred my call, then the president of NYU came on the line. "Mr. Miles? I didn't expect to get a call from you. I was just watching your press conference."

"Ah, then you know everything. It's been...wild, to say the least." I shook my head. "Anyway, I'm calling for a personal reason. It's on behalf of Taylor Kennedy. She applied to NYU a few years ago, correct?"

"What is this concerning?"

I sighed. "Please, I owe it to Ms. Kennedy to do this. Can you check your system?"

"All right, Mr. Miles. Only because your father is a good friend," the president replied, then I heard clicking on her computer. "Yes—Ms. Kennedy applied to the NYU fashion program three years ago. And she was accepted."

I frowned. "No, no...that can't be possible. She never heard back."

"That's incorrect. We sent her a letter of acceptance in the mail. When she didn't respond, we assumed she wasn't interested. Her spot was given away."

I rose to my feet. "Something isn't right here. Anyway, thank for you this information. If Ms. Kennedy's still interested, would you accept her again?"

"Yes, of course. Her application was very impressive. The fashion directors were in awe of her sketches. She's a talented, talented girl."

"I know—her fashion shows are a hit back in Bridgewood. Anyway, thank you for the information. Have a nice day."

I hung up, reaching for my things. Taylor could hate me forever—that was her choice—but I was going to make her dreams come true. That was the least I could do for her.

I got into Mom's car, sidestepping the journalists and heading to Cheyenne's apartment. She and her fiancée had seen the press conference. While Cheyenne was a little nervous about taking over the company, I did my best to convince her.

"Come on, you can't be worse than my brother," I begged. "You're brilliant, kind, and hard-working. My father's company needs you to help them rebuild, Cheyenne. What do you say?"

A smile grew on Cheyenne's face. "I think you have a deal, Ethan. And thank you. It won't be easy, but I'm up for a good challenge. Anytime you come to LA, let me know. The company will personally put you up in a hotel."

"Good, because my brother totally stole my house. That jackass." I pulled a contract out of my pocket. "Anyway, we'll both sign here and it'll belong to you. I have complete faith you'll make the company successful again."

After Cheyenne signed, she gave me a hug. She promised she'd get to work on hiring new employees and reaching out to clients. It would take a while, but I knew she would get our business back to where it was before my brother took control. I even gave her access to the family fortune and left that life behind me.

I just had one last thing to do to make everything right. Well, as right as I could make it.

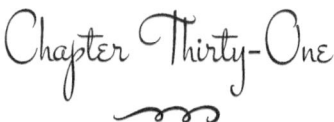

Chapter Thirty-One

After saying goodbye to Cheyenne, I headed to the airport, buying a ticket for Portland, Maine. I had to rent a car and drive to Bridgewood to reach the inn. After I pulled into the familiar parking lot, feeling nervous, I entered through the front doors. There were even more guests and tourists checking out the place.

When Sharon saw me—just one of many in a sea of eyeballs—she smiled. "Ethan, you came back! Oh, we're so happy to see you. We saw your press conference. Thank you for exposing Oliver Vaughn."

She ran through the crowd to hug me, then Mark walked over. "Yes, we're deeply grateful. And our bank informed us of the money transfer. With all of that, we can afford to expand the inn. And we paid off your truck debt."

I smiled. "Thank you. But...you aren't mad I lied to you about my past?"

"We don't care about that, Ethan," Sharon insisted. "We care about who you are now. And from what we've seen, we think you're an incredible man."

"And so did the guests," Mark added. "They checked out earlier but told us you sent them money as well. Mrs. Cabot cried tears of joy—she can keep her house now. So did Sophie and Eric. She's putting the money in a trust fund for her son. Eric can stay in the US after hiring a caretaker for his parents back home with the money you sent. Breanna is using it to start a new life, Abigail is enrolling in another program to combat her eating disorder, and Madison is grateful too. She's helping her father save their house. You changed their lives for the better."

"That's good to hear. But what about Taylor? Has she forgiven me yet?"

Sharon paused. "I don't know, Ethan. She's been hanging out with Drew a lot again. He's been comforting her ever since the fashion show, despite our concerns."

Of course he would swoop in. "Well, I need to talk to her. I have good news about—"

When the door opened behind me, I spun around, noticing Drew and Taylor entering. Taylor's eyes widened when they landed on me but she kept silent. Drew was the first to speak.

"What the hell is *he* doing here?" Drew demanded.

"Calm down," Mark scolded. "Ethan is our guest—and he's given us money to expand the inn. He's a hero in our books."

"You think a liar is a hero?" Drew crossed his arms. "How pathetic."

I shook off his comments, stepping toward Taylor. "Look, I know you're still mad at me and I don't blame you. But I wanted you to know I called NYU. The president knew my father. Anyway, I got you into the fashion program."

Taylor gasped. "You...you what?"

"Maybe I shouldn't have meddled, but you deserve a spot. Besides, the president told me you got accepted years ago. That they sent a letter of acceptance but never heard back."

"What?" Taylor frowned. "I never got a letter."

Drew looked guilty, his eyes flitting to the floor. I crossed my arms. "Do you know something about that, Drew?"

Taylor turned to him. "Why would Drew know anything?"

Drew stammered. "I...I don't know. You know Ethan—a typical liar. He's just trying to turn us against each other."

Taylor scanned his face. "I don't believe you. You know something, don't you?"

Drew looked like he was going to deny it, then sighed. "Fine, fine. Three years ago, your acceptance letter arrived when I was working at the inn. Your father had me fixing a broken light in the hall. Anyway, I greeted the mailman and told him I'd pass it along. I opened it out of curiosity. When I realized it was an acceptance letter, I...kinda threw it out."

"You *what*?" Taylor shrilled. "Why the hell would you do that?"

"Because then you'd leave and become some famous fashion designer. And I didn't want to lose you!" Drew cried. "Taylor, we belong together. It's fate. And I wasn't going to let some stupid fashion school or Ethan get in the way. It's why I did everything I did. Tracking your phone, teaming up with Madison, stalking Ethan. I just wanted us to be together, no matter what—"

Taylor slapped him, making it echo around the foyer. All the guests looked over in shock. For a moment, I saw a look of pride on Mark and Sharon's faces.

"Get out," Taylor growled. "I never want to see you again. I should've told you that as soon as I found out you were stalking me, but I was naïve. Well, not anymore."

Drew looked shocked, clutching his cheek. "Taylor, please. Just hear me out—"

"Get out!" she yelled. "Or I'll call the police and have you arrested. Out, out, out!"

He looked afraid at her screeching, turning toward the door and vanishing outside. Sharon and Mark gave me a small smile and rushed to the front desk to distract the guests. They still looked concerned while staring back at us.

I sighed, watching Taylor's chest heave as she leaned against the door. I figured I should say something to break the silence. "Well...like I said before, I'm sorry about Drew. He shouldn't have done all that. But NYU is waiting for you, Taylor. They're lucky to have you."

Taylor turned to me. "What about you? I heard your press conference on the radio. You're giving your company to a friend back home?"

"That's right. You showed me I'm done with that life—that I want something real, something authentic. I don't know what I'm going to do but I'm never going back to LA. And I mean it this time."

Taylor stared at me, wordlessly. It hurt knowing I'd never hold her again.

I cleared my throat. "Anyway, good luck at NYU. I'm hitting the road—trying to find another place. I won't ever bother you again, Taylor. Goodbye."

As I turned, she grabbed my arm. "Ethan, wait. You should stay."

"I...what?"

"You heard me." Taylor sighed. "Yes, I'm still upset you lied about who you are. But you've proven you're a good person, Ethan. It wasn't fair of me to compare you to Oliver. For that, I'm sorry."

I shook my head. "You have nothing to be sorry about. God, you've been perfect. It's why I fell in love with you."

"And I love you too," Taylor whispered with a shy smile. "I was just too scared to say it. And I'd love for you to stay here and help out with the inn."

"You don't have to ask me twice. I love this place—it's

like my second home. But what about you? Aren't you heading to fashion school?"

Taylor glanced out the window, then shook her head. "No, I'm not. I'll thank NYU for the opportunity, but I don't need them. The fundraiser and fashion show proved that. Besides, why would I want to leave Bridgewood when I have everything I need right here?"

When she reached for my hand, squeezing it three times, I smiled. "Do you mean that?"

"I sure do. And with all your marketing experience, you can become a partner in the inn *and* help me launch my fashion line. You can be my official marketing director."

"Sounds perfect to me," I sighed, squeezing her hand back. "I'm just...I'm so glad I didn't lose you. Trust me when I say I would give up all the money in the world to be with you."

"Well, you kinda did," Taylor joked. "Now, what do you say we start over? Maybe grab some food?"

"Oh, I'm in. Just lead the way—"

Taylor grabbed my shoulders, pulling me in for a passionate kiss. And everything was right in the world again.

The future? Now that was something I was looking forward to. Helping Taylor with her fashion company, marketing the inn to become more popular. *And* putting a ring on Taylor's pretty finger.

That was priceless—and better than a billion-dollar company any day of the week.

THE END

THANK YOU FOR READING

Did you enjoy this book?

We invite you to leave a review at the website of your choice, such as Goodreads, Amazon, Barnes & Noble, etc.

DID YOU KNOW THAT LEAVING A REVIEW...

- Helps other readers find books they may enjoy.
- Gives you a chance to let your voice be heard.
- Gives authors recognition for their hard work.
- Doesn't have to be long. A sentence or two about why you liked the book will do.

About the Author

Dana Gricken is a multi-genre author from Ottawa, Canada, writing stories since she was old enough to hold a pencil. She has been published in fantasy before with *The Dragonwitch Chronicles* and *The Soulless War Trilogy* and  has more books coming out in 2024 and beyond like the *Jessica Prince Mysteries* series.

In her spare time, she enjoys reading, playing video games, mailing letters to friends, spreading kindness, educating about mental health struggles, and watching *Star Trek* with her cats. She hopes her books bring joy and make people feel less alone. She wants to write over a hundred novels in her lifetime.

You can connect with her @DanaGricken on all social media or her website:

danagricken.com

facebook.com/dana.gricken.7

x.com/DanaGricken

instagram.com/danagricken

Also by Dana Gricken

Satin Romance

Novels
Riches to Rags

Fire & Ice Young Adult Books

Novels
Chatter

The Soulless Trilogy
The Dark Queen

The Dark Evolution

Dark Cage

The Astrid Trilogy
Coming of Age

The Kingdom of V Trilogy
The Kingdom of V